THE LAST LAW
THERE WAS

**Center Point
Large Print**

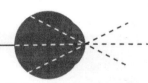

**This Large Print Book carries the
Seal of Approval of N.A.V.H.**

THE LAST LAW THERE WAS

BILL BROOKS

CENTER POINT PUBLISHING
THORNDIKE, MAINE

This Center Point Large Print edition
is published in the year 2008 by arrangement with
Golden West Literary Agency.

The text of this Large Print edition is unabridged. In other
aspects, this book may vary from the original edition.
Printed in the United States of America.
Set in 16-point Times New Roman type.

ISBN: 978-1-60285-095-8

Cataloging-in-Publication data is available from the Library of Congress.

For my new grandson Kaleb Mikel
A young cowboy

ONE

Took me out of an orphanage in Dallas, the old man did. Come down there one day when it was ice and snow on the ground and the horses were blowing steam out of their noses and pawing at the frozen grass trying to find graze. It was uncommon brutal weather, I remember that.

One minute, I am an orphan without kith or kin to watch over me, none but the Little Sisters of the Sacred Heart Industrial School for Orphans to provide me with moral guidance and learning of life's cruel ways, and the next minute I'm riding beside the old Mexican bouncing up and down on the seat of a spring wagon heading north into the Texas Panhandle.

I remember it as a long tedious trip without comfort.

The whole while, the old man worked hard at a bottle of tequila he kept stashed inside his coat and grumbled much about the hundred dollars he had paid the Sisters at the orphanage for me. Asked me if I ever dug a grave before, or mucked out a stall, or if there was anything at all I could do?

I told him I worked plenty hard at the orphanage and it wasn't all reading and writing and arithmetic thank you. He gave me a cross look, snorted through his nose, and kept at the bottle of greasy-looking liquor.

That was the year previous to when the riders came and killed Mr. Sand.

I was either fourteen or fifteen when that happened.

All these years later, I can still close my eyes and recall it like it just did happen yesterday.

The riders come in on the west road, come riding directly out of the setting sun so that when you first looked at them coming, they looked like they was on fire and the dust their horses kicked up was like smoke rising from their hooves. Fire and smoke, like they was coming out of hell itself.

Of course it was later, after they killed Mr. Sand that we all learned it was Rufus Buck and his gang. Killers and thieves and blackguards every last man. Little did I know that soon, their fate and my own would be tied together.

Rufus Buck was an uncommon ugly man. I know that because when he and his band of murderous trash passed me by that dreadful day outside of Otero's livery, he hauled back on the reins of his horse and let his evil gaze fall on me as hard as cold rain.

Mostly what struck me about his treacherous looks was the long welt of bone-smooth scar that pulled down on the corner of his right eye and seemed to connect up with the lower part of his jaw. His mouth was grim, his teeth yellow as a dog's, and his large white eyes were like boiled eggs floating around in his coal-black face. He was the first colored man I had seen in Deaf Smith County since I had arrived except for one or two cowboys who passed through that way on trail herds and at a distance.

And, the way he sat up there on that big bay horse

of his staring down, I reckon I was the first colored boy he had seen himself in Deaf Smith County.

"What yer name, child?" he said in a manner that reminded me of distant thunder.

"Ivory Cade," says I, too afraid to lie or tell any other untruth.

"What's a black child like you doing in a pig-hole place like this?"

It wasn't something that I could answer. For who can know the fate that guides us?

I thought for a moment that he might plug me out of spite with one of the several pistols that were stuck down inside his belt or hanging from the horn of his saddle. His bad eye roved over me like a hound searching up quail in tall grass.

"Ivory seems like a funny name for a child as black as you," he said with a twisted parting of his lips that didn't hardly come close to a real smile. And that was all he said before he and his band of brigands spurred their rough mounts down the street. From what I could see, they were mostly men of mixed blood: Mexican and Indian with one or two whites among their bunch. Comancheros, maybe, for such were common in Texas at that time, trading stolen properties between the Comanche and the Mexicans.

Later, there was trouble at the cantina. Trouble always came after dark in Last Whiskey, except for the time the dutchman, Mr. Shirtz, lost his mind and murdered his wife and children, then rode to town naked and sitting backward on a mule and confessed

9

the crime. That was the middle of the day and everyone that saw it will never forget it.

When the trouble at the cantina started, Mr. Sand got called down there, because it was his duty to go.

He was a tall serious man who always wore a white shirt and string tie, even on the hottest days. I liked what I knew of him. He never had anything but kind words toward me.

When some of the men in town came carrying Mr. Sand's body to the livery I was surprised to see so many bloody wounds staining his white shirt. His head hung limp, and even though he was not a heavy man, those carrying him were stained with sweat.

Otero told them to lay him in the bed of the spring wagon. Puddles of his blood collected beneath him and dripped down through the boards of the wagon and into the straw.

One of the men told Otero there had been trouble down at the cantina and Mr. Sand had been summoned. And that when he arrived, there had been harsh words thrown back and forth between Mr. Sand and Rufus Buck and his pistoleros.

"All of a sudden," said the man waving his arms in the air in an attempt to demonstrate the trouble. "Shots were fired from every angle. "They shot him to ribbons . . . he had no chance at all."

I remember not wanting to look into the bed of the wagon anymore, but the more I didn't want to the more it seemed I had to. Terrible things have a way of holding our attention.

He had lost all his color, drained out in his life's blood that had collected in puddles beneath the wagon. He was the first dead man I ever had to look at and it lent me no comfort to do so.

It was nearly ten o'clock in the evening when the men brought Mr. Sand up to the livery and laid him in the spring wagon. Ol' Otero worked late into the night sawing and hammering together planks of pine. Some so fresh, the sap seeped out and stuck to his fingers and the sawdust clung to his forearms.

In spite of all his shortcomings as a benefactor (and there were plenty), Otero Chavez was an expert at coffin building, just as I had got to be an expert at mucking stalls and digging graves. If a body does a thing long enough, it's hard not to become an expert at it, even if it is something common as digging graves or mucking out stalls.

Some women from the Free Methodist Church came with fresh clothes and offered to see to the care and cleaning of Mr. Sand's corpse and Otero and me stepped outside into the cool night air in order to offer them the needed privacy for their work.

Right away Otero starts pulling on his tequila and the air's blowing so fresh and clean, that it just naturally gives me a whiff of Otero's breath which is as harsh as coal oil.

The hour was late, and the streets of Last Whiskey were quiet except for down in the "South Section" where you could hear pianos being played in the hurdy-gurdy houses and the laughter of what Otero called "painted ladies." And twice there was the sound of gunfire, but who was there to go and investigate? For the town constable lay dead inside the livery with Christian ladies washing away the stains of his demise.

Otero made several noises while we waited. Each time he took a pull of the juice, he grunted and said something in Mex which I didn't understand. He wasn't much on talk, Otero wasn't. Mostly he'd just say what it was he wanted, or come up and smack me alongside my ear if I wasn't doing what he wanted.

It got to be all right with me after a while, the fact that he didn't talk much. But, I can't say's I ever got used to being smacked alongside my ear.

About the longest speech he ever gave me was that if I did right, worked hard, and did what I was told, I might someday take over his business after he passed on.

"You must learn to build a good coffin by the time I am ready for *la muerte*," he warned. "I want a fine funeral, as fine as any that this place has ever seen. You must not disappoint me or I will come back from the grave and trouble your dreams!"

Otero Chavez had a way of crawling down in your bones.

After about an hour, the ladies of the Free Methodist Church came out. One was carrying a bundle of bloody clothes, and they all were sobbing something pitiful.

I followed the old man back inside. I was amazed at the wonderful job the church ladies did, for Mr. Sand was lying there in fresh clothes with his hair neatly combed and parted in the middle. He might have been asleep for all anyone would have knowed.

"Come, take his feet," Otero ordered. If you ain't never touched a dead man, then you cannot know what an unpleasant experience it is. Otero didn't ever seem troubled about such work, but I confess that all along it caused me nightmares and was a leading cause of my eventual decision to strike out on the vengeance trail of Rufus Buck and his gang of low characters. You will see what I mean.

Once done, Otero took a couple of swipes at the lid with a plane, then placed it precisely atop the coffin and hammered it in place with ten penny nails sprouting from his mouth.

Soon's he finished, the widow and her boy, Albert, came. I knew Albert some. He'd come around now and again with one of their horses for shoeing or to have a saddle repaired. He was about a year older, I guessed, than myself. He was tall and lean as his daddy, and had his daddy's dark eyes. We got to be somewhat friends, for I found his company agreeable and once or twice we went fishing. Otero didn't afford me many days off.

I never did know Mrs. Sand, although I'd seen her several times. She was wearing a black dress that caused her skin to seem perfectly white. She had large hands and auburn hair, as did Albert, and a long, thin nose, as did Albert. It was plain to see by her reddened eyes that she had been crying a great deal.

"I want to see him," she said. "I want to see my Joe."

"But, señora . . ." Otero's oily breath seemed to fill up the stable.

"Please . . . remove the lid so that I might see him once more." How could he refuse those stained eyes?

Otero took his claw hammer and pried open the lid. It sounded like men crying out from the grave the way the nails screeched coming out.

The widow stepped gingerly up to the open coffin; she had to hold onto it with her gloved hands to keep from swooning over. I kept watching Albert. It seemed like as though he didn't want to look down on the cold silence that had become his daddy. I sure didn't blame him.

"Oh, my poor, poor Joseph!" The words came out of her like startled birds flying out of a bush. I could see she was going to swoon, so could Albert. We both come and took an elbow and held her steady. Her sobbing was loud and awful and the horses skitted around nervously inside their stalls. I don't know whether it was the terrible sounds of grief she was making or that the horses could smell the death.

"Oh, Albert . . . !" she cried. "What will we ever do without him?"

Albert whispered something to her and took total hold of her and led her toward the doors.

She kept repeating over and over again: "What will

we ever do without him? What will we ever do without him?" Then they was gone, swallowed up by the black night. The old man slumped himself down on a three-legged stool and took the tequila bottle from his pocket.

"It's a very sad thing," he said in the first true kindness I had ever known him to demonstrate. After two or three swallows that left him with a dazed look in his eyes, he stood and put the lid back on Mr. Sand's coffin and hammered it shut.

Early the next morning, Otero roused me from a sleep in which I had been dreaming of eating peaches. I always favored the ones packed in tin cans because of their syrup. At Christmas and once or twice during the year at the orphanage, we had peaches for desert. It's where I obtained my fondness for them.

"Come," said Otero, looking as though he had not slept a wink for his clothes were the same rumpled wear he had on the day before. "We must go dig the grave." It was grueling work.

Once we had finished, he made me dress in a clean white shirt and the single pair of woolen trousers I owned. They were stiff and scratchy and I did not care for them. But, the old man insisted that his business— that of taking care of the dead—was one of respect, and that we should show it by our good appearance. He, too, had put on a clean shirt, but his trousers remained the same stained and oily ones he always wore.

We waited outside in the pearl light of morning for

the widow and Albert and the other mourners to come. The sky was streaked gray and it might rain and the wind came out of the east. It was always a poor thing for the wind to come out of the east, Otero said. I tended to believe him for whenever I did have the opportunity to go fishing in the little branch of the Canadian, I was always skunked when the wind blew out of the east.

Otero and me had loaded the coffin in back of the wagon. (It was my misfortune, being of lowly position and the only helper Otero had, to scrub away as much of the bloodstains as was possible with cold water and a yellow bar of lye soap and an old horse brush.)

We waited maybe an hour for the widow and Albert and the others to come. The wind worried their clothes and the men had to hold on to their hats to keep them from flying away.

I counted fifteen folks in all; it did not seem like many.

I whispered to Otero that there sure didn't seem like a lot of folks had come to mourn the passing of such a good man as Mr. Sand had been what with all his concern for their welfare while in life.

He told me to shut up. I reminded him that asking questions was not a sin. He growled that the others were afraid to show themselves.

"Because of the killing?" I wanted to know.

"*Si*. Now shut up!"

A man in a dark coat and white collar stepped out of the small crowd and said, "If you would lead us to the cemetery, Mr. Chavez . . ." I knew that man's name to be Martindale and that he was a deacon at the Free Methodist Church. He had a large nose full of busted veins, the mark of a heavy drinker. But then, I shouldn't be the one to pass judgment for some day it will be passed on me and I'd like it to be by the Lord Almighty himself and not some poor little pecker-wood of a grave digger.

It was then that I saw Albert looking my way. I believe that I understood what he was feeling for he had a look in his eyes that showed all his pain and anger at once. A look like that don't hide much of what a body's feeling.

It took maybe ten minutes for the whole procession to reach the cemetery north of town. It sat on a small little rise that was unusual for that part of Texas—as though it was created special for burying people so's they could be a foot or so closer to heaven than the rest of us.

Some of the men that had come to mourn, helped me and Otero take the coffin out of the back of the wagon and place it next to the open grave. Then me and Otero stepped back aways, Otero reminding me to remove my hat which was naught but a floppy old black felt that had seen plenty of better days.

Then, Martindale stepped forward holding a small Bible and took to speaking loudly against the buffeting wind and the widow's sobs. After a few minutes, his words just got lost between the two and he gave up.

The widow plunged forward and threw herself on the casket. Several men, Albert not included, went to her aid and gently pulled her up.

Then for the second time, Albert's eyes drifted across the crowd and came to meet my own. Without saying it, I told him I knew, that I understood and I felt sorry for what had happened to him. Then he sort of just looked away, back toward the casket of his daddy and let the wind tug at his clothes and auburn hair.

Then, it was just me and Otero standing there after the rest had gone off back toward town.

"Get the shovels," said Otero with no more ceremony than that.

It started raining halfway through our labors and turned the earth into mud which was heavy upon our shovels and made the work all that much more difficult.

All the rest of that day, it rained and Otero sat out 'neath the overhang of the livery and worked on a fresh bottle of tequila and smoked cigarettes. As it turned out, it was Sunday and I reckon he figured he deserved to take it off now that our earlier work had been completed and no more awaited us.

I found a chair with the back busted off and mended a bridle and watched the long silver rain fall from the sky. How was I to know that the very next day, I'd be party to vengeance and easy prey for Rufus Buck and his band of killers?

TWO

Otero had a habit of rising before the chickens and was already swallowing his second cup of coffee before the rooster crowed. As was usual, he didn't bother to make any breakfast. The old man did not know what breakfast was. Seemed like, he never slept and never ate and I don't know from that day to this what kept him alive other than his tequila and hard ways.

He was setting up his mule, Oliva, a cautious-eyed beast that brayed her displeasure over the disturbance. Between her braying and his cussing her skittishness, a body could not get an ounce of rest (for my bed was directly in the stall next to Oliva's). I think them two got along so well because of their mutual sour disposition. Once, I tried to ride her and she tossed me into a trough. I never bothered trying again. Give me a gentle mare any day.

"I will be gone one day, maybe two," he said.

He put a knee up against Oliva's ribs and pulled up tight on the cinch and she brayed some more. I didn't say anything, I figured he would tell me where he was off to. Finally, satisfied that she was set to go, he said, "I am going to Ulvade to buy a fresh string of ponies and have some lumber shipped up."

I saw that he was wearing his best sombrero and figured it wasn't all business, the reason he was going to Ulvade. Seemed like every previous trip he had ever taken to Ulvade, which was every other month, or thereabouts, the old man came back bawling drunk, his pockets empty, and him wearing the fragrance of "painted ladies" about his person. And for three or four days afterward, his mood would shift between that of a happy trickster (he once tried to give me a hotfoot) and that of sorrowful sinner (for he sometimes wept openly over his transgressions) before finally settling in to his regular mood: that of joylessness.

Occasionally, he'd feel the need to tell me of his adventures, but always doing so in his native tongue, a lingo of which I only understand five or six words (mostly of the cussing variety). I could only imagine the mischief he'd strayed into when journeying to Ulvade. Having witnessed Otero's fallen condition upon his return each time, Ulvade seemed to me a cauldron of sin and low living. I promised myself that I'd go there as soon as the opportunity presented itself.

"Make sure you take good care of the stock," he grumbled. "Feed and water them but not too much, eh? Muck the stalls and clean that sorrel mare's feet."

I brought Oliva around whilst Otero climbed up on a three-legged stool in order to mount her. He had short banty legs, bowed and arthritic, which forced him to mount her that away. She gave a short buck and a hard bray, then settled into the fact that her and Otero were going to Ulvade to buy a string of ponies and some lumber. I watched them take the south road until they were clean out of sight. Oliva's tail switching round like a crank handle.

It had give up raining sometime during the night and the morning dawned bright and clear.

It seemed like when the old man left, Texas felt peaceful and pleasant again.

I gave the mare oats and cleaned her feet. She did not look well in the eyes and had little gumption to her. I watered the rest of the stock and turned them out into the corral so's I could muck out their stalls.

As I have said, it was not glamorous or easy work and did little for the disposition.

I was the whole while thinking about the mean life that some are assigned, when I come across the grain sack containing Mr. Sand's pistols: twin Navy Colts of a large caliber with walnut grips. One of the men who had helped carry him over that fateful evening must have brought them.

They were long-barreled and still fully loaded; I couldn't help but take one up in each hand. Dangerous things are curious things. They felt heavy as bricks. I did not toy with them long for it pays to know that luck only smiles on a fool but seldom. It did not escape my memory: the dark and bloody wounds such weapons could cause a body.

It was my rightful duty to return them.

I knew the house in which Mr. Sand and his wife and Albert lived: a small white clapboard near the north end of the town.

Last Whiskey wasn't but three blocks either side of

a wide dusty street. Course, as I have alluded to earlier, there was also the "South Section" which contained several saloons, hurdy-gurdy houses, and other low establishments of entertainment. It was another place I couldn't wait to visit soon's the opportunity presented itself.

Several folks waved and said: "How do, Ivory" as I passed them by, all wondering what it was I was carrying in the grain sack. I have to admit, looking back on it all, that the folks of Last Whiskey was, for the better part, decent and kind citizens and never once was abusive to me on account of my color or status as Otero's apprentice (a fancy word for slave if you ask me).

The little white clapboard had a sagging roof, but other than that, looked as fine as any in Last Whiskey.

I knocked on the door and waited some, then knocked again. Albert answered it, seemed surprised to see me, and said, "What're you doing here, Ivory?"

"I brought your pap's pistols," I told him and handed over the grain sack.

He held it out in front of him for a time like a fellow might hold a dead chicken by the legs, then said, "You're welcome to come in."

I said I better not, then soon's I did, I spotted a long table covered with platters of meat, bowls of salads, biscuits, pies, cakes, and a whole turkey.

He saw me staring and said: "The kindness of our neighbors. It's more food than me and Ma can ever hope to eat. You might just as well come in and have some. You are hungry, ain't you?"

Even a blind pig could see that I was. Ol' man Otero's idea of a feast was powdermilk biscuits and a few strips of greasy side pork fried brown and tough as shoe leather, and that was more seldom than often. More usual, I lived off bread dipped in milk, and sugar when I could get it. That and Otero's black-as-mud coffee.

It was the tequila that fed his appetite; my own suffered greatly under such poor victuals. So when queried as to whether or not I was hungry, was like asking a drunkard if he could stand a beer.

"Help yourself," said Albert. It was the first truly kind gesture offered me since Sister Agnes back at the orphanage gave me a set of toy lead soldiers of which I spent countless hours setting up into mortal combat and thus helping me to not notice so much the loneliness of not having parents or other loving kin.

I will always remember her as a kind woman; a true and faithful saint.

I must be honest in saying that I set upon the table of comestibles with all abandon, loading up my plate with turkey and kraut, Irish potatoes and beets, and every other delectable I could manage to stack up without spilling and thereby seeming hoggish.

Albert said, "You ain't shy, Ivory, I'll give you that."

"No sir, I guess I ain't," says I, for hunger can be an overwhelming thing and the sudden sight of so much food was enough to cause a body to swoon if he wasn't careful.

"Well, dig in," he says and I did not wait for him to say it twice.

Between chomps, I give the house the once-over. It had nice furniture and flocked wallpaper above the wainscoting. A small wood stove, a cast-iron Monarch cooking range, a horsehair settee, a red velvet rocker, the big oak table I was sitting at and several heavy oak chairs, and plenty of pictures in pewter frames on one wall.

Among which, I spotted a picture of Albert's daddy, Mr. Sand, holding on to one of the Navies in his right hand and him dressed up in a dark suit and tie. His hair, neatly combed. Albert sees me staring at that one particular photograph and informs: "That was taken the day my father was elected town constable."

I studied it some and determined it to be a true likeness of the man.

"I remember how pleased he was," said Albert, going over to the photograph and taking it down from the wall. "Ma wasn't any too happy over it. She told him that if he didn't know how she felt about men and guns, he didn't know a thing about her. It sort of took all the starch out of the moment of his triumph."

Albert then set the photograph down and picked up his pap's pistols.

"I don't understand why he didn't lay low three or four of those men," he said. "He was a terrible good shot."

Then, I saw the face of Rufus Buck sneering into my brain from just behind my eyeballs and knew right off why Mr. Sand had not used his pistols. It was plain common logic that such an evil-doer as Rufus Buck would have never have given Joe Sand the opportunity to pull his weapons.

"I'm afraid they christened your pap in a hail of lead before he could even train his guns on them," says I, not realizing how awful that might have sounded to Albert. "I seen the dark devil that shot your daddy as close as I and you are now, and what I seen was nothing more than pain and misery for any man that went up against him. Probably shot him first in the back, like most murdering cowards would do."

"I have been thinking long and hard about it, Ivory," Albert revealed, his dark eyes brimming over with tears; whether of anger or sorrow, I could only guess. "I am going to avenge my pa's murder."

Now some might forsake the idea that a fifteen- or sixteen-year-old boy would have it in him to go out on the trail after a band of killers as skunk low and dog mean as Rufus Buck and his bunch. But, I seen the pitiful hard look in Albert's eyes and knew that he meant business.

"How?" I wondered aloud.

"Got these for a start," says he, holding up the Navies. "I am a good shot. Pa made me practice until the banging made my ears hurt."

"Still . . ."

"I know," he said. "There are maybe eight or ten of them and only one of me, but it don't matter."

"Why not?"

"Because I don't plan on taking them on entirely by myself."

"Who you planning on helping you?"

"A fellow my pa used to talk about all the time. A man of great skill with a gun and courage to match. An old acquaintance of my father's back in Kansas. I've been up the whole night thinking about it and the answer came to me just at dawn."

I swallowed down a mouthful of apple cobbler curious as a yellow-eyed cat.

"Who?"

Then, with a pained smile of satisfaction at having solved how he would bring to justice Rufus Buck and his murderous bunch, Albert announced his man: "Augustus Monroe!"

The name swept chills up my spine. Anyone alive those days had heard of Augustus Monroe, a man whose fame had spread all over the West—and East— like wildfire. Friend to presidents, companion of Pawnee Will, killer of Standing Bull in the battle of Yellow River, that's who Augustus Monroe was. Lawman, gambler, scout, and Indian fighter. That's who Augustus Monroe was. Killer of men and rescuer of women. That is *who* Augustus Monroe was.

"He'd be up to the task all right," I managed to say between bites of rhubarb pie. "But, how do you know he'd do it?"

"Cause he knew my pa back in Topeka and because he stands for justice."

It had seemed to me that I had read that part about Augustus Monroe standing for justice in one of DeWitt's Dime Novels. (*Augustus Monroe—Prince of the Plains*, as I recall.)

Albert stood there holding his pap's pistols—one in each hand—and it sure looked like justice just might get done.

"I could stand your help, Ivory," he said. "You look like a good fellow to me and one that would not faint from danger."

It was high compliment and one meant to weaken whatever resolve I may have had. But, the scarred brutal face of Rufus Buck staring down into my soul was not something so easily forgot.

"I reckon you'll have to go it without me, Albert," I said. "I am not a killer, nor have I ever shot a pistol at a feller. I would be useless to you—a stone around your neck." I figured if I had to quail, I'd do it with face and not so's it'd make me out to be cowardly (which I wasn't) or afraid (which I was).

"You could learn," he said.

"Couldn't," I said.

"Could, too."

"Nope, not me."

Then Albert asked me a question that changed everything.

"Is it because you have such a great life being Otero's stable boy and grave digger and stall mucker, and that you get so well treated and well fed and that you have an easy life and that things couldn't ever get no better for you and that you'll someday wind up rich and owning the old man's business and you'll wear a monkey suit and tip your hat to all the ladies and that you'll get married and have a bunch of children and die an old man, that you wouldn't consider anything else, like going with me and seeing my pa's murderers brought to justice and perhaps having a damn high adventure along the way?"

Well, that called for an answer I did not have, 'cause it sure wasn't the case that my life thus far in the employ of one Otero Chavez had been what a body would call romantic. And at the rate the old man was feeding me I'd grow to bones long before I'd grow up. And it was true that he never did pay me one red cent for my labor. Nor were my accommodations luxu-rious: each night I'd bed down in the stable with the horses and got woken up every morning nearer to five than to six and with practically no days off except to go fishing once or twice a month. And as for the rest of Albert's question, I already had forgotten half of them and honestly could not pick my way through.

All Albert's excited talk was putting a fever in my blood that I did not want to be there. Especially that part about high adventure. While I was thinking of all them things, Mrs. Sand, the widow, appeared from a small room off the parlor.

"We have a guest?" she said, blinking through bleary eyes.

"It's Ivory Cade, Ma," Albert said. "He come and brought back Pa's pistols."

Her gaze fell on the twin Navies Albert was still holding on to.

"You will divest yourself of those foul instruments." (Albert had once told me that his mother had been a schoolteacher in their home town of Quincy, Massachusetts, and that it was often her habit to use "four-bit" words, as he'd put it.)

Albert shoved them inside his waistband.

I thought she might fly across the room and lay a lick on his head from the hard stare she gave him. But before she could say anything, or do anything, Albert said, "They are all I have left of him, except a few photographs. I have determined to keep them and to use them in helping me bring his murderers to justice."

Then the widow gave a great sigh and I thought she might sag to the floor, but instead she looked at Albert with her watery eyes and said, "It isn't enough that your father has brought me so much pain, now you must bring me more."

That sort of took some of the stiff out of Albert's backbone, for I saw his shoulders slump a little.

"It's something I *must* do," he said.

"You are just a boy and those men who murdered your father will murder you as well if you try to pursue them. I won't allow you to consider such foolishness."

"I am old enough," said Albert, jutting his chin forward. "There is no one to see that Pa's death is avenged but me. He was all the law this town had. Now, I am all the law there is as far as he is concerned."

For a moment, she neither moved nor spoke. Briefly, she bore her gaze upon me and it was a hurtful thing to stare into her troubled countenance.

Then, she looked at Albert and said, "You are all I have left." And I saw how that got to Albert real quick but he did not do more than flinch as though she had hit him with a stone.

"I have made up my mind," he said, but softly. She crossed the room to him, placed her arms about him, and said, "Please don't . . ."

"I have to," he said.

"Then I shall grieve for you terribly," she said, and kissed him on the cheek before turning, looking once more in my direction as though I might be the one responsible for all her suffering, and disappeared back into the little anteroom.

Albert said, "She's probably right."

"About what?" I said.

"That Rufus Buck and his boys will air me out first chance they get unless I can locate Mr. Monroe first. Are you sure you won't change your mind and go with me, Ivory? I could pay you twenty-five dollars, a portion of the money I have saved up from years of chores. I'll need the rest for expenses to reach Mr. Monroe."

Twenty-five dollars sounded like a world of money,

and I must admit that there was a certain attraction about setting out with Albert on the tracks of them ruthless killers (the way the widow's tears streaked across her cheeks had screwed up my courage; just how long it was to stay screwed up, I failed to consider).

I thought about Otero and how mad he would be if he was to come back from Ulvade in his usual low condition and find me having fled the coop. He would rant and rave (I imagined) and start out immediately on the trail after me. He would do this, I told myself, not because I had short-changed him so much, but because he missed me dearly and knew what a good and faithful helper I had become.

It was all fitting together pretty good: I could tell Albert that I'd go with him, thereby proving my moral courage. And Otero, realizing what a terrible mistake he had made by not treating me better, would come retrieve me home again before Albert and me could fall prey to the scourge of Rufus Buck. And in the process, I'd increase my stock with Otero, forcing him to pay me real money.

It was a wonderful plan.

"Albert," says I. "You can count me in."

THREE

I never thought I'd miss Last Whiskey—or Texas—for that matter, but once me and Albert crossed over into Oklahoma (what was then called the Indian Nations, or the Indian Territory), I realized that all the safety and comfort I ever had (meager as it was) had now been left behind.

Albert said we had to travel on the *cheap* because of our lean funds. He had give me ten dollars as down payment in part of what he promised. He said that once we got hold of Rufus Buck and seen justice done, I'd get the rest.

I spent a dollar of the money on two big cans of peaches and tucked the rest down inside my shoe. By the time we got to the Nations, the peaches was gone, but the money was still riding safe inside my shoe.

Albert rode a little piebald gelding, and me a paint named Swatchy, which I had *borrowed* from Otero's string of ponies (having left him a note to the effect that I had gone off in pursuit of the notorious Rufus Buck and was in need of a sound mount and was sure that he would not mind so much seeing as how it was for a good cause. I also indicated the direction which Albert and me were riding). This last, I added in high hopes that Otero would be mad enough at losing his investment (me and the paint), to come and bring us back before we could fall into the foul hands of the ungodly—as I have stated earlier.

However, ten days on the trail, and no Otero. I can't say I was all that surprised (except for the paint, which I was certain Otero would take exception to having been *borrowed*). I spent a lot of time riding looking back over my shoulder, but all in vain. All I saw was the wavering heat, and my neck grew sore from the effort.

On the morning that we left Last Whiskey, Albert handed over to me one of his pap's Navies and a repeating rifle. He was equally equipped.

"What do you expect me to do with all this armament?" says I. "If I fall into a river, I will be weighed down by it and drown for sure."

That brought a wide grin to his face, but it wasn't meant to.

"We cannot hunt down killers with willow switches," he replied. "I have plenty of ammunition in case we need it."

Now, riding through the Nations (which were at that time notorious not for the peaceable Induns that lived there, but for the many bad actors that such territory naturally attracted to its borders), I was feeling a little more than glad to be wearing such heavy *equipment* as the Navy Colt and the repeating rifle Albert had provided.

There were plenty of tales about such men as China Jimmy, Little Dick Truehart, Bloody Bob Francis, and Jesus January (a murdering madman with a mouthful of gold teeth—or so it was rumored) having taken up refuge in the Nations. I was sure that any minute,

Albert and me would become acquainted with one or all of the above mentioned.

So far, we hadn't.

I looked forward to the day when we would cross over into Kansas. If it had been the day before yesterday, it wouldn't have been too soon to suit me.

As a matter of caution, me and Albert agreed that we would sleep up during the day and do our traveling at night so as to avoid trouble. The worst part about our plan was the mosquitoes which tended to seek a body out in droves and ride him the whole night through. Our hands and faces swole up something awful.

After a week of this, me and Albert daubed mud on our exposed parts in order to ward off the ravenous insects. It made us look ridiculous in the whole, but worked out well enough.

Somewhere toward the latter part of our two-week journey, we found our first trouble.

It was an uncommonly warm night with a full moon with which to see by: nearly light as day, and therefore making travel somewhat easier (riding at night with no moon in such dangerous territory is just something you'll have to experience for yourself).

Both of us had learned to nap in the saddle and not fall off our horses. (Having learned after several incidents of doing so; it is quite a start to one minute be riding along fine as you please, and the next thunk your head against the ground, or worse, a rock!)

We was riding one behind the other like that, our heads bobbing like fish corks, half asleep, when we heard the sound of several voices: rough and mean and cussing.

"Get the damn rope up on that limb there, Burt!" said one.

"Bring that sombitchin' Indin round here!" yelled another.

"Looks like he's lost all his red and turned white!" shouted another.

Then there was a general roar of laughter that sounded like dogs barking, come up out the copse of trees directly ahead of where me an Albert reined our mounts to a sudden halt.

Albert looked around back at me without speaking a word, and I looked at him in the same silence. He motioned for me to come ahead, and I did so.

There was some more cussing and shouting and the sort of hard horse laughing drunken men will do.

Albert whispered: "It sounds like they're going to hang somebody—an Indian."

"Maybe so," I whispered back.

"We can't just sit here and let them," he whispered back again.

"It sounds like maybe there's a bunch of them," I said.

"Don't matter," he said.

"I thought we was just going to Kansas," I said.

"We are," he said.

But I could tell he wasn't earnest about going just yet.

"Pull out your Navy," he whispered.

"What for?"

"Cause we are going to put a stop to a hanging."

I could feel nine one-dollar bills pressing into my foot and it did not feel like all that much money just then.

I pulled the Navy, and he pulled his and we spurred our horses forward.

There in the ghostly light of moon in a small clearing with but a single blackjack tree—its branches as tangled as the hair of a witch against that pewter skyline—was a group of men standing around another astride a gray mare. The man aboard the horse sure enough was an Indun or I missed my guess. He wore long braids, and a rope around his neck.

Albert shouted: "Leave off!" and brandished about the big Navy so that everyone could see.

At first it seemed like no one heard, then he fired off a shot into the air, and several of the men fell on their bellies and covered up their heads.

My little paint, Swatchy, danced around in a nervous circle and was ready to spring through the brush because of the noise Albert's pistol made; it was all I could do not to get tossed overboard.

The man holding the other end of the rope that was looped over the Indun's neck dropped his end of it.

"That's better!" said Albert.

Then that fellow holding the rope got his nerve back and said: "Who the hell are you?"

"You don't want to know," said Albert.

"Well, who's that you got with you?" said the man. He was about a foot taller than a big rock and just as round and wide.

"That there is Ivory Cade, most terrible killer of men in seven states," said Albert. I could tell he was enjoying this playacting. Maybe too much.

"Never heard of him!" said the man.

"He killed China Jimmy and Jesus January. You've heard of them, ain't you?"

"He ain't nothin' more'n a kid," declared the man, "a tar baby!" Some of the others laughed but stopped short when I threw down on them with the big Navy. I never was one to take offense easily, but that ugly cuss calling me a tar baby was too much.

I leveled my Navy at him and said, "You are hardly worth the price of lead, mister. I'd watch who I was calling names. This here pistol will put a hole in you the size of a dinner plate!"

Then one of the ones lying on the ground growled: "Shut up, Burt, they'll kill us all!"

Albert urged his piebald forward and took the noose off the Indun's neck, then took his pocket knife and cut the bonds of the Indun's wrists and said: "Let's go."

The whole while, the Indun never once changed his expression. It was sort of like he was bored with the whole affair. He looked like maybe he was a hundred years old and had seen everything there was to see in life and that the business of being hung up by a rope was nothing new to him.

"Maybe you ought to shoot one of them fellers in the kneecaps, Ivory," said Albert over his shoulder. "Just to show them we mean business if they are thinking to follow after us and give us any trouble."

I thumbed back the hammer of the big iron, but I had no intention of shooting anyone for I had got on pretty good to Albert's act and was sort of enjoying the whole thing myself.

"Which one do you reckon?" says I to Albert.

"Oh, any will do. It won't matter," he calls back.

By now, him and the Indun are clean out of camp. Then Burt begged me not to shoot him, said if I was going to shoot anyone it ought to be, ". . . ol' Harly Bean, standing over yonder next to the tree . . ."

Harly Bean was a simple-looking fellow wearing a tall-crowned hat and bib overalls.

"Harly ain't even married," said Burt. "The rest of us is all married and got kids that need raising. We can't do none of that if we's shot in the kneecaps."

Harly was whining out his protest of having been selected the sacrificial goat.

"Don't shoot me, Kid! Not in the . . . knnnneeeeessss!"

"Tell you what, Mr. Bean," says I. "You pick up them fellows' pistols and rifles and bust them up against the tree, I'll let you walk another day."

I didn't have to say it twice, Harly jumped right to the task and began busting up good serviceable weaponry (including one six-gun that had mother-of-pearl grips) against the tree with such eagerness that it

38

didn't take more than five minutes to complete the job.

He was sweating, but had a pleased look on his face, when he finished.

"How'd I do, Kid?"

"Fine enough, Mr. Bean, now go slap your hat across the rumps of the horses," I said.

He did and they run off into the night.

"Now you have no reason and no temptation to follow us," I said.

I could hear them grumbling amongst themselves as I rode off after Albert and the Indun. I must admit, that even though the Bible teaches that a man's pride will bring him low (Proverbs), I was feeling blowed up and sassy as a Shanghai rooster.

FOUR

We rode till daylight come creeping up over the eastern horizon. Mornings was always a pretty sight that time of year with the sun rising up out of the dark land, spreading its golden light across the grasses, showing itself off the waters, and generally chasing away the low moods that night can bring on a body.

We pulled up near a small tributary of clean trickling water and good grass for the horses to graze on. We didn't even bother to hobble them poor creatures because they was all wore out from the full night's ride without stop and wasn't in any shape to run off; neither was we, and it was good fortune that the hanging committee had not taken it in their heads to seek us out.

The whole ride, the Indun hadn't said a word; he simply rode along with us like we was old pals.

Albert climbed down off his piebald and removed his saddle. The Indun was riding bareback. I climbed down, too, but thought, even after several minutes, as if my legs was still wrapped around the paint's ribs.

Albert pulled out some beef jerky from his saddle-bags and some hardtack biscuits.

"Do you want some?" he asked the Indun. But the old fellow simply stared at him.

Then Albert made a motion of putting the food to his own mouth: eating.

When that didn't seem to do no good, Albert looked at me and said, "Do you know how to speak the lingo? Mex. Maybe he understands Mex?"

I tried what little I knowed, but it was clear he hadn't ever learned to cuss in Mex (which as I have said before was all I ever learned from Otero).

Albert said, "How old do you figure he is?"

"Looks like maybe he was here before the buffalo," I tell him and half meaning it. For it was true that there in the first real light of having laid eyes on him, the old man's wrinkled flesh was more like dried-out hide with all the hair wore off and stained dark brown from many applications of grease and smoke and soot (it was hard to tell where his buckskins ended and his own meat began). I imagined that was how he got to be that way: leaning over so many campfires for so many years and eating greasy dog and hump ribs and antelope.

His eyes were narrow and sloped downward at the corners and his eyeballs looked like small wet brown marbles folded inside little parfleche pouches. His nose took up most of his face, and his mouth the rest.

"Maybe they was just drunk and being extra mean and didn't have anything else to do," says I, as way of answering Albert's question, for I've seen whiskey steal a man's brains before.

"I knew you would come," the Indun said of a sudden. It had the same effect on me and Albert as if the sky had up and spoke to us.

"What?" said Albert.

"I knew that you would come and save me from those men," he said.

"How?" says I.

"I had a vision of it."

"That's true," says Albert. "Indians have visions of all sorts of things before they happen."

"What tribe you with?" I asked him.

"I am of the Antelope Eaters: Comanche. My people fought the Red River war but we got rubbed out. It was the last good war for us."

I didn't see anything good about a war where you got rubbed out, but then, Induns look at things different than most everyone else.

"Why were those men trying to hang you?" Albert asked him.

41

"I am not sure. They didn't say."

"It is probably like you figured, Ivory, they was just drunk and being mean," said Albert.

"They asked me to drink their whiskey with them," said the old warrior. "At first they were pretty good about it. But after awhile, I could see they just wanted to kill another Indian. I knew there was no use fighting with them. There were too many and I had no weapons. If it had been the old days, I might have taken coup on them . . ." His voice crackled like dry twigs over a fire.

"Where'd you learn to speak such good English?" I asked, for I surely did admire any man that could speak more than one language. (The Sisters had tried their best to teach me Latin, but it was as hard as trying to crack walnuts with your teeth.)

Instead of answering my question, he sniffed the air for a time. Me and Albert sniffed, too, but neither of us detected anything unusual (although neither of us had had a bath in nearly ten days, we had grown accustomed to our own gaminess and thereby did not count ourselves as smelling unusual).

Finally satisfied as to whatever it was he was seeking out with his nose, he let his aged countenance rest on me.

"Traders taught me your language," he said. I noticed how keenly he was studying me.

"You are a *nee-gar,*" he pronounced.

I wasn't too keen on being called names, especially by a man whose life I had just helped save.

Then he smiled, shuffled forth and rubbed his hand on my hair. "The traders call you *neegar,* but you are more like the young buffalo. *Heeenah, heenah, heenah.*" He laughed through his nose and his breath had the stench of decayed teeth.

Albert laughed, too. "I think he's taking a shine to you, Ivory."

"I reckon I wouldn't mind so much if he didn't," says I.

"Buffalo Soldiers were pretty good fighters," says the Indun. "They rubbed out plenty of us people in the old days and were hard to kill. I killed one or two myself, but it wasn't easy. Later, I was sorry that I had to kill them because they were pretty brave, those men."

I didn't doubt that he done what he said he done because of the way he said it: sort of matter-of-fact, like he was describing a meal he had just eaten.

"Where's your tribe at now?" Albert asked him.

"I don't know," says he. "Last winter I walked out to die. It looked like I might. It was a pretty bad winter. Some of the people had to eat their extra moccasins. I went to sleep for a long time. Maybe I died, I don't know. But then I woke up again and they were gone. They couldn't wait to find out if I would die. That's all right, that's the way we are when it comes time for someone to die. Then an old buffalo came by where I was waiting to die and laid down and let me kill him for his meat. I made a robe out of his hide and it kept me warm. I was able to live off him the whole winter and drink the snow."

"That's a pretty incredible story," says Albert. (I had to admit, I thought it was, too.)

"Yes, maybe so," said the Indun. He didn't act like he cared one way or the other as to whether we believed him.

"My name is Albert Sand," said Albert sticking out his hand for the Indun to shake. "This here is Ivory Cade. He's my partner. What do you call yourself?"

The Indun took Albert's hand in both of his and shook it with some vigor, then he commenced to grabbing mine and doing the same.

"Before I died, I was called, Man Who Likes Horses. But now that I have gone to that other place, I am not so sure that is still my name. I guess I don't have one anymore."

Soon as he said that and realized its meaning, he let go of my hand and took on a look of a sad old hound.

"I've heard it said, that an Indian is named after something that happens when he is born, then later, he is given another name for something he is or does," said Albert. "That the way it is?"

"That is pretty much true," said the old man.

"Then it sounds like you need a new name. What have you been doing lately, since you died and come back and found your people gone?"

You could see his wet marble eyes searching for something inside his soul, the way they moved back and forth without looking at anything directly while he was thinking about Albert's question.

Finally, he shrugged his shoulders and said, "Waiting for the next winter to come. Maybe that is when I will die again."

"Then that is what we'll call you," said Albert. "Man Who Waits for Winter." The old man's visage brightened considerably at the pronouncement.

"That sounds like a good name. Now, I will eat some of your beef."

Albert and me removed our boots and plunged our feet down into the cold running water of the little tributary while Man Who Waits for Winter sat nearby sucking on a piece of jerky happy as an infant.

"You see there, Ivory," said Albert with a wide grin. "We've been gone a little more than two weeks and we've already tasted adventure. We saved that poor fellow from getting hung and at the same time, met a man who died and come back to life. I'd say that's something."

I had to admit that once I got over the notion that Otero was going to come and rescue me (if that is what it could be called), I was quickly growing to like my newfound freedom.

I liked waking up in the morning, each time in a different place, and crossing over land that I had never seen before, and leaving one place and going to another. I liked eating the rabbits we shot and cooked over an open fire and eating all that I wanted, all that there was. And, I liked sitting around the fire afterward and talking to Albert about everything that come into our heads.

I guess I knew down deep, that if we ever caught up to Rufus Buck and his gang, we was going to die a brutal hard death. I trained myself to pretty much avoid thinking about what was going to happen if we ever did catch up with Rufus Buck. But, even hard as I tried, I wasn't entirely successful a hundred percent of the time.

"What are we going to do with him?" I asked Albert, regarding Man Who Waits for Winter.

Albert glanced over his shoulder whilst chewing on one of the several hard biscuits he had produced from his saddlebags.

"We could take him along."

"Another mouth to feed," I cautioned.

"Don't look like he eats *that* much," Albert says.

"Still . . ."

"I have heard that Indians are the best trackers there is," Albert informs.

"If he's such a good tracker," I say, "then how come he couldn't find his people after he died and come back?"

"That's a real smart question, Ivory. I will ask him."

Before I could offer second thoughts about it (for I immediately wondered if asking a fellow that had died and gone to that other place and come back, might not be some sort of transgression that could get you into real trouble—spiritually speaking. I still was carrying around inside me a lot of catechism forced there by the Sisters and was thereby subject to such considerations as tampering with the world of the dead. No one of reason could blame me), Albert walked over to Man

Who Waits for Winter and says: "How come you never did find your people after you died and come back?"

Without evening blinking an eye at the question, the Indun said: "I wasn't looking for them."

"Oh," said Albert.

"The men you are looking for are not far from here," said Man Who Waits for Winter.

"What?" says Albert.

"I know that one of your people died and did not come back and that you are looking for the men that killed him. I saw it in the vision I had that told me you would come and save me from those men that tried to hang me."

Albert swallowed hard like he had a chunk of crab apple stuck in his craw. Then he turned pale and rolled his eyes until they showed mostly white.

He said to Man Who Waits for Winter: "Excuse me," and then came back over to where I was sitting.

"Did you hear that? Did you hear what he said about my pa and Rufus Buck being close to here?"

I didn't want to admit the truth to myself, even though it was staring me hard in the face: the old Indun truly must have died and crossed over to a place where he could see things normal human beings could not. Only thing was, I wished he hadn't of seen where Rufus Buck and his men had went to, or once he had, if he hadn't of said anything about it.

"There ain't no denying it, Albert," says I. "He is a strange bird with uncommon powers and I don't mind saying it gives me the spooks. I'd just as soon we

47

shake loose of him."

"You ain't afraid are you, Ivory?"

"I reckon it's more a case of being superstitious." (That might not have been the entire case, but was close enough.)

"Ivory, there is a reason, I believe, that we saved him from the hangman's rope: he's the trick card we need to catch Rufus Buck. He's got the powers to tell us where he is."

"Well leading us and helping us is two different things," I argue.

"True enough, Ivory. True enough. But, I still am going to ask him to go with us. At least until he can tell us exactly where Rufus Buck is at."

"What about Augustus Monroe and Kansas?" I ask.

"Oh, we will need every bit of Augustus Monroe," said Albert. "We'll go there first, just as we had planned, but we'll take along Man Who Waits in order to give us a leg up on our mission."

"What if he don't want to go?" I said. I was feeling as uncomfortable as a boiled dog about the prospect of traveling any farther with a man that had already died and could see things that had not happened yet. There was just something plain unnatural about it.

But Albert was just the opposite, he couldn't wait to walk over and ask Man Who Waits if he'd go along with us.

"We could stand your help in catching my pa's killers," he said.

Man Who Waits for Winter looked up through the

wrinkles of his face and said, "Do you see my horse standing over there eating grass?"

"Yes."

"Ever since I died and came back from that place, I have learned that he is my spirit guide. Wherever he takes me, is where I should be going. So far, he has taken me with you. If he wants to keep taking me with you, that is okay with me."

Albert looks my way, and I shrug my shoulders. "Well then," says Albert, "let's all get some sleep and leave at dusk."

Man Who Waits smiled broadly and lay down in the grass and went promptly to sleep.

"It's a Christian thing," says Albert just as I am myself drifting off to sleep.

"What is?" I ask.

"Taking him along with us. If we was to leave him, he'd probably die of starvation in another week."

"No, I don't believe he would," I say.

"What makes you think not, Ivory?"

"I think he would eat that old mare first," I tell him, feeling the warm soft grass beckon me. "That's why we'll probably be stuck with him the whole while—that mare will follow us to kingdom come just 'cause she won't want that Indun to eat her."

I was already sliding down into the dark funnel of sleep when I could hear Albert mutter: "You don't reckon Comanches eat humans do you, Albert?"

I never did answer, but that night I had some terrible dreams.

FIVE

Two days more, and we was in Kansas: at last! I was glad to have left the Nations with my hide intact.

We come to a town called Buffalo Jump, and it sure enough looked like salvation to three straggling souls such as ourselves. It was the first town we had seen in nearly two weeks, having preferred to skirt other such communities in the Nations for fear that we would get our throats cut, or worse.

But, we had run out of the basic provisions and had not shot a rabbit in the last two days. Even Man Who Waits for Winter was looking more gaunt than usual. Several times I saw him eyeing his worn-out moccasins with what could only be described as desire.

Our arrival was greeted by a pack of mangy hounds who barked and bayed and snapped at the fetlocks of our ponies.

"That yellow dog would taste good," said the Indun, referring to one especially ugly hound whose head was laced with old black scars. "I could knock him in the head and have him fixed up pretty quick if you wanted me to."

"No thanks," I tell him, for I have not sunk so low in my habits as to eat a cooked dog.

Then, without warning, the air around us was shattered by the crashing roar of some unknown origin. We all three laid low across our ponies' necks in an attempt to avoid disaster.

I saw the yellow dog do a cartwheel and flop dead. (I knew the Indun had uncommon powers, but not so much so that he could simply talk about killing the dog for eats and then have it happen just like that, without lifting a finger!)

The sudden event was followed by the shouting and cussing of a man wearing a stained apron who had emerged from what could only be described (as it had once been described to me by Otero Chavez after one of his return trips from Ulvade), as a bagnio. Several (again, I'm referring to Otero's vivid descriptions) painted ladies stood within the establishment's doorway.

The man's head was either shaved clean, or he was bald, and he wore garters on his sleeves. His galluses hung from his waist as though he had not finished dressing, and his trousers were punched down inside a tall pair of riding boots.

"Got damn you, Henry Shortbread, you have killed my best hound!"

Coming across from the other side of the street was a tall fellow in a plug hat wearing a dark coat with a five-point badge pinned to it. He was carrying a large pistol in his left hand; blue smoke was curling out of its barrel.

"Dutchy, I have warned you about violating the town ordinance on stray dogs." The lawman's voice had the slow deliberate drawl of a Texan, a kind of noise you ain't apt to forget once you've heard it, and if I was guessing right from what I knew about Texas

51

men, you did not want to fool with or intimidate one unless you was willing to fight. And that held double for one carrying a gun.

Some of the painted ladies standing in the doorway of the bagnio giggled and chittered among themselves like nervous parrots. They was dressed gaily in pretty bright dresses that showed much of their "charms." I must admit that my fascination was more with them than it was on the scene right in front of me.

"I vill make you pay for dis, Marshal!" declared the Dutchman.

"Then go and arm yourself now!" ordered the lawman.

Among the painted ladies was a young negro gal of light cinnamon skin and glittering black hair. She was wearing a red velvet dress and laced-up shoes and combs in her hair. And when she saw me staring at her, she tossed me looks from behind a paper fan she held up to her face.

"You are a damned son of bitch!" said the bald-headed man. I knew that the Dutchman had made a mistake by offering such an insult.

The lawman took several quick steps toward the shorter fellow, slapped him hard across the face two or three times, then laid the barrel of his nickel pistol across the man's scalp hard enough so that it sounded like a melon being thunked. The result was that the man's eyes rolled over white and blood spilled from a long gash just above his ear. He sunk to his knees, then fell over on his side next to his poor late hound.

"Some of you men clear the streets of. this h'yer trash," ordered the lawman to a group of rubber-neckers. He then took a small notepad and a stub pencil from the pocket of his coat and made an entry before replacing each.

At the sight of the bald man being laid out cold by the marshal's long-barreled pistol, several of the painted gals standing in the doorway of their establishment shrieked in unison and ducked back inside. All, except the temptress that had been peeking over her paper fan at me.

I did not know beans about women, or love, or what a fellow was supposed to do in the company of such a pretty dove, but I did know that I was feeling something I had not ever felt before and that something was a most powerful and debilitating thing. Like fire running through my blood. A sort of wild fever.

I was still staring at her when one of the other gals came and pulled her back inside.

Albert said: "Ivory, you look dumbstruck, ain't you ever seen a dog shot before, or one man lay a lick on another one's noggin?"

Man Who Waits for Winter offered a soft grin of his wide mouth and said, "Young Buffalo has had his eyes plucked by a sweet bird and he now lives in the land of the blind."

"Huh?" said Albert.

I felt the blood rush up into my temples at having been caught in my act by the old Indun.

"Heenah! Heenah! Heenah!" Man Who Waits's

laughter blew out through his large nose causing him to sound like a honking goose.

Marshal Henry Shortbread come over to where we sat our ponies and introduced himself: "I am Henry Shortbread, town marshal. I ain't never seen you fellers before so you must be strangers. It is best that you know something right off. If you have come here to make trouble or cause a disturbance, you have come to the wrong place. If you have come here to rob or to take advantage of innocent ladies, you have come to the wrong place. If you are shirkers and no-accounts or other forms of trash, you have come to the wrong place. If you are Yankee sympathizers, you have come to the wrong place."

It was quite a speech and left an impression.

"We just come to replenish our store," said Albert. I had to give Albert his due, for he was not shy or retiring even while staring into the hard, narrow face of lawman Henry Shortbread.

"How long, exactly, are you planning on being here?" asked Shortbread.

"Just long enough to buy some supplies and sleep one night in a bed," said Albert. "We are on our way to Topeka to find Augustus Monroe. I reckon you have heard of him?"

"What would a tallywacker like you be wanting Augustus Monroe for?" The Texan's voice was as hard and sharp as a flint arrowhead; it sort of prickled my skin when he spoke.

"You've heard of Rufus Buck and his bunch?" said Albert.

"Low nigger dogs!" he declared, squinting at me in a hard uncaring manner that let me know he didn't give a spit about my feelings as to the use of the word *nigger* and that if I was to set up a protest, he'd be willing to give me the same treatment as he had given the Dutchman. Some men are easy to dislike. I found him to be one.

"That still don't tell me what a pair of children and an old buck Indian are doing in my town," insisted Shortbread.

"It was Rufus Buck and his men who murdered my pa fourteen days ago and left me an orphan and my mother a widow. Ivory here, and this Comanche and I, are on our way to Topeka to hire Mr. Monroe in order to find the Buck gang and bring them to justice."

Marshal Henry Shortbread let out a howl that sounded like the sharp barking of a dog. It was the sort of laugh that made you wish you hadn't heard it.

Soon as he was done enjoying himself at our expense, Marshal Shortbread narrowed his eyes in looking at us.

"Well now, that ought to be some posse: two kids, a hundred-year-old Comanche, and a half-blind drunk!"

Albert said: "You should not cast aspersions on them who ain't here to defend themselves." Albert could be well-spoke when he chose to be, just like his ma.

"Don't get sassy with me, boy!"

"No sir, wasn't meant that way!" said Albert, but I could tell that it was, and so could the marshal, I believe.

The lawman took a small brass watch from his pocket, snapped open its lid, and studied its face.

"It is past two now, I expect you to be gone before daybreak. I don't want to have to wake up and see any of your faces in my town. You look like trouble to me." Then he put the watch back in his pocket and walked on down the street just like we wasn't any more concern to him than soap and water was to a miner.

"That man has the grumpiness of a badger," said Man Who Waits. "My sister was once married to a man like that. He would go around causing everybody trouble and could not get along with anyone. He would wake up in a bad mood and go to sleep in a bad mood and stay in a bad mood all the time. He was pretty mean, too. Everybody was afraid of him except me. But because he was married to my sister, I did not say or do anything to him for a long time.

"But then finally, I grew tired of his business and I waited for him one day to go squat in the bushes. When he did, I went and caught a rattlesnake and tossed it down there where he was squatting. It bit him in a pretty bad place. He came close to dying because of it, but I did not feel bad about it. After that, he left us people and disappeared. Maybe he died and has come back as that man," he said, pointing toward Marshal Shortbread.

There was a brief silence among us while we considered the possibility. It had got so that anymore, neither me nor Albert questioned some of Man Who Waits's logic or views on matters. Too often, he had proved to be right.

"What do you reckon he meant in calling Mr. Monroe a half-blind drunk?" says I, for it gave me no comfort to suspect that our waiting hero was flawed.

"Don't know," says Albert, "other than Mr. Shortbread is a hardcase with a bad sense of humor." A man that would shoot another man's dog, would find no difficulty in laying a cloud on another man's reputation. At least not in my book, he wouldn't. We would learn later that it was common practice for frontier marshals to earn extra money (twenty-five cents apiece was the usual going rate) for shooting stray dogs. Augustus Monroe also supplemented his income from this practice, as did Bill Hickok, and Wyatt Earp in other years.

"Maybe we have stepped in it," I say.

"Maybe so," said Albert. "But right now, we must concern ourselves with gaining fresh supplies, a good meal, and a place to sleep for the night."

We bought our supplies easy enough. I bought two more cans of peaches and was now down to only eight one-dollar bills left in my shoe.

We found a livery run by a one-armed man and Albert paid him one dollar and fifty cents to feed and water our horses and put them out in his corral until our return. He did not say a word to us, but took our money in his only hand and went about his business.

Albert said that we should forgo eating in a restaurant because of the expense. I still wonder to this day, if it wasn't his way of avoiding me and Man Who Waits further embarrassment than what we had already suffered at the hands of Marshal Shortbread, because many of the restaurants of that day had signs clearly posted: NO COLOREDS OR INDIANS SERVED IN THIS ESTABLISHMENT! NO EXCEPTIONS!

Instead, Albert went into a butcher shop and come out with a package of sliced blood sausage, some cheese and crackers. We went into an alley and ate until everything was gone. We was all pretty well worn out afterward and put our backs against the wall of a vacant building and took siestas there in the warm late sun.

I fell right to dreaming about the negro gal I had spotted in the doorway of the bagnio.

By the time we awoke, it had grown dark and the air cool.

Albert suggested that since we was planning on staying the night, we might just as well walk around and see the sights. I made it a point to suggest we start off in the direction of the sporting house where I had seen the gal I had spent that afternoon dreaming about.

Albert grinned like a possum and said: "Ivory, you are as bold as brass and more than I expected."

On our way, we passed several saloons that were

doing a lively business, and once or twice we paused in the open doorways in order to bear witness to the activities within. In one, a place called the Alhambra Club, we saw a man wearing a bulldog on top of his head.

We reached the bagnio, and the hard clinking of piano keys greeted our ears. Man Who Waits for Winter asked what made that noise. Neither Albert or me could explain a piano.

The door was open and the air greeting us from within was warm and thick with cigar smoke. We could hear the clack of a roulette wheel and the gay laughter of several gals. I strained to see if I could spot *her:* the honey-skinned dove of earlier that day.

She was sitting on the lap of a man wearing a tall-crowned hat and a long walrus mustache. He looked pale in the kerosene light. They looked like they was having a swell time together and my heart sank down into my boots, a lump pressed into my throat.

She was pretty as a picture and had a heart-shaped mouth and large sweet eyes. I could see her knees because of the short fancy dress she wore, and my own knocked together.

Something about that gal had a hold of me. Her hair was long and black and straight. When she laughed, her teeth showed white against her red mouth. I could not stand the thought that she was now in the arms of a drunken cowboy. It was the first time I ever tasted the bitter bile of jealousy.

Before we could stop him, Man Who Waits for

Winter stepped inside. Nobody bothered noticing him for they were all too busy having a good time.

"We better get him," said Albert.

I wasn't opposing the idea if it would bring me closer to her.

Somehow, the old Indun just disappeared into the crowd and smoke that filled up the entire room, wall to wall.

"You go that way, I'll go this," said Albert.

I soon, too, got lost in among that bunch of celebrators. The next thing I know, there she stands, right in front of me.

"You sure are a purty-looking thing," she says in an all breathless sort of way. "And a man of color, too. My my."

I nearly lost my balance.

"What's a child like you doin' in a den of sin like this," says she, sidling up close enough I could smell the rosewater on her. (It had the familiarity of that comely scent of Otero used to come riding home from Ulvade with.)

I could not find my tongue.

"What's the matter, honey? Cat got your tongue?" She was now standing so close, her breath was warm on my face. Warm and sweet as lilacs on a summer evening.

"If you've got yourself a dollar, you could buy me a drink," she breathed, for now, her words were low and whispery, more like she was breathing them out than saying them.

"My name's Charity," she said. "What's yours?"

"Ivory," I finally managed.

"Well now, ain't that a funny name for a boy as black as you." Her laugh was like the tinkling of small bells. Then, she kissed me on the cheek and said, "I think it's a sweet name and unusually handsome. I like the way it sounds. *Ivory.*"

She took my hand and asked again would I buy her a drink. I was about to take the money out of my shoe—my last eight dollars and buy her all the drinks that eight dollars would buy in a place like this when suddenly appeared the cowboy I had seen her with.

"Charity, what ya' doin' with this here colored boy?"

He was a tall stringy fellow pretty well liquored up and he spoke through his teeth as a way of showing me he was tough and not one to be fooled with.

"Ain't doin' nothin' but what I want to be doin'," she told him, and I admired her grit in the way she gave it back to him.

"Don't give me sass, girl!" he said, taking hold of her by one arm.

She hissed and kicked him in both legs and commenced to fighting him like a wildcat he had reached in a dark hole and grabbed a hold of without expecting to.

But, he was a big cuss and soon had her well wrapped up and began his rough ways on her by cussing and calling her cruel names.

I never did know that I had it in me to jump to another's defense (not including when Albert and me saved the Indun from hanging, and that was mostly at Albert's insistence), but I could not simply stand by and watch this cowboy take unwanted liberties with the girl that had stolen my senses.

Before I could even think it, I was giving it to him in the ribs with both fists. It did the trick, for he turned her loose and turned all his attention on me.

She said: "Hit him a good lick, Ivory!" It screwed up my courage to hear her say that. I popped him a quick one to the jaw and it felt like I had struck rock. "Hit him again, honey!" Charity cried out. So I give him another lick and staggered him some.

But the results were not what I hoped for, for he simply rubs his jaw, gives me a grin, and wades into me all arms and elbows and big bony knuckles.

We crashed to the floor and a good bit of eye-gouging, knee-kicking, arm-twisting, ear-biting, and name calling ensued, me now fighting not so much for Charity's honor as my own survival.

We each had our cheering sections, the cowboy and me. His, mostly drunken men in big hats and tall boots and wide neckerchiefs such as he wore himself. To my credit, there was Charity shouting and hopping up and down, Albert, and Man Who Waits.

"You don't need to just stand there!" I yell out, for the cowboy was now on top of me slapping my head this way and that. Whiskey had stolen his brains and turned him into a demon of uncommon strength.

Albert and the Indun can see he is getting the best of me and finally join in and when they do, the cowboy's cheering section commence to join in as well. Now, instead of suffering one cowboy on top of me, I have several; the Indun and Albert included.

Two loud bangs of a pistol and everyone gives up the fight.

I find myself looking up into the stormy countenance of Marshal Henry Shortbread.

"I knew you was trouble the minute I laid eyes on you three. Now you have gone and bought yourselves a bad time!"

Welcome to Buffalo Jump and Kansas, I say to myself.

SIX

A frontier jail is a depressing place to be. Marshal Shortbread's proved to be one big room with bars and no bunks and plenty of other troublemakers such as me and Albert and the Indun (although I do not believe for one minute that men who would jump to the aid of an abused woman should be labeled trouble-makers).

"You'll stand hearing before Judge Puddymaker in the morning for disturbing of the peace. I hope you boys brought money with you 'cause Buffalo Jump ain't no good town to be found disturbing the peace in and Judge Puddymaker ain't no friend of the malcontent!" He had that seesaw laugh that could be heard even after he closed the iron door on us.

Man Who Waits for Winter seemed in wonderment of having been placed in the "can."

"This is the first time I have ever been locked up," says he. "I can see how a man would not care for it too much."

Several of our criminal brethren were drunks and vagrants who Marshal Shortbread had rounded up before he got us. Most were curled up on the floor asleep or trying to be.

Albert went to the one small window that looked outward to the night and wrapped his fingers around the bars that kept us from our freedom.

For the first time since the burying of his pap, I seen that sad, sad look wash over him. I couldn't help but believe that it was because of my own foolishness that we had landed in this new trouble.

Man Who Waits found himself a spot on the floor large enough for him to take up residence and settled in like some old hound that had found him a pretty good spot to lie down.

I went over and stood next to Albert.

"I'm sorry I got you and the Indun locked up," I say.

For a long time he just stared out at the night, at the many stars that streaked the heavens.

"I was just thinking about my ma," he said at last with a sigh. "Pa's dead and she's alone and I'm here. Two weeks ago and we was all sitting down to supper together. Now, we're as scattered as leaves in the wind."

His talk had a lonesomeness to it, like the howl of a coyote, or the whistle of a train passing through the night.

"I think about Pa lying in that cold dark grave all alone," he said. I could see it in my mind, Mr. Sand and the pitiful way he had met his end and where he was forever going to be up on that little rise lying in the ground with the wind sweeping over the grass above him.

Albert's lonesome words fell on me like a cold rain and chilled me to the bone. I tried to think hard of something good to say to him, something to lift his spirits, and my own.

"Albert, the Latins had a saying," I tell him. (Of course the Latins had a lot of sayings. They was famous for their sayings, and I figured I ought to be able to remember at least one the Sisters had learned me—one that might bring some cheer and hope to our predicament.)

He rolled his eyes round toward me. "Don't try to cheer me up, Ivory, I don't think it can be done."

"Caveat emptor," I said with a firmness of knowing something important, for it was the only Latin phrase I could remember from all my long days of schooling in that large stone room with the icy cold floors in the wintertime and the gray light coming through the high windows. There ain't nothing harder, I believe, than trying to study Latin or learn the ways of ciphering when a body is cold and always hungry.

"What's that mean, caveat emptor?" he said, only somewhat curious.

"Well . . . it means . . . in a loose sort of way, that

darkness falls on the poor man as well as the rich, but so does the sunshine."

"Huh?"

"Yes sir, when times is at their worst, they can only get better!"

"Those Latins were pretty smart people, were they?"

"Smart as they come," I say. "They were known for their ability to think."

"Caveat emptor," says Albert, rolling the words out of his mouth in a soft easy manner. "Caveat emptor. That's a pretty good saying." Course, I didn't have the heart to tell him I wasn't so sure that caveat emptor meant anything like what I had just said it meant. But, what did it matter as long as Albert took some cheer from it.

We found us places on the floor amongst the sleeping, snoring, scratching, grunting populace and hunkered down with our hands tucked between our knees and our hats for pillows.

Again, I dreamt of Charity. We was riding a white horse together through fields of ambrosia where the air smelled of honeysuckle and she had her arms around my waist and the wind was lifting her hair and the horse was rocking slow beneath us.

It was as swell a dream as a fellow could hope for but it all come to a crashing end when Marshal Short-bread come marching through the cell area banging his tin coffee cup off every single one of the bars that held us within.

"Rise and shine my darlings!" he calls. I notice how

his dark curling mustache rides the corners of his mouth like a wooly worm clutching to his face and the cocky manner in which he has his hat tipped back.

Clang! Clang! Clang! Clang! Back and forth he raps his cup until all are on their feet.

I can see by every eye, other than Albert's, the Indun's, and my own, that these men are still suffering the effects of hard liquor and low living from the previous night. It ain't likely there's a married man among the bunch. They are all bachelors.

I spot the Dutchman uncurling up from the floor, still holding his head from where Marshal Shortbread laid the barrel of his big pistol there. A considerable knot has formed just above the Dutchman's ear and old dried blood painted a painful sign of the violence the man had suffered.

Shortbread opens the door with a twist of his key and herds us out to where a deputy, a man whose belly hangs over his belt, stands with a double-barreled shotgun lying in the crook of his fat arms.

Shortbread makes us stand all in line until the last of us is ready and then he and the deputy march us across the street for our destiny with Judge Puddymaker.

The judge's court is set up right there in the bagnio where me and Albert and the Indun got arrested. Only now, it is a quiet, solemn little house where the heavy velvet drapes are pulled back so that light may find its way into the room and spread itself over the large Brussels carpet and unto the little table that the judge sits behind. The table has carved legs and clawed feet.

At his left hand, a Bible five inches thick and gold leafed. At his right, a gavel of hard maple, big enough to cave in a man's head.

We are marched to a corner of the room and one by one called before Judge Puddymaker. He has glorious white hair and plenty of it flowing from a pretty large head whose face is round as a harvest moon. He has resting eyes that give the appearance he is bored with the proceedings. His coat is of black broadcloth.

Marshal Shortbread goes and stands next to the judge and one by one, calls out our names:

"Red Carson, step to the front!"

A man with red hair steps forward.

"Charged with drunkness, you honor," says Marshal Shortbread.

"How do you plead to the charge?" says the judge.

"Not guilty, sir," says the prisoner.

That got the judge's attention, for he lifts up them heavy eyelids of his revealing watery blue eyes that bug out like a frog's, and glares hard at the man before him.

"Not guilty?"

"Yes sir. I wasn't drunk, I was just drinking."

"You was raising hell and drinking," declared Shortbread. "In this town, that's the behavior of a drunk."

"Guilty!" said the judge and slammed down his gavel so that the sound of it rang in our ears sharp as pistol fire.

"Ten dollar fine for being drunk, and ten more for perjury!"

"But . . ." The man had no time for protest, for the fat deputy come over and stuck the end of the shotgun in his ribs and said, "Move out."

Then, Judge Puddymaker looked at the rest of us and said: "I hope you all have learned not to lie to this court for I won't feel generous long—it is too hot a day! Next man!"

Marshal Shortbread called out names, one by one, and those that stepped forward entered only one plea: Guilty as charged. They were fined (mostly five or ten dollars) and led away.

Just before me and Albert and the Indun were called up, Shortbread called his old friend the Dutchman forward and he came meekly.

"What's the charge?" said the judge.

"Assaulting a peace officer and resisting arrest," said Marshal Shortbread.

"He kilt my hound!" declared the Dutchman.

"Did you shoot Dutchy's dog, officer Shortbread?" asked the judge.

"Did, your honor. He was a stray and running loose with a pack of other strays. And as such, fell under the ordinance that prohibits strays within the city limits. I shot him and expect to collect on him as I do others."

"Dutchman," said the judge in a kindly way. "Does that gal what calls herself Hootchy Kootchy Sal still ply her trade here in your establishment?"

"Yas, she is upstairs right now, I believe. Her and the udder girls, probably still sleeping."

The judge lifted his head up toward the second floor and the several doors that lined up behind the banister there. Each had a brass number plate on it and I wondered which one was Charity's room.

Finally, after a short time of quiet reflection, the judge taps down his gavel lightly and orders that the Dutchman be set free and no fine given because he's a local and honest businessman that provides the male citizenry with a good and needed service to say nothing of lending his establishment for the purpose of holding court.

Marshal Shortbread and the Dutchman exchange angry looks but nothing more is said.

"You three, step forward!" Shortbread yells out. Albert, me, and the Indun do as told.

Judge Puddymaker looks at Albert and me and states: "They ain't nothing but boys, Shortbread. What the hell are they doing in my court? And who is this Indian and what's he got to do with things?"

Shortbread tries to explain the row we were into with the cowboys, tells it mostly from the cowboys' point of view as far as I was concerned.

"That correct?" says Judge Puddymaker. "You and this Indun jump on a cowboy and beat his head in?"

At first we are all tongue-tied, but then I cannot stand it anymore and have to tell the truth of it, the part about how we was protecting the honor of one of the girls.

"Which one?" asks the judge.

"A girl named Charity," I tell him.

"Charity," says he with a great sigh. "I had almost forgotten about that lovely child."

"Yes sir, your honor," I tell him. "That cowboy was insulting her and pulling on her arm and that's when I let him have it and the row began."

"That true, Shortbread? That what started the ruckus?"

"Don't know, Judge. All's I know is that when I first laid eyes on this trio, I knowed they was trouble. I am convinced that they are."

"Well someone go on upstairs and bring that winsome child forth to stand as witness to this court." We all waited holding our breaths as the fat deputy climbed the long staircase, knocked on several doors, and then come back down again with Charity in tow.

She was wearing a plain cotton dress that showed neither her shoulders or her knees like the one she had been wearing the night before. She had red ribbons in her hair. Marshal Shortbread cast her a hard look of warning.

"Charity," said the judge in the softest manner.

"Howdy do, Judge," she says with a happy smile on her face.

"Charity, these fellows here, that colored boy in particular, says he was defending your honor last night from a rough cowboy—that true?"

Charity then looked my way for the first time since she smiled and kissed me on the cheek and asked me to buy her a drink of whiskey not more than ten hours earlier.

"Oh, yes, Judge. He was right brave and manly in going up against that big of boot of a drover. Why, that puncher grabbed hold of my arm and began pulling me when Ivory here jumped on him like nobody's business. Gave it to him good, too!" She smiled so sweetly at me I thought my heart was going to pound out of my chest.

The judge leaned back in his chair and ran his fingers through the thatch of long white hair. In so doing, his gaze wandered over Charity's beauty like an old buffalo searching for sweet grass.

"I only get through here once a month, Shortbread," he declared, sitting up straight again and finally taking his eyes off (my sweetheart?) Charity.

"Once the business of this court is conducted, I expect, like every other unattached male, that I am able to take some pleasure and relaxation during the remainder of my stay here. It is up to you to see that the gals of Dutchy's establishment, as well as all others of its nature, are protected from the assaults and insults of cowboys and other low types—is that understood!"

Shortbread leveled his hard stare at me and Charity, for our testimony had put him into a box and made him seem unreliable, either as a lawman, or a witness.

Judge Puddymaker rapped his maple gavel down hard and declared: "Case dismissed! Clear the courtroom!" And, "Bar's open for business!"

Albert shook my hand and the Indun gave a bored smile.

"Charity, would you come have a drink with an old man?" said the Judge. "You boys don't mind do you?" he asked without expecting none of us to answer that we would and then took her by the arm and led her over to the bar. It was only nine in the morning!

Marshal Shortbread brushed by us and said: "Leave town if you know what's good for you!"

"We've worn out our welcome," said Albert.

I reckoned we had. Charity tossed me a final longing look as me and Albert and the Indun walked through the doors of the Dutchman's bagnio.

I turned one last time and read the little sign that had been tacked up above the door.

COLOREDS, INDIANS, CHINAMEN, WOMEN & HORSES NOT WELCOME!

That pretty much seemed to sum up the flavor of Buffalo Jump.

SEVEN

We met the preacher halfway to Newton. He was wearing only his underdrawers and was walking. We reined up out of kindness—a man afoot on the prairie, wearing only his underdrawers, is an unusual and pitiful sight in anybody's book.

"Hello brother," he says, smiling in a pleasant enough way. He had a pretty harsh cough as well. *Consumption,* thinks I, for I had seen folks with it before, either that or he has caught a chill from being improperly dressed.

He was slab sided and gangly, had the eyes of a young man, but looked altogether older because of the deep lines that creased his face like furrows in a field and the lank silver hair that splayed about his head. He was also barefooted.

"I could use a drink of water if you have any?" he said.

Albert, being the kindest of the bunch reached down and unwrapped his canteen from where he kept it tied to his saddle horn and handed it over to the man.

"Kind of a long ways from nowhere to be walking," says Albert in that curious manner that is his.

"Is indeed, friend," says the man as he gulps down about half the water in Albert's canteen. Then, he looks at the Indun and myself and gives us each a kindly smile.

"Truth of it is," he says, "road agents come up on me and plucked me clean as a chicken. They even took my Bible. What is this world coming to?"

None of us knew.

He swallowed some more of Albert's water, said, "I don't suppose you boys would be toting anything stronger in the way of drink?"

"You mean liquor?" said Albert.

"Yes son, that is what I mean."

"No sir," says Albert.

"Well, that is just how my day has been going," says the man. "Name's July Sunshine—preaching's my profession," and he sticks out a hand with long bony fingers for us to shake. We do, all around, including

Man Who Waits, who, as I have said earlier, enjoys the activity.

"I'm Albert Sand, this is Ivory Cade, and that there is Man Who Waits for Winter. He is a Comanche, of the Antelope Eating band."

"Well, pleased to make your acquaintances," says the preacher. I can see him eyeing our pistols which we wear butt-forward sticking out of our belts. But, he makes no fuss over it.

"How far you reckon it is till the next town?" asks Mr. Sunshine.

"Next town's Newton, mister," says Albert. "I guess twenty or so miles."

The preacher stares out toward the horizon for a good long spell and says: "That's quite a ways. I was hoping for something closer."

Albert said, "Did you get a good look at those fellows that robbed you? Was one of them a big black fellow with an ugly scar across his face?"

"No," said the preacher. "They were white men with freckles, redheaded—looked like maybe they could have been brothers. There were three of them, not much older than you and him," he indicated nodding toward me. "But mean cusses none the same—some are born that way, no accounting for why, they just are." His gaze drew up to the sky as though he was looking for the answer.

"I had taken a morning break from the tribulations of this world, and was reading a chapter of the good book under the only cottonwood I could find when they appeared out of nowhere—like as though they come up out of the very grass itself."

"They must have been truly low of character to have robbed a preacher," said Albert with a sad shake of his head.

"They was son, they surely was. Left me near naked, as you can see. Would've taken even my under-drawers I suspect, except as you can see, they are worn thin and faded out and not much good—even to thieves."

"Which way did they go?" I ask. (And as soon as I did, I knew I shouldn't have, for what business of it was mine?)

"Oh, they went right that way," he said, pointing in the direction we had been heading, Newton.

"Well, hop aboard," said Albert, "you don't mind riding double?"

"No son, I don't mind," said the preacher, and off we went to Newton. Not unlike Buffalo Jump in most respects, Newton was a town of wide dusty streets and businesses—mostly established to serve the cowboys who drove in the herds to the railheads there—and little else.

It rose up out of the prairie—a clutter of buildings, a haven from the lonesomeness that was Kansas (and still is, in my book).

We must have been a sight to the citizens of that town: two boys, an Indun, and a near-naked preacher. But none the same, we did not let our appearance dis-suade us. For we were on a mission.

Two women in large calico bonnets paused long enough to watch us and whisper to each other. A man riding a mule swiveled his head around in order to give us a good stare.

"Put in at that saloon yonder," said Sunshine. "I could stand a libation. I'll stand you boys a drink as well for your kindness."

"I thought you was robbed?" I say. (Some of Albert's curiosity was beginning to wear off on me.)

He offers me a knowing smile and says, "I've a bit of paper money pinned to the inside of these here drawers—rainy day money. I reckon this is a rainy day."

The Indun looks skyward but can't understand why he sees no rain.

"Well," says Albert, "I reckon that'd be all right with us, if you was to stand us a drink." Then, he turns and winks my way. All I knew about whiskey was what I had seen left in the disconsolate face of Otero upon his return trips from Ulvade. That, and the way it could get some men to kill each other—like the cowboy in Buffalo Jump that had tried bashing my brains out on the floor of the bagnio.

Remembering the incident instantly caused me to remember Charity as well. Her beauty washed behind my eyes like cool water. I promised myself someday I'd write a poem about her.

The sight of us hardly raised a stir inside of Ned Apple's Cattlemen's Club. It made me wonder what they *had* been used to seeing.

The preacher discreetly unpinned several bills from inside his union suit and ordered us all a whiskey. I said make mine a beer figuring that it might do less damage to my sensibilities than straight up whiskey. Albert stood fast on hard stuff, and the Indun said he'd have one of each. It all came to two dollars which the preacher peeled off and slapped down on the bar.

I must admit that my first taste of iced beer came as a pleasant surprise and that I have never since lost my liking for it. It cut the dust in my mouth right away and had a calming effect on me overall.

"You ain't cowboys," said the barman, pouring himself out three fingers' worth of whiskey into a short glass.

He could have said anything. He could have asked the preacher why he didn't have any clothes on but his union suit, or what was we doing with an old Indun, or why was *they* traveling with a colored boy, or who we were in general and where did we come from. But instead, all he said was: "You ain't cowboys," and then walked down to the other end of the bar to enjoy his juice.

"Well," said the preacher. "One thing I will say about Newton, Kansas, it sure ain't a place of busybodies."

We took our refreshments to a table in a quiet corner of the establishment and watched a game of monte being played by several men at another table. There was a warm and pleasant feeling about being inside a saloon, a place where a man might relax and let the world pass by him and not worry so much that it did. I was beginning to understand the attraction of such places as saloons, bagnios, and other establishments of low repute. Places where men could enjoy themselves and one another's company. Places safe from decent women, small children, and the righteous.

We lingered less than an hour, for Preacher said what little of the paper money he had left he needed to buy clothes to put on his back and shoes on his feet.

Albert said we should be going anyway, because Topeka wasn't getting any closer by us just sitting in a saloon and cooling our heels.

Preacher thanked us for carrying him to Newton and said he wished us well in our journey. We walked outside into the sharp glare of midday sun and Preacher offered to shake our hands once more there on the sidewalk. Man Who Waits was the first one to stand in line and shook Preacher's hand like he was trying to remove it from his arm.

Then Albert, then me. But he never finished with me, for he stopped of a sudden and said: "I'll be goddamned!"

"What?" said Albert.

"There's them three red-haired sons of bitches that waylaid me on the road!"

We all turned to see. All we caught were the heels of men entering what looked like a parlor house several hundred yards down the street.

"What are you going to do?" asked Albert.

I wanted to know that one myself: one man in his

underdrawers going up against a trio of redheaded brothers. (I only knew one red-haired person in my entire life, and that was a gal by the name of Pedora Osborn who lived there in the orphanage in Dallas. Pedora was what you would call hateful mean and homely to boot. In her case, I pretty much came to the conclusion that one went hand in hand with the other as far as she was concerned. She could outbox any boy in the school, and other gals shrieked and ran off for safety whenever she came near. She was eventually adopted by a stern, but rich man and his large-eyed wife from Pittsburgh and taken off to live the life of the pampered. At least that was the story that haunted her departure. Was none of us unhappy that she was adopted and taken away.)

That's what I knew of white people with red hair: they was unpleasant to deal with.

"Give me your pistols!" said the preacher. Me and Albert traded looks.

"Well, I can't very well go up against them three in just my union suit," he cried. "I'll need your pistols!"

Before we could protest or give it any real thought, he plucked the Navies from our waistbands and was off down the street, his bare feet spanking up the dust as he went.

"What do you think?" said Albert.

"I think that fellow ain't everything he represents himself to be," say I. "For what religious man do you know, would speak so profane, steal our pistols, and seek revenge on his fellow man with the flap of his union suit half undone and no shoes on his feet?"

The Indun stood there smiling that half smile of his like as though life was growing personally more pleasant for him by the moment.

"It is good to see that there are still some warriors among your people," says he. "For a long time, I thought we Comanche had killed all of them. *Heenah! Heenah! Heenah!*" It was not a mirthful laugh so much as it was the sound of a punctured windbag (I described it previously as sounding like honking geese, but I may have been too poetic in my description).

We had not hardly time to think when the pop and bang and crack of pistol fire sounded from the parlor house quickly followed by a rush of humanity from within: gentlemen in shirttails, ladies in their bloomers—or less—and members of a five-piece band toting their instruments. They was hot-footing down the street like the devil was on their heels.

More gunfire! More high-stepping souls seeking sanctuary!

"He's killing them all!" shouts Albert as a bare-shouldered blonde runs past holding her shoes in one hand and her corset in the other. I can't help but notice she has sky-blue eyes and a small dark mole on her right cheek. (Sister Pious back at the orphanage often commented to her fellow Sisters that I possessed uncommon powers of observation. "Blessed in an odd way," she referred to me.)

Suddenly there is a crash of window glass, a man

riding a shower of slivers out through the front of the establishment. He has red hair: one of the brothers that the preacher has gone to seek justice on.

He lands on the boardwalk, his clothes in ribbons, his hide bloody from the glass. He staggers around a bit like a horse that has been clubbed in the head and then drops to his knees, no doubt stunned beyond redemption.

A couple more pops of the pistols from within, and then all falls quiet. A quiet so great, we all can hear ourselves breathe. It stays like that for maybe a full minute before the preacher comes charging through the doors, his hands full of clothes and hats and boots (some of which is stained bloody).

He pauses briefly before the red-haired man that took the window exit and even from where we are standing, we can hear him say: "If them are your kin inside, I'm sorry. They left me no choice. They were foolish men to begin with and have paid the fool's price for their wanton ways."

Then he paused long enough to take good stock of the bloody fellow kneeling before him and said: "You don't look so well but better'n them inside, considering. I reckon we are even."

Then the bloody fellow looks up at the preacher and says back: "Do you know who you have just shot all to ribbons?"

"No," says Preacher. "Who?"

With great and painful effort, the bloody man spits out: "Ray and Elrod Flymaster. Me, I'm Billy Flymaster. Our daddy's the county sheriff, Red Flymaster! Dangerous Red Flymaster, most folks call him! He'll hunt you down and cut your head off and hang it on a pole for what you did to us!"

I can see how the announcement has no effect whatsoever on the preacher.

"Never heard of him," says he, pulling on a pair of trousers from among the bundle of clothes he is carrying.

"You will . . . you son of a . . ." The man bent double and let out a great moan of pain and studied the streamers of blood flowing from nearly every part of him.

Then the preacher, having put on a shirt, a battered hat, and a pair of tall boots, leaned down to the man and in a kindly, near whisper, said: "I hope this experience has been a lesson to you about your outlaw leanings. It is not too late to change your ways."

With that, he strolls over to us and hands us back our pistols. I notice the barrels are still warm from the shooting.

"You better find yourself a good horse and git," warns Albert.

"Oh, why's that?" says he.

"Because Red Flymaster is about the second most dangerous man in all of Kansas and it sounds like you just pruned his family tree by a good bit."

"*Second* most dangerous?"

"Augustus Monroe is number one. Ivory and me and the Indun are on our way to Topeka to meet with him.

But I was you, I wouldn't tarry around here. From what I read of Red Flymaster, he is meaner than anybody and would not hesitate to shoot a man in the back, and once shot a man who was sitting in a privy."

"Well, from what you have told me, Albert, I reckon to avoid further violence and seeing's how the score has been settled, I best take your advice and leave this place."

"I think it would be a good idea, Preacher."

"That was some show," said the Indun with a pleasant smile on his aged face. "I would have given two ponies to have been in there with you when the shooting started."

"It was all hell and brimstone, Chief," said the preacher. "Lead was flying everywhere . . ."

"We better git!" I say, for the last thing I want to see, if what Albert has stated is true, is Red Flymaster coming out of nowhere and turning us all into crow bait, or (if what Albert also says is true), filling up the bottom of a privy with our remains.

"You mind if I tag along for a ways?" says Preacher of a sudden.

"No, not at all," says Albert. "We can always use another man."

"For what?" says Preacher.

"I'll tell you on the way. Right now you better round up some sort of horse to ride."

Oh Lord! We are beginning to seem like a traveling side show.

EIGHT

We camped that night on Cottonwood Creek, me, the Indun, Preacher, and Albert. It was pitch-black, the sky was, and full of faraway stars but no moon. It was the kind of lonely night that is common on the prairie. We gathered cow chips and built them into a fire and threw our blankets and saddles onto the ground for our beds.

We'd had no time to buy provisions in Newton due to the unfortunate circumstances between Preacher and the Flymaster brothers. That name: Dangerous Red Flymaster, still haunted my thoughts, for all that afternoon's ride, Albert proceeded to go into great detail about his knowledge of Red Flymaster's notorious background (as revealed to him in old issues of *Police Gazette* and *Harper's Weekly* that his pa used to bring home).

"He once bit off a man's nose for delivering an insult to Dangerous Red's mistress," offered Albert earlier that afternoon in his litany on the gunfighter.

"And killing for little cause is nothing foreigner to him, nor is hanging suspects without a legal trial. The Police Gazette referred to Red Flymaster as a Walking One Man Jury!"

"And now you've gone and killed some of his people," said Man Who Waits with a soft smile of satisfaction. "It is a good thing to take revenge on an enemy's people. It has a way of stealing the thunder from his heart."

"Well, Red Flymaster don't mean squat to me," said Preacher. "And though I regret having laid them two boys low and leaving the other in poor condition, it was of their own doing, calling down the calamity upon themselves. All I can do now is pray for them—the living and the dead."

It was dark and unwelcome talk that I heard swirl around our little camp that night. I longed to be in Charity's arms, surrounded by her warm sweet breath. Her swarthy beauty visited me there in the darkness of night with the yellow lick of flames dancing up off that pile of dried cow dung (not as unpleasant a scent as you might think, a burning cow flop).

I imagined her and I off somewheres private, just the two of us—a picnic, maybe. We'd be feasting on fried chicken and potato salad and pickled eggs and fresh pie and buttermilk. And afterward, we lay on our backs and give names to the shapes the clouds made.

Then, after a long while of holding back, we'd be in each other's arms and her sweet kisses would rain down on my face like warm sugar rain . . .

"Ivory!"

The sudden urgent sound of my name caused me to blink away my thoughts of Charity and me. It was Albert, leaning over and asking me was I all right.

"You look like you was struck dumb," says he.

Then, when I rolled my eyes round toward him, he grins wide and says, "You was thinking about that colored gal back in Buffalo Jump. The one that testified on our behalf."

I denied nothing, but said instead, "I hope that Red Flymaster has not found out about today!"

The Indun stared across the fire at me, his small wet eyes catching all the light of the yellow flames like there was a tiny fire burning inside each one.

"He won't be no good now until he gets a chance to be with a woman. I have seen young men of my own band with that same look as he has."

I feel like I want to swallow up the night and disappear inside myself 'cause the old warrior is getting under my skin with the truth of his words and letting everybody know in the process what I'm thinking in a private way.

Such talk leads to a general discussion between the Indun and the preacher about boys and men and women, most especially of women of stained reputations.

"I must confess," said Preacher, "that I was as young as these two companions of ours the first time I ever did taste of the carnal flesh."

I am not sure the Indun understood the preacher's words, but by the keen look in his beady eyes, he sure understood the gist of what the preacher was saying.

"She was a three-toed gal over in Ellsworth. Mowing accident while still a little girl, she said. Part of the reason she left her daddy's farm in Indiana and ran off to the West. She smelled like lilacs and had cornsilk hair and knew everything there was to know about pleasing a man." The preacher leaned back across his saddle and gnawed on a piece of beef jerky and stared up at the faraway stars as he talked.

"At the time, I did not know a thing about women. She taught me everything. She was the kindest sweetest soul I ever met on this earth. It cost me a dollar to have my eyes opened to the ways of the world. And even though I no longer indulge in such sinful behavior—except on occasion when the flesh grows weak—I still think of her with love in my heart."

"What was her name?" asks Albert.

"Madam Blue, but some called her Three-Toed Alice, a cruel appellation by rough men that did not understand the kindness of her soul."

Preacher gave a great sigh, then looked over at the Indun, and said, "What was the first woman you knowed, Chief?"

Man Who Waits leaned forward, warming his brown hands near the fire and smiled broad enough to show the remnants of what few teeth he still possessed. They were as yellowed and curved as those of a horse.

"Her name was Wandering Mouse and she was big and fat but I didn't care. I remember that us boys use to practice on her when we were ready to become men. She didn't care that we would practice on her. She laughed and squeezed us and took us into her and that was all there was to it. Her uncle was a medicine man who had pretty strong powers. And sometimes whenever we would start acting a little foolish with her, teasing her, she would say that her

88

uncle would turn us all into hairy spiders. I believe that he could have done that to us if he wanted to, but she never told him on us. She was not much older than us boys and later married a white man who used to come and sell us whiskey once in a while even though it was illegal to do so. I never saw her anymore after that."

There was a pretty long silence after the Indun quit talking, for me and Albert had nothing to contribute in the way of "First Time" stories and both the preacher and the Indun were kind enough not to ask. I reckon they were both worldly enough to know that me and Albert hardly looked seasoned enough to have had such experiences. Although, I reckoned we was both looking forward to them—at least I was!

Seemed like all four of us watched that fire for a long time; Preacher and the Indun, no doubt thinking about their first times, and me and Albert wondering about when ours was going to be.

Finally, Preacher says, "I reckon we've had a long day of it and should turn in. Ivory, are you sure the horses are all hobbled?"

I had volunteered to care for the animals and had put on their hobbles and let them graze there along that little creek.

Before I could even answer, Preacher's eyes were closed and his head resting on the seat of his saddle. The Indun dozed sitting upright, his saddle blanket draped over his shoulders. They were an uncommon pair, our travel mates.

Albert said: "Do you reckon those stories they told us were true?"

"I suspect so, for I have heard similar tales from Otero sometimes when he would come back from Ulvade and be in a talkative mood. Men get a funny sound to their voice when they are talking about wanton women."

Albert smiled that good smile of his and said, "It has been some adventure so far, huh?"

"More than I reckoned it would be," says I. For in the little more than two weeks since we have left Texas, we have saved the Indun from a hanging, been involved in a barroom brawl and jailed, and witnessed murderous revenge. It was my hope that things would settle to normal until we at least reached Topeka and found Mr. Monroe. It seemed to me, there was still plenty of adventure to come after that. Right now, I only wished to dream of Charity and keep her in my thoughts the live long day.

A pleasant ride to Topeka would do me just fine.

NINE

One day more found us coming upon an abandoned soddy. Some of its walls were crumbling, and most of its roof caved in. We took the occasion to pause for lunch such as it was. Mostly warm water and some hard candy I had been carrying with me since leaving Last Whiskey but had been keeping to myself. But, it was all we had among us to eat, and so I shared.

The Indun plopped a piece of it in his mouth and smiled.

While our little group rested on the shade side of the soddy, I took it upon myself to explore the inside of what was once somebody's dear sweet home. Having never known a home of my own, I was curious as to why someone would have taken all the trouble to wander this far out on the prairie, cut blocks of sod and build them into a home, and then simply abandon it and leave it in ruin.

It was a bittersweet place to look upon.

Inside, I found among the crumble, some old newspapers, yellowed and falling apart. One scrap talked about the rising price of hogs, and another talked about the exceptionally dry weather of that year.

I found a piece of red ribbon and a headless rag doll. A rusted razor and a man's brogan shoe, its toe curled up, its leather dried and stiff with a spider living inside.

One busted chair lay tipped over in a small room that had been blocked off from the rest.

I reckoned they was probably white folks that had lived here. Thousands had come west in the migration. So had families of coloreds, but somehow it struck me as the folks that lived in this house were white.

I leaned halfway through an open window, a piece of isinglass lay on the ground below it, all the real window they must have had to keep out the bugs and flies and still let in the light.

I walked outside and all the way around the soddy

and saw there, forty or fifty yards to the rear, a collapsed privy—a pile of weathered boards caved in on themselves. I also saw a pair of wooden markers not far off to the side.

I walked over to where they stood and read the difficult carving in each: JUDITH GRIMES BORN 1851 DIED 1875 ANDY GRIMES INFANT DIED 1875 BLESSED LAMB.

It could have been anything that took them: Cholera, smallpox, dysentery—they was all common killers of the plains.

Or, maybe it was wild Induns, or a twister, or starvation. Or, maybe it was just heartbreak. There was no way of knowing what tragedy had befallen them.

Little wild blue flowers grew up out of the grass that covered their graves and the wind blew gentle.

I went back and sat in the shade along with Preacher, the Indun, and Albert.

Preacher and the Indun were taking a nap using their arms as pillows. Albert was airing his feet.

"I saw some graves out back," I tell him.

"No fooling?"

"Most likely the folks that lived here, at least some of them. One was just a baby. It was scratched into his headboard: 'Blessed Infant.' "

Albert looked sad.

"Their names was Grimes. Judith and Andy."

He looked sadder still.

"I wonder how my ma is faring?" he says.

"She's probably grieving yet."

"I know I broke her heart by leaving."

"You did what you felt needed doing," I say.

"I hope Mr. Monroe is still in Topeka," says he.

"What if he ain't?"

"Then we'll just have to find out where he is and find him."

"What if we can't?"

"Then, I guess we'll die trying to do what we set out to do—kill Rufus Buck and his cutthroats!"

The thought brought me no cheer.

"I think I will grab a piece of shut-eye," says Albert stretching out on the tall golden grass. "It's such a pleasant afternoon." It was true: the wind was warm and gentle, the sky a pretty blue, streaked with dozens of mare's tails. I reckoned there was no need not to let my guard down.

We were all awakened by a rumbling sky that had grown dark and dangerous by the way flashes of lightning streaked back and forth across it. (Later in life, I was to learn that the long wispy clouds known as mare's tails were an ominous sign of bad weather to come. The vagaries—a word I learned from Albert—of the prairie can kill you just as quick as a six-gun.)

We had hardly sat up when the first cold drops of hard rain smacked against our faces. Far out on the horizon, marching in our direction, was a wall of rain like some great black curtain being lit up from behind by jagged bolts of lightning.

"We can't outrun it," says Preacher.

"Not even a rabbit could escape from it," says Man Who Waits.

"We better git inside the soddy," says Albert. "Least-ways the wall will offer some protection."

I suggest we take the horses in, too. "That storm will run them clean out on the prairie and the lightning will strike them dead. We'll be left afoot."

The horses were skittish about going in through the narrow little doorway, but we finally managed them and ourselves and crowded up as best we could behind the west-facing wall. Luckily, the roof had not caved in over that part of the house.

We took off our bandannas and tied them around the horses' eyes to help keep them calm. Man Who Waits said his horse didn't see so good anyway and that it didn't matter if he had a rag tied around his eyes or not.

The lightning grew louder and the rain heavier as the storm came on. Once, a bolt of lightning passed directly overhead and lit up the darkness surrounding us so brightly it hurt our eyes and the sound of thunder caused our ears to ring for several minutes afterward. The horses, in spite of having been blindfolded, stamped and reared and screamed out their fear. It took all we had to hold them.

Rain drummed against the side of the soddy and atop the roof and eventually began to leak in on us. Muddy chunks of water and dirt.

Soon, a small portion of the roof over our heads gave way and nearly knocked the Indun to his knees. Through the hole above us, the sky boiled black and rolled over us like the devil's anger. Albert's piebald broke free and knocked out a hole in the wall where the window had been.

I figured he had purchased his death by doing so. Sometimes horses can be awful dumb! We could do nothing to save him.

It kept up like that for less than a half hour more, then slowly and gently the main part of the storm gave way on its march to the east. I pitied any of the poor folks that might be living in its path farther out on the great prairie.

The rain had pretty much give up and was now only a light drizzle. But the day had grown late and soon enough it would be nightfall.

"I should go and look for my horse," said Albert, water running off the brim of his hat and down the tip of his nose.

I didn't have the heart to tell him that the piebald was probably done in by the lightning. "I'll go with you," I volunteer, for what with the smell of wet horse and one another, crowded as we all was together in that small space, I was glad for the relief of fresh air, no matter that when we come upon Albert's horse it would most likely be a gruesome sight.

We had barely cleared the soddy's small frame door when, in the distance, riding hard in our direction, are men in yellow slickers.

Sometimes danger don't need a calling card, you can just smell it. Like we could smell the rain and the air now that the rain had mostly passed, or the sweat of our horses.

"Maybe they're just running from the storm," says Albert.

"The storm's went thataway," I remind, pointing off toward the blackness in the east. He knows and I know and so does Preacher, and maybe the Indun don't know, but what we saw riding down on us was danger.

"Red Flymaster," says Albert. "I have never seen the man before in my life, but that is Red Flymaster out in front of the others!"

"How do you know?" says Preacher.

"Look at the size of him! He is known for his size according to *Harper's Weekly*!"

Preacher strains a look, lifting his hand to his brow to see under it.

Man Who Waits said: "It looks like we will have a fight between two good warriors. I am looking forward to it."

I count at least ten riders. It's plain by now they have spotted us, for they alter their path slightly and head right toward us and the soddy.

"How can you be so dang sure it's Red Flymaster?" says Preacher still looking under the palm of his hand.

"Can't," says Albert.

A puff of white smoke rises from among the riders and something whizzes past our ears and slams into the. wall of the soddy spraying up mud.

"I reckon there's your answer," I say and lead the run for the safety of the soddy. Albert, the Indun, and Preacher are stepping on my heels.

We only have the twin Navies and the single

repeating rifle I have jerked from the scabbard of my horse (Albert's repeater is somewhere out on the prairie along with the piebald).

By the time we have hunkered down behind the thick sod walls, we can hear the lead slugs slamming into it from the other side.

Preacher takes my rifle and returns fire from the window.

"Well are you boys going to fire off them pistols!" yells Preacher from above the sharp banging of the Henry. "Or, will you have them come riding down here and kill us all?"

"We didn't have anything to do with the death of Red Flymaster's boys," Albert reminds him.

"He don't know that!" argues Preacher.

Albert looks over at me with his eyes full of questions.

"I remember once when some of us Comanche were out on a raiding party and we come across four or five white men who were living in a little shack like this one, only it was made of wood," said Man Who Waits for Winter.

"We hadn't been very successful until we found those white men living in that little house near a creek. It looked like an easy time to us so we attacked them." The story seemed all very interesting, but wasn't any one of us knew why the Indun had chosen right this minute to tell it what with the possibility that a slug could come through a crack in the wall and blow out our brains!

"We had a pretty good fight with those white men. It lasted until the sun made long shadows along the ground. They had repeating rifles, but they weren't very good at shooting them straight. We had pretty good medicine that day."

The lead bullets of the riders was eating away at our protection: *Thud! Thud! Thud! Thud!*

But the story had a point to it, and I figured I might as well know it: "What happened?" I ask the Indun.

Man Who Waits smiled in that manner of his that drew all of his wrinkles up at once.

"We killed them. This sort of reminds me of that time."

"Thank you very much," says Albert in an ungrateful way.

I don't have to be told twice to save my own skin. I join Preacher at the window and aim the big Navy and for the first time ever, I fire a pistol. It nearly jumped out of my hand and I had to catch it to keep it from falling in the mud.

Preacher grins and levers still another shell into the breach of the Henry.

"Keep both hands wrapped around the butt, Ivory. That way, you'll hold her steady and more likely hit something."

Soon enough, Albert joins the fray and we are pouring lead into the charge of Dangerous Red Flymaster and his posse of riders.

One of them is snatched from the saddle and lands in a heap. (Which one of us was responsible for that poor fellow's wound, even to this day remains unknown, but it turned the trick.)

A hundred yards out, and the riders haul up on their horses.

By now, Albert and me are getting the feel of it and find that a good fight can be an enjoyable occasion (the possibility of death aside). Preacher has to tell us to cease our fire.

"We don't have that much ammunition and they are too far distant for us to do any real damage."

The air around us is filled with heavy blue smoke so thick and acrid it stings our eyes and causes our noses to water. The Indun seems disappointed in us for having silenced our guns.

By now, it is getting too dark to see one another. "What now?" asks Albert.

"We'll have to wait to see what their next move is," says Preacher. "But, you boys did real good in standing and fighting and I want to say that I am proud to be with you boys, even if this is our last fight."

The thought of being back in Last Whiskey mucking out stalls and watching Otero coming in from a week-long drunk from Ulvade, seems to me now to have a certain attraction that it lacked before. Until this very moment, I never did once think about dying on the open prairie at the tender age of fifteen years.

The memory of those two little graves out back flashed through my thoughts. At least their final resting place had been marked, mine would not be. What would there ever be present to signify that I had ever once lived on this earth, if Red Flymaster and his boys had their final wish?

It was a dreadful piece of thinking.

Albert poked me in the ribs and said: "Look there!"

The man that Albert said was Dangerous Red Flymaster had tied a white bandanna around the front sight of his rifle and now rode forward, leaving the rest of his bunch standing where they were.

"If you will give me your rifle, I will shoot him for you," says the Indun with a look of old glee on his face.

"Can't Chief," says Preacher. "It wouldn't be a Christian act."

The Indun offered Preacher a pitiful look. It was plain to see that he did not approve of Preacher's tenderhearted view of matters.

Coming through the late gloom and misty air, rode Red Flymaster on a big chestnut horse, the kind the Army preferred because of their deep chest and stamina. It took a big horse to carry Mr. Flymaster because he was a big of cuss himself wearing a pinned-up hat, a brace of pistols, ammunition belts, knives, a hand ax, and possible other instruments of death hidden somewhere inside his coat or boots.

He pulled up about ten yards from the soddy and shouted:

"I've come to git the son of a bitch that killed two of my children and left the other a bloody mess! The son of a bitch that I have come for was described to me by my boy, William, as a skinny, silver-haired bastard who wasn't wearing no clothes other than long drawers. If there is a man of you inside there that fits such description, I advise that you come out now and face your medicine!"

We all looked at Preacher and he looked back.

"Well sir," he hollers through the open window, "I reckon that would be me."

Red Flymaster shifts his bulk and the leather of his saddle creaks.

"Well you'd be the son of a bitch I am after, then! Come on out and take what's coming to you!"

"Those youngsters of yours, as you call them, robbed me of all I had and left me afoot on the prairie," calls out Preacher. "Still, I did not have it in my heart to take the lives of your boys except that they would have it no other way. Your boy, Billy jumped through a window and saved his own life by doing so."

"He was cut to pieces!"

"But alive to live another day."

"It don't wash with me!"

"Well, what do you suggest?" says Preacher. "For I would be a fool and well deserving of whatever fate you have in mind for me if I was just to lay down my arms and surrender."

"You have no choice. I'm giving you a chance to come peaceful and let me take you back to Newton and hang you. Now I can't get no fairer than that!"

"All my men inside here are sharpshooters," says Preacher. "It will be one hell of a fight if you insist.

And now that you are well within our sights, you will get first consideration."

It was only then (I believe) that Dangerous Red Flymaster realized what a fix he had ridden himself into. His long red mustache twitched back and forth as he chewed the insides of his cheeks in consternation over the dilemma.

"I've come under a flag of truce," he finally says. "It would take a low dog to shoot a man under a flag of truce!"

"I've nothing to lose," says Preacher, "and neither do my men."

It was tough talk coming from our side considering the fix we was in. While Preacher and Dangerous Red had been carrying on their tough talk with one another, me and Albert counted up the remainder of our bullets: Four.

"Tell you what," says Preacher. "You climb down off that horse and we'll have it out—you and me—no pistols, guns, knives, axes, or other instruments of death. Just using the parts the good Lord give us. However, no biting nor no eye-gouging."

Red Flymaster looked forlornly back at his men, a hundred yards distance.

"Well, you skinny son of a bitch," says he, dismounting from his chestnut, "I'll take your challenge. And if I win, we'll skip the trial altogether and find us the nearest tree and I'll hang you there and then!"

"And if I win," says Preacher, "we'll call it even and my men will not shoot you dead!"

Albert whispers: "You might just as well let me or Ivory shoot you, Preacher, for look at the size of him!"

"The Lord is on the side of the righteous, boys, don't be fainthearted!"

We watch as Dangerous Red stacks up his weapons in a nice little pile on the ground, I guess forty pounds worth of steel and iron, not including a double-barreled shotgun he leaves tied to the saddle of his horse.

Preacher hands us the Henry, and leaps out to greet his foe.

They circle one another like wary dogs, Preacher and Dangerous Red. Red has a murderous look in either eye (for he is somewhat wall-eyed and it is hard to tell with which he is looking at Preacher).

Me and Albert and the Indun take up positions as spectators, but make sure that the distant posse does not ride down on us.

Dangerous Red makes a sudden swipe at Preacher and lunges forward in a bull's charge, but Preacher leaps high in the air and kicks him with both feet in the face, knocking him several steps backward.

"Look at that!" shouts Albert, and I must confess that I had never seen anyone perform such a trick either.

Dangerous Red regains his senses and charges once more, but Preacher sidesteps him and whirls around on one foot, swinging the other hip high and plants it on the back of Red's skull, knocking him facedown in the mud.

It goes on like that for the next several minutes, with

Preacher kicking Dangerous Red Flymaster this way and that with as much ease as a man beating his dog with a stick. Dangerous Red's only threat is the string of cuss words coming forth from his puffed and bloodied lips. He has the print of a boot on his forehead.

Once more, Red lifts himself from the mud and grunts and roars his final frustration at having been beat by the "Goddamndest skinniest son of a bitch in all of Kansas," as he puts it, and throws himself in Preacher's direction only to be greeted by several more swift kicks that lay him out cold as a restaurant duck.

"Come on boys, and let us take our leave before he comes around," says Preacher with no more fanfare than that. "I don't believe I would trust him to hold to his promise, but then, maybe he is a man of honor and will do so. Either way, it seems judicious that we go now."

We rode off, found Albert's piebald—amazingly alive and calm with no outward signs of wear for the worse—and lit out for Topeka.

If it was true what Preacher said, "That the good Lord looks out for fools and children," then surely he was looking out for us.

TEN

Topeka was filled up with cattle and cowboys: thousands of the former, hundreds of the latter.

We ride past the pens of long-horned steers that watch us with wary yellow eyes as though they already know what is in store for them once they head east, as though they know they will wind up on some rich man's dinner plate. It makes me exceptional hungry to look at all them beeves. We have not had a decent meal in several days and our bellies are scraping our backbones.

Jug-eared cowboys wearing tall-crowned Stetsons hang around the stock pens with their hands stuffed down in the pockets of their blue jeans.

Wind drifts in from the west and carries with it the smell of all them cows, both in the stock pens and farther out on the prairie surrounding Topeka itself. It is a town of cows and cowboys.

Albert wants to go right away and find Mr. Monroe, but the rest of us vote on buying a good meal at the first restaurant we encounter.

Man Who Waits for Winter says: "These are the white man's buffalo; they are scrawny and do not look much good to eat."

"Just you wait and see, Chief," says Preacher.

The talk of food and eating makes me faint-headed. Albert reluctantly agrees to go along with us to the nearest restaurant.

Cowboys ride up and down the street on either side; some look drunk; they all wear grins and offer sloppy "how-do's" to every gal that passes down the sidewalk. Some of the gals giggle, and cover their mouths with their fingertips. Others, cast back flirting looks. The married ones—them holding babies or small children by the hand—make it plain, by screwing up their faces and walking stiff-necked, that such attention from the jug-eared cowboys is unwanted and unappreciated.

Every other building that we pass by is a business set up for the cowboys: saddle shops, chop houses, haberdashers, barbershops, Chinese baths, tobacconists, gunsmiths, horse traders, beef buyers, musical instrument makers, boot makers. And, saloons. I count more than twenty on our pass through town.

We rein in in front of one of the restaurants, the Kansas Beef Club, and wearily dismount. Inside, we are greeted with curious stares as we take our place at an empty table. It is covered in a red-checked cloth and there ain't so many flies buzzing around as you might of thought.

A menu is posted on the wall behind the counter. It offers a variety of dishes, all served with beef steak. The Indun can't read; I can tell by looking at him.

"Do you like potatoes?" I ask him.

"Don't know," he says. "What are potatoes?"

I scan on down farther and see that there is a dish offering beef liver and onions. I figured he had at least et liver one time or the other.

"Liver?"

The smile fills up his face and causes his ears to rise a notch.

"Liver is a good thing," he says. "I once ate the liver of some Crows." I'm thinking he means a crow, a black bird that is so common in these parts, only it is referred to as ravens. Then, he states: "We caught two or three of them riding their ponies along Mud River; they had stolen some of the white man's buffalo and a few of our horses two days before that. When they saw us, they tried to run, but we caught them and killed them and ate their hearts and ate their livers. It wasn't as good as some things I have eaten, not as good as the tongue of a buffalo."

When I realized he was talking about having et the livers of other Induns, some of my hunger went down into my shoes.

But when I heard the sweet song of voice ask us what it was we'd be having, I looked up and into the angelic face of Jasmine Winfred Lucille Pettycash (of course, it was only later that I learned her name).

She had creamy brown skin and large round eyes and a mouth the shape of cupid's bow. She was wearing a gingham dress and crisp white apron and wearing it all real good. When her glance fell upon me, it took my breath away.

She was the fourth black girl I ever met. (Winona Washington and her sister Fairly were the first two. They lived at the orphanage and was eventually adopted by a family of black folks with seven or eight other youngsters. Winona and Fairly was big unattractive girls and so I never did have any *sweet feelings* for them in that way.)

Charity, of course, had been the first to make the blood in me rush hot through my veins, but now that I had laid eyes on Jasmine, the memory of Charity dried up like a Texas waterhole in August.

Preacher said, "I'll have a steak and make it a big one and some cowboy beans and a black coffee."

The suddenness of her pretty presence made it hard for me to say anything.

"Well, what you going to have?" says she after awhile and not the least enamored with my staring and acting like a mute.

"Come on, boy, I's busy."

Finally, I find my tongue, for she is giving me a cold impatient stare that has the feel of a winter frost.

"I . . . I'll have the same as him," I say, nodding Preacher's way who is grinning over at me like a fish eating possum.

She turns and takes Albert's order, which is beef steak, potatoes, and collard greens, and makes me wish I had ordered collard greens as well.

Man Who Waits said: "Liver," and then offered her up a mostly toothless grin that caused her to give a little gasp and take a step backward. She sort of sniffed the air around us and rolled her eyes before taking our order off to the cook. I couldn't help but watch the way her skirts sashayed and the wonderful way her feet took small quick steps.

When I returned my attention to our little group, they was all looking at me.

We ate in what Preacher called: "Near lust." He mumbled a prayer, but we was all into our food before he could get out the *Amen.*

The Indun had a hard time with the liver, cooked as done as it was, which had the shape and thickness of a boot sole. And, the way the Indun was struggling with it with the few teeth he had in his mouth, I imagined it was just as tough.

Nonetheless, the Indun sucked at the liver's juices and swallowed down—whole—the small round onions that came with it.

"It's about the same as the liver of the Crows that I ate," he commented with a high amount of satisfaction.

If eating like hogs was a sin, Albert, Preacher, and me would have all been cast into hell right then and there. Several times, Jasmine, our waitress, came over with pitchers of coffee and buttermilk to replenish our cups. Seemed like every time she graced us with a visit, she turned up her nose a little higher at our low behavior. But was none of us seemed to care, except me, secretly. I tried wiping my mouth of buttermilk before offering her my best smile, but she only glanced down at my stained sleeve and rolled her eyes some more. First things first, thought I.

We was close to finished, sopping up our plates of red grease with chunks of hard bread when our attention was drawn to a deputy city marshal that entered the little cafe.

He was dressed in a somber manner: Black sugar-loaf hat, black broadcloth coat, and checked trousers. He wore a brass badge pinned to the lapel of his coat and a big Peacemaker Colt was tucked inside his waistband.

He seemed to know everyone in the cafe except us, for he greeted most in a serious, but friendly fashion and one or two he shook hands with. But all the while, his attention was on our table.

He finally meandered over to us as casual as a magpie looking for worms on a hot day.

We kept our eyes glued on our plates.

He smelled strong of tobacco. Pipe tobacco. And, looking down, I noticed how large his shoes were.

"I don't believe I have seen you boys around before," says he.

"No, we just have arrived," says Preacher.

The deputy gives us a little snort through his nose and says, "Well, I can sort of see that."

Jasmine comes over with more coffee and butter-milk. I take it as a sign she is warming to my attentions of her, all these trips to our table. The deputy warns her off with a hard look and my heart slides a little further down in my chest.

"We haven't broken any ordinances have we, Deputy?" asks Preacher.

"None so far," he says, "unless there is a law against slovenliness." That sort of brings a half smile to his lips for he has made a little joke of our lowly condition.

"You look like vagrants to me," says he, returning his features back to that of the serious-minded.

"Well, we are not," says Albert, jumping right into the inquisition.

"Is that an Indian?" the deputy wants to know, his gaze now on Man Who Waits.

"It's plain to see that it is," I say (for now that I have helped to save the Indun from hanging, I feel somewhat responsible for his future—at least till the coming winter).

"Why you're a mouthy little nigger, ain't you," he growls, casting both eyes down on me, and I see that he is wall-eyed—a common condition it seems among many of the men of that day—and am not sure exactly which gray eye to look into.

Preacher says, "There is no need for hateful talk, Deputy. These are my friends."

Without taking the staring eye off me, the deputy's other eye, the roving one, sort of moves round to where Preacher is sitting. I am at once amazed and somewhat envious at the feat.

"I wasn't talking to you, I was talking to this sassy little nigger!"

Preacher gets that same look in his eye that he got just before he grabbed me and Albert's Navies and cleaned out the Flymaster brothers. Albert sees it, too. I figure I better act before the deputy goes the way of the Flymasters.

I have been sipping from my cup of buttermilk, and

holding a little in my mouth, I toss myself to the floor and begin rolling around and letting the buttermilk foam out of my mouth.

"Good gawd!" shouts the deputy and steps back just in time for me to miss his shoes with some of the buttermilk leaking out from between my lips. "What the hell is ailing him!"

"He's got the fits!" shouts Albert. "Comes on him now and then when he's afraid of something. I guess you done scared him witless!"

Rolling around on the sawdust floor, snapping my jaws open and shut, and kicking my feet, has an appalling effect on the cafe's patrons. So much so, that some even quit eating long enough to stare at me.

"How long's he stay like this?" the deputy demands.

"Don't last long," says Albert. "Doctor back in Saint Louis says its the demons got him when he's like this. Get's powerful strong. Can break a man's neck with his bare hands if he was to get hold of you." The deputy takes two or three more steps backward.

"Get him the hell out of here!" shouts the nervous lawman, tugging out the big Peacemaker that he has tucked inside his belt. Soon's it appears, I start to lower my act, for I don't want to be shot through the skull by the wall-eyed deputy.

"Looks like he's coming out of it," says Preacher, with an admiring glint in his eye for he knows—being in the preaching business—good acting when he sees it (for all itinerant men who earn their keep by their wits, like the preacher, has to be good actors. It is a trait that I have come to admire ever since I saw how fat and well fed the Padres were back at the orphanage).

Albert, the Indun, and Preacher grab hold of my. limbs and carry me out, followed at a safe distance by the deputy.

"That boy ought to get treatment!" hollers the deputy. They carry me around a corner and down through an alleyway and set me atop a rain barrel. We laugh till tears roll down our cheeks. Man Who Waits for Winter laughs, too, but's not sure what the joke is.

Soon's we catch our breath again, Albert says, "We must go and find Augustus Monroe." Then he looks at Preacher and says, "I reckon we'll be saying good-bye to you, Preacher. Me and Ivory have our business to attend to."

"I'll pray for you boys," replies Preacher. "I know that you're hearts are wholesome and that your minds are set right and that you have been good company to me."

With that, Preacher turns to the Indun, and says, "Someday, I'd like to discuss religion with you, for the heathen gods has always been a curiosity of mine," and then shook the Indun's hand warmly to which Man Who Waits derived a great deal of pleasure.

"You could come with us," says Albert. Albert was the kind that just naturally couldn't let go of a new-found friend and took in folks like some take in stray cats or dogs.

"You boys are headed for violence," says Preacher. "I can see it in your faces. I'd ask you not to continue your vengeance trail, but I know it would do no good. And normally, I'd sermon you on turning the other cheek, but you'd only think me a hypocrite and who could blame you. But, I hear the flock calling me to other things and therefore must say goodbye and good speed."

It was a sad end to a short friendship and we all watched as Preacher strode down the alley toward the main street and disappeared into the sharp glare of sunlight.

"Do you think you might fall down again, and have the white water flow from your mouth?" asked the Indun, staring down at me with his mischievous eyes. "There was a man in our village once when, I was just a boy, who used to fall down and roll on the ground, shake all over like you did. Some of the people wanted to kill him by beating him with sticks the first time it ever happened, but some of the others persuaded them not to because they believed that that man was a special man who had great powers and the reason he was rolling on the ground and shaking like that was because all the powers was coming into him and taking over his body. There was a big council about it among the old men who pretty much ran things and they decided that this fellow was having his body entered by the spirits and so they left him alone when he'd get like that. They'd all come and watch hoping that maybe one of the spirits would jump out of his body and into their own. It never did happen, though. Not that I remember."

"No," I say. "I ain't gonna roll around on the ground no more. I only did it to save that deputy from going the way of the Flymaster brothers, for I could see the way Preacher was growing angry over that deputy's surly manner."

Albert offered me a gentle smile.

"You are of good heart, like Preacher said, Ivory. I always did know that about you from the first time my pa brought me by Otero's stables. You was in the corral putting liniment on a mule's foreleg and talking sweet to it. Anybody that will talk sweet to a mule has to be of good nature." (The mule was Oliva and the only reason I was sweet-talking her that day was so that she would not kick out my brains, or reach around and try and nip a chunk out of my shoulder as she sometimes had a habit of doing. I had no love for that animal, and was I to be judged on my feelings that particular day, it would no doubt be a mark against me in the book of life.)

"Well thank you, Albert," I tell him with all humility.

"It is a big town, Topeka is," says Albert. "Where should we begin our search for Mr. Monroe?"

ELEVEN

A man with Augustus Monroe's reputation ought to be easy to find, Albert reasoned. But to save time, he suggested we split up: him and the Indun going in one direction, me in another. That was okay with me, for I had my own reason for wanting to be on my own for a time. I said I'd head up the street that-away, and him and the Indun could go the other.

"We'll meet back here in an hour," said Albert.

I found myself standing right in front of the cafe, staring through the plate-glass window. It didn't take but a minute for me to spot Jasmine, weaving her way through the tables of customers carrying platters of food. I still had eight dollars left over from the ten Albert had spotted me the first day of our journey. A piece of pie and coffee cost two bits. I figured it was worth it and went on in and sat myself down at the counter.

I was waited on not by Jasmine, but by a large German woman who looked like she had a pair of pillows stuffed in the top of her dress. Her cheeks were as rosy as apples and her arms were wings of heavy flesh.

"Yas," said she. "Vat can I get for you?"

She was big and round and you could feel the warmth coming off of her like as though you was standing in the kitchen itself, and she smelled of baked bread.

"I reckon I'll have a slice of that blueberry pie yonder and a cup of coffee," I tell her, sitting up straight.

"You got money? You don't look like you got no money to me!"

I reached down in my sock, after having made sure I wasn't being watched by strangers, for I have heard plenty of stories about how someone will come up and knock you in the head with a poke full of rocks and rob you blind given the first opportunity. Upon seeing that I was not being watched, I pull out a dollar of what I have left and place it on the counter in front of her.

It seems to satisfy her curiosity and she goes and cuts a slice of pie and brings me steaming coffee with it. The whole while I watch Jasmine pass in and out of the kitchen's doors with empty plates and full plates, and never once does she acknowledge my presence.

The pie was warm and sweet and the coffee hot, and so I have good reason to linger longer than I should. The fat German waitress, who some of the cowboys sitting inside the cafe call Hilda, comes over once or twice and looks at my progress but don't say anything when she sees I've still some crumbs left on my plate and a swallow or two of the coffee still remaining in my cup.

"You gonna just hang around here all day?" The voice is that of Jasmine, the tone, unfriendly.

I turn slowly to look at her; she's just as spellbinding as before.

"I thought you wouldn't even notice," I say.

"Oh, I noticed," says she.

I give her my best smile (I have always been blessed with perfect white teeth and will gladly show them to anyone at the drop of a hat, pretty gals included).

"Ain't no use offerin' me your possum grins," says she. "I ain't impressed!"

"Why'd you notice then?"

"Hard not to notice you. Lord! You and them others you was in here earlier with! Eatin' like rootin' pigs, falling out on the floor and rolling around with Lord knows what spilling out your mouth. Mercy, but it sure would be hard not to notice you!"

It wasn't exactly the way I was hoping to make an impression.

"Oh that," I laugh, slapping the top of my knee. "That there was just an act."

"Is you a fool?"

"Oh no, miss, I surely am not."

"You acts like a fool."

"Sometimes I do, yes'm."

"Is there somethin' wrong with you? The way you rolled around on that floor with foam comin' out'n your mouth, it looked like somethin' was wrong with you."

"No, that was buttermilk was all."

"Why on earth . . ."

"If you'll take a walk with me after you get done working here, I'll explain it all."

"Why in the world would I do a crazy thing like that?"

" 'Cause I know it just ain't my foolishness and low manner of dress that you been noticing about me," I say with a wink. I am surprised at what is coming out of my own mouth.

My boldness causes her to roll up her eyes and nearly drop the tray of dirty dishes she is carrying. "You is crazy!"

"No I ain't."

"Are."

"No," I shook my head slow.

"I gits off at six in the evening. You could meet me out front if you want. They sell ice cream down at the drugstore. I'd let you walk me maybe that far."

My face was starting to hurt from the grinning I was doing.

"Lord, I must be crazy my own self for lettin' you come on around back here this evenin'," she says with a big sigh and then disappears into the kitchen before I can get off another word.

The big German waitress comes over and stands before me.

"It looks like you are done vid your pie and coffee, ya?"

It is warning enough for me not to loiter. I ain't eager to run into that deputy again.

Outside, it don't hardly feel like my feet are touching ground, I am so elated over the prospect of meeting Jasmine later that evening. I pass in front of a haberdasher's store and notice my poor condition in the reflection of plate glass. I consider what I see for a time and realize there is little to be done, at least not with a little over seven dollars left to me.

I have completely forgotten the reason I am on the streets of Topeka: to look for Mr. Augustus Monroe.

It doesn't matter, for Albert and the Indun are tromping down the sidewalk in my direction; Albert's appearance does not look hopeful.

"Ivory," says he. "Me and Man Who Waits found some acquaintances of Mr. Monroe. He is indeed residing here in Topeka, but is currently out of town." Albert's gloom wells up in his dark eyes.

"He has taken a party of dukes and a Russian Prince on a hunting party. They will be gone several days. They left just yesterday. It looks as though we will have to kill some time here in Topeka until his return. I'm sorry for the delay."

My own heart soars over the prospect of having some leisure time to pursue my newfound interest, but I let on that I, too, am disappointed.

"Well, we've come this far," says I. "I reckon we'll just have to tough it out until Mr. Monroe returns. It won't be so bad, Albert. We'll just lay low, is all. Cool our heels."

"I don't know what I'd do without your good cheer at times like this, Ivory. I couldn't have picked a better partner than you. I know it was fate that sent you to our house that day, and I knew right off that if anybody could help me avenge the murder of my pa, it was you. When we catch up to Rufus Buck, he won't stand a snowball's chance in Hades!"

I waved off the praise, for I certainly wasn't deserving of it. Albert had a blindness to him in the way he saw some things that most normal folks wouldn't. I understood, looking at him now why his poor mam was so troubled about his going off on the vengeance trail. He was just as innocent as peas.

"We had better go and find us a room," he says at last. "This town is plenty crowded with cowboys. We will be lucky to find a place to lay our heads."

We traipsed up and down the street checking in at several hotels but were told they were full up. Finally, at the very edge of town in a run-down looking she-bang calling itself Dick's Emporium Hotel, we find us a room.

The clerk had a false eye—I could tell by the way it didn't move around with the other one—and he sort of tilted his head at an angle in which to look us over with his good eye when we stated our request. Several rough types sat around the small lobby reading yellowed newspapers and old copies of the *Police Gazette*.

The clerk made Albert sign a register and put up three dollars and seventy-five cents in advance for the night. Albert passed him a ten and said we'd take three nights for that amount and not a cent more.

"Take it or leave it," said Albert. "We have to, we'll sleep out on the prairie with the cows."

"There's only one bed," said the clerk. "You'll have to share it."

"Is there a bath included?"

"End of the hall. The water's changed once a day. You want more than that, it'll cost you fifty cents extra."

Albert was furnished a skeleton key and told we had room number nine. It wasn't any bigger than the jail cell we had been locked up in in Newton and nearly as poorly furnished. An iron bed with tick mattress and two cheap moth-eaten blankets adorning it, stood against one wall. An armoire with a cracked mirror stood across from the bed. There were no windows in the room, and therefore nothing to look out on. There was no sort of carpet on the floor. A sign tacked up on the back of the door read: NO SPITTING ON THE FLOOR—MANAGEMENT.

We threw down our bedrolls and sat on the edge of the bed.

It was a small warm room and our journey had been tiresome to this point. The Indun stretched out on the floor, while me and Albert laid across the bed. There was little to do but wait. I remember for a long time staring up at the stamped tin ceiling, at the squared patterns, and thinking just how far away I was from the orphanage and from Otero and from the Texas Panhandle.

Something wakes me. Something awful and fearful, for my heart is pounding and beads of sweat trickle down my sides. Albert and the Indun are snoring away and no one else is in the room. In less than a minute, I know what the fear is that has brought me from the fitful dozing sleep: My appointment to meet Jasmine in front of the cafe!

I slip quietly from the room so as not to disturb my companions and make my way down the hall to the lobby. The glass-eyed clerk cocks his head in my direction. I see a Regulator clock above the desk. It reads five minutes past six!

I fly through the front door and down the street, almost bumping into three or four soldiers who cuss me and call me names I won't bother to repeat for they are foul and distasteful and would only bring me to fighting anger if I was not in such a hurry.

The cafe is at the far end of town from where Dick's Emporium Hotel is situated. I take to the street for it is less crowded than the sidewalks and am nearly ran over by a teamster's wagon.

I finally arrive at the cafe, breathless and bent over from a side ache. There is no Jasmine waiting for me. I am too late! I lean on the sill and draw air into my aching lungs while fighting back the bitter taste of disappointment.

I am standing thus when suddenly approached by the big German waitress, Hilda, who is carrying with her a tote from which protrudes several loaves of bread.

Upon spotting me heaving like a winded horse, she states:

"If da deputy catches you loafing around here, he will hit you on the noggin wid his pistol and put you in da jail, ya!"

She seemed to take some pleasure in telling me this.

"You come looking round here for Jasmine, I can

tell," she further states. It was the first time I had heard my sweetheart's name (for even though we had only met, and not under very good circumstances at that, I already considered her my sweetheart).

I was just about to inquire of the fräulein the whereabouts of my beloved when out of the cafe she steps. She is still wearing the gingham dress but the apron is gone.

"What's wrong with you, breathing so hard like that?" she inquires, noticing my labored condition.

I didn't bother to explain but instead proposed we stroll down to the drugstore and have an ice cream. That seemed to please her more than anything else I could have said. I tipped my hat to Hilda and wished her a good evening, but she only grunted hard enough to cause her big bosoms to rise and fall and strutted down the street in a stiff manner that caused the bustle of her skirt to dance choppily like there was critters inside trying to fight their way out.

We ordered lemon ice cream and sat outside on a bench provided for that purpose and watched the long shadows of late day creep down the street as we ate.

She tells me her full name: Jasmine Winfred Lucille Pettycash. "My mamma couldn't decide which name she liked best of the three," she said, with a dab of ice cream on her chin. "So she named me all three. Jasmine was my grandmother, Winfred was my great-grandmother's name, and Lucille was my aunt's name, only she died as a baby."

She had the sound of meadowlarks in her voice when she talked.

"My mamma dead now, and so's all the rest of the wimmen she named me after. Seems like death dogs the wimmen in our family. All is sadness. My poor daddy ain't of good health neither, that's why I works like I do. So's we can get by."

She reminded me of Albert when she spoke of her tragedy. They both had that same soft manner when speaking of their pain.

I thought a brighter note might be in order.

"I could afford you another ice cream if you wanted?"

She smiled sweetly and said, "That's awful kind of you. What is your name?"

I told her it was Ivory Cade.

"That's a nice name, Ivory is," she said. "What you doin' here in Topeka? I ain't never seen you or them mens you was with before neither, so I know you ain't from around here."

I explained to her we was on a mission of justice, Albert and me, and maybe the Indun if his horse decided to keep on following us. And that we had come to Topeka to enlist the aid of Augustus Monroe.

The name causes her to stop working on her ice cream and offer me a large-eyed look of concern. "Lordy! That gentleman's a killer! Talk has it, he's murdered a hundred men! I seen him once in the cafe with some other gentlemens and he had the coldest eyes you'd ever want to look into. He wasn't mean or nothin'. Wasn't rude or course talkin'. Fact is, he's got sort of a high voice, somewhat like a gel's. Course there ain't nobody hereabouts would make fun of him—he's well respected and much feared. You do business with him, you do business with the devil's own kind!"

"He's exactly what Albert says we need," I explain. "For the men we are after are a murderous bunch who will only understand an eye for an eye and a tooth for a tooth."

"Ain't you awful young to be doin' such business, Ivory Cade?" she asked with an honest tongue. (How could I tell her that I was caught up in the dreams of righteousness and justice and that I didn't know a thing about dying other than what I had seen in my days of working for Otero, but that such witnessing couldn't possibly be the same thing as my own, possibly violent, death. And that such a prospect was beyond the pale of my thinking, as it might have been any fifteen-year-old boy's. How could I confess that to her and in so doing make myself seem mature enough to woo her and cause her in return to see me as an object of her desire?)

"Old enough I reckon," was my simple answer to her question.

"My, but maybe I have misjudged you, Ivory Cade," she replied.

My heart felt like it tripped over itself.

I went on to tell her that Mr. Monroe was currently

out of town and that me and Albert and the Indun would be staying on a few days until his return.

"Well now . . ." she sighed.

"I'd sort of like to see you again," says I.

"You sure have a flattering tongue, and make it hard for a girl to resist your advances."

"I was hoping that would be the case," I state.

"I got to be goin'," says she. "My poor ol' daddy's waitin' at home for me to come make his supper. I'd invite you along, but he'd sure enough see what you are."

"What is that?"

"A wild-eyed rascal that's out to steal his only daughter's heart."

"He'd be right in thinking so," I say.

She tilted her head a little and smiled her prettiest smile.

"How long you say you is goin' be around town?"

"Three or maybe four days," I tell her. "It all depends on when Mr. Monroe returns."

That seems to please her as she backs up still holding the last of her ice cream.

"Well, Mr. Ivory Cade," says she. "I reckon if you was a mind to, you could stop tomorrow and see me again. If you don't want to, it don't make no never mind to me." But, I could tell by her eyes that she wanted me to, and I was feeling pretty full of myself when I heard her warn: "You better git on now, here comes Deputy Muddbottom." I turn just in time to see my nemesis coming in our direction, his big heavy boots clomping out a dirge upon the boardwalk.

With great reluctance I bid Jasmine farewell: "At least for now," I tell her, and find myself quickly crossing to the other side of the street and heading for Dick's Emporium Hotel.

TWELVE

For three days more, I pursued the object of my affection: Jasmine Winfred Lucille Pettycash, while Albert and the Indun took in the sights and we all waited for the return of Augustus Monroe.

"I ate oysters today," Man Who Waits announced proudly on our second afternoon in town. "At first I wasn't sure I wanted to eat such things for they looked like what comes out of little children's noses. But after I tried one or two of them, I thought they were pretty good."

"We went to an Oyster Bar," Albert explained.

By that time, Albert and the Indun had caught on that I was spending every possible moment with Jasmine, whose work at the cafe carried her from six o'clock in the morning until six o'clock in the evening with one hour off for lunch. When I was not spending the little time available with her, I was lingering close to the hotel, for I did not want to try my hand a second time with Deputy Muddbottom (a good actor knows when his play is over).

I purchased, for a nickel, a small writing pad and a pencil. I had decided to record my feelings for dear sweet Jasmine, and possibly try my hand at poetry in order to better impress her of how serious was my affection for her.

It was an endeavor that I vowed to keep secret from Albert and the Indun. True friends that they were, they might not understand or appreciate a partner that had strayed so far from his origins as to have taken up the practice of writing love poems. I did not want to seem unmanly in their sight.

"Dear Jasmine," I began the first one. "Tis you who has . . ." *Who has what?* Already I was stuck and not even well underway. This poetry business was going to be harder than I first imagined.

Our room was too crowded, for Albert was being spare with the funds saying that he had to have enough cash on hand in order to sway Mr. Monroe in joining our cause, which in turn kept everybody staying close to our accommodations at Dick's Emporium Hotel. So I mounted up Swatchy and rode out onto the prairie. I rode until I was beyond the grazing herds of cattle that the cowboys had drove up from Texas and were awaiting their turn to be shipped off on the railroad to the east.

The sweat and stink of so many restless cows on a warm day had a way of disturbing the senses.

I found myself a little stream that meandered along through the tall grasses and along whose banks grew many large cottonwoods. I picked one to sit under, its shade spreading out on the ground like a cool green blanket, and let Swatchy graze freely for he proved to be a dependable horse and had never before run off on me.

Dear Sweet Jasmine. You are the fairest of the fair, the comeliest of the comely, the dearest of the dear. Well, now, that was a good beginning in my book. I sort of doted over the words for quite some time reading and rereading them.

Maybe I do have a leaning toward the poetical after all. I continue: *Dear Jasmine, will you be mine? Dear Heart, why remain apart? Dear . . .* Again, I find myself stumped and chewing on the end of my pencil. None of the words are saying what I want them to. I lie on my belly, take up a stalk of grass to chew instead of the pencil, stare up at the clear blue sky that has maybe all of two clouds floating around in it. It seems like a perfect day to be a poet, but I'm not having any success.

I am positioned so, thinking only of Jasmine, when a cowboy comes riding up out of nowhere.

He's a rangy type, like most cowboys are, young, jug eared. He is dressed in the usual cowboy fashion (which is no fashion at all unless dusty clothes and sweat soaked hats are considered fashion): wide-brimmed hat, big swipe tied around his neck, home-spun shirt, canvas pants, mule-eared boots, and a large lariat draped around his saddle horn. He is riding a good horse of bay color.

"What you doin' out here?" he asks.

I am not inclined to tell him the truth. Instead, I ask him the same question.

"Herdin' the cows," says he with a look on his face that says I ought to know better than ask what a cowboy is doing on the prairie. He waits patiently, leaning his forearms upon his saddle horn while his horse stamps at the ground.

"You still ain't said what you're doin' out here."

"I reckon its a free range," says I. "And I reckon a body can go wherever he chooses without being asked as to his business."

"My name is Deeds," says he. "Julip Deeds, and I am with the Triple Bar X and we just finished bringing our herd up from Texas. Have you ever heard of Texas?"

"I am from Texas myself. And yes, I have heard of it."

He takes on a look of pleasant surprise.

"Texas?" he states. "What part?"

"Most recently of the Panhandle. Last Whiskey." He squints one eye the way some do when trying to recall something.

"Last Whiskey. Is that up near Ulvade?"

"About a full day's ride," I say and immediately think of Otero and his forays to that sinful place.

"Yes sir, I believe I have heard of it. Me, I'm down along the Brazos, a little place called Chili Pepper. What'd you say your name was?"

For a cowboy, he is taking a lot of liberty and asking a lot of questions. Most cowboys I know only grow talkative when they are drunk or dying. He seemed harmless enough, however, sitting up on his horse with his hat pushed back and so I was inclined to be agreeable with him.

"Ivory Cade," I tell him. "My name's Ivory Cade."

With that, he gives a wide grin.

"I know," I say. "Ivory is supposed to be white and I ain't so don't make jokes about it. Besides, they wouldn't be any that I hadn't already heard, so nothin' you would say would sound funny to me."

"Naw," says he in that long drawn out way that Texas cowboys have of speaking. "Anyone can see that you ain't white and the name seems to somehow fit you. I once had a trail partner that was black. Called him Ace of Spades he was so black. His real name was Henry Tillman. One of the best hands I ever knew."

Then, the cowboy shook his head in a slow manner and a sad look come on him and he stated: "Ace drowned crossing Red River, him and his horse. Swept away. Never even found him to bury him. A poor end to a good man."

"Well, that is a sad tale," says I, hoping maybe the cowboy would move on so that I could get back to composing my first love poem to Jasmine.

"Are you lookin' for work, boy? Mr. Bevis, our trail boss is goin' to sell off the cows and purchase a big herd of bosses to take back down to Texas with us. We will be short a few hands and could stand the help."

"Ain't interested," says I.

"Hard to see why not?" he says. "Judgin' by the skinniness of you and the poor way you are clothed,

I'd say you'd do well to join on with us and get regular wages and regular grub."

My own patience had grown thin with the cowboy and his open observation of my condition, although I cannot say that he was telling a lie, or being in any way untruthful about what he saw before him, for as I have earlier stated, I would not have qualified—either in dress or physical bearing—to have gone to a dog fight.

"Ordinarily," I began. "I would not discuss my business with a stranger. But, seeing as how you seem convinced of my low condition and lack of immediate future, I will tell you the reason for my being here in Kansas: I am on the vengeance trail of one of the most ruthless killers in all of the West!"

"Who might that be?" he said with a grin wide enough to spread to both his jug ears.

This drover just wasn't about to give up.

"Rufus Buck! That's who!"

The cowboy's smile dissolved into a look of disbelief.

"Rufus Buck!" says he in the same way that a dying man might whisper the name of our dear sweet Savior at the last moment.

"That's right."

Then the grin comes slowly back and when it does, he leans from the saddle and spits a brown stream of juice that causes a grasshopper to seek refuge.

"That's some story there, Ivory Cade. I reckon I almost bought into it for a second. You had me goin' pretty good. I guess maybe I crossed the line of politeness in askin' you all about your business. Rufus Buck! That's a good one! Hell, I was you, I wouldn't even mention that feller's name for fear he'd pop up in one of my dreams and murder me just for having thought of him!"

The cowboy caused his horse to do a little sideways dance step—I don't know if was for my benefit to show me that he was a good horseman or not—then backed him up two or three steps by pulling on the reins.

"If you decide to change your mind and join us," he called, as he started away, "we're staying just over that way on the edge of town. You show up, and I'll put in a good word for you with Mr. Bevis."

Then, as a matter of show, I suspect, he gets the bay to do a couple of crow hops before breaking into a gallop that kicks off black clods of prairie and flings them high in the air. I ain't impressed all that much, but must admit he was pretty fair in his riding skills, and overall cannot help but like his disposition.

I tried for an hour more to write a love sonnet to Jasmine, but only wound up with several pages of *Tis*'s and *Thou*'s and *Love me not*'s! I finally gave up and stretched out there on the wide open prairie, for the gentleness of the wind and the warmth of the sun had a way of making a body sweetly tired. I slept all that afternoon and awoke (dreaming of who else but Jasmine) to a slanting sun that burned red above the endless landscape of golden grasses.

I was also suffering from hunger, realizing that I had forsaken both breakfast and lunch, so caught up in my desire to pen love poems for my sweetheart. I was only now beginning to learn the lengths that the male creature will go in order to draw the attention of a female. I have seen the mating dance of the prairie chicken—quite elaborate—and listened to the calling through the night of coyotes. I have witnessed the stiff-legged hop of antelope bucks around the female herd, and seen stud horses bite and kick one another nearly to death in fighting over a mare.

Again, I thought of the old man, Otero, and what women had cost him in the way of his lonely existence. But still, I could not help but spend every spare minute thinking about her. Jasmine. I guess it is true what they say, that there is no fool like a fool who is in love.

I wandered back to town, taking my good sweet time and in no hurry to bunk down one more night three to a room. Neither Albert or me could convince the Indun to try the copper bathtub at the end of the hall.

Most things new, the Indun was captured by, but not the bathtub. He was beginning to take on a fishy smell to him.

I returned without fanfare. Albert and the Indun were dozing out front of the hotel, having taken up the only two chairs set there for the purpose of doing nothing more than watching the traffic as it passed up and down the street.

"How do," I say as a way of greeting.

Albert opened one eye and looked at me sheepishly.

"I guess I must have nodded off," he said.

Man Who Waits sat up and looked at me with those curious wet eyes of his.

"I think maybe you are getting close to becoming a man," he said. Albert and me trade looks. "I think maybe your time is drawing near."

"I guess he means," said Albert with a grin as wide as the Canadian River, "that you and that gal are going to lose all your innocence." Albert's laughter carries out onto the street and causes several passersby to turn their heads and toss us unapproving looks. (To the casual eye, we would seem little more than loafing juveniles—with the exception of the Indun—waiting for trouble to come our way.)

"I reckon not," I say glumly.

"Sure. It's bound to happen sooner or later," says Albert with all certainty.

It is suppertime and we decide that our constitutions cannot afford to eat another lard sandwich, which has been our meal for the last three days running due to Albert's close watch of the funds. I have agreed that I will go our meal as long as the cost does not come to more than a dollar each. My own generosity escapes me.

It is near time for Jasmine to be off duty at the cafe and I am anxious to meet her on time. However, Albert suggests we go to the Jezebel Cattle Company Saloon where for the price of a beer we can eat a free meal from their buffet. "It would cost less than the three dollars," he states. I am torn between being on time with Jasmine, and being a slave to my hunger.

"It ain't all that far from the cafe," he further states, having read my thoughts.

I agree, but with trepidation.

The place is full of rowdy cowboys all hoisting glasses of beer that look amber in the dull smoky light. There is plenty of food, however, spread atop a long table: sliced meats, deviled eggs, baked beans, cornbread, and stalks of celery kept fresh in glasses of water.

We shoulder our way to the bar, order three beers (for which I pay one dollar and fifty cents) and are given plates with which to load up, which we do, and find a corner to stand in for there are no free tables to sit at; all are taken by the cowboys.

No one would have figured it for trouble: our eating in a cowboy saloon.

"That there's a goddamned Injin!" The voice was so sudden and barking loud, that it caused me to spill some of my baked beans onto the toes of my shoes.

The cowboy was plainly drunk. He was a slight-built man no taller than my shoulder, but he wore a big hat and big spurs and a brace of pistols strapped up high on his waist.

"And that there is a nigger boy! What the hell are they doing in here!" It was plainly an insult to him, our presence.

Once again, I was witnessing what whiskey will do

to a man, especially one that already has a mean streak in him to begin with.

He was backed by several other drunken cowboys who screwed up their faces into menacing smirks.

"I reckon this here ain't no place for an Injin and a nigger boy!" shouts the cowboy, his right hand pulling one of the pistols he is wearing.

Another cowboy steps from the crowd and states: "You are just a mean drunk son of a bitch, Kelly!" It is none other than Jullip Deeds, the cowboy I met on the plains earlier in the day. I am at once surprised and relieved that some one has taken up our defense.

"What business is this of yours?" demands the drunk.

"That there is a friend of mine's what," replies Julip Deeds. I notice he is now wearing a small pistol inside his belt, the butt of which faces forward.

"You talking about that nigger or that Injin?"

"Let's just say you ought to leave trouble before you find it," states Deeds. A cooler head I can't say that I have ever seen.

The drunken cowboy looks disturbed at the unexpected defense of helpless men trying to eat a simple sandwich and some beans.

There is a softening of the knotted features that has collected on the wind-burned face of the drunken cowboy. He grins enough to show that his front teeth are missing. Then, just as quickly as he began, he appears to give up the argument and turns back toward the bar. I take my first breath in a full minute.

The Indun, the whole while, never once did stop eating, but continued to do so, watching as though a distant spectator to the entire affair. He was still eating and watching when the drunken cowboy suddenly turned, bringing his pistol round fully cocked and aimed it at Deeds.

Julip Deeds, in an instant that was almost too quick to see, drew his own pistol and shot the drunken cowboy through the face. The drunken cowboy's own gun fired harmlessly under the pressure of his dying finger and together the two loud reports shattered the revelry of the room.

The man, Kelly, caved in and landed on the floor on his back, a small dark hole just below his right eye, but a pool of blood collecting behind his head in a crimson halo.

For a moment, you could hear the breathing of every man gathered. Then, slowly, as though little or nothing had happened, men went back to whatever it was they had been doing. Some of the drunken cowboy's companions carried his body out of the establishment, and one of the bar keepers came over and began washing away the bloody stain that was soaking into the floor.

It was all done in a manner of casualness that sent a cold chill through my veins. I suspect Albert felt the same. The Indun seemed not at all disturbed by the shooting and made his way to the food buffet for second helpings. I had lost all appetite.

Deeds said nothing more, but went instead to the bar and drank.

Soon enough, the deputy, Muddbottom, came rushing into the saloon followed by several other deputies; they all carried shotguns.

It was demanded by Muddbottom as to what took place, this followed by a general discussion as to what *had* happened, with Julip Deed's friends siding with his story and those of the dead man's taking up his cause.

Finally, it got around to our involvement in the affair: Albert's, the Indun's, and my own. Muddbottom seemed terribly unhappy to see us again and eyed me warily as he approached. (I was fully prepared to have another fit on him if need be.)

"Some of them boys over there say you was the cause of all this," he growled. "You and that Injin!"

"We was only having a meal and a glass of beer, bought and paid for," I replied honestly.

"Well, you was witnesses, wasn't you?"

Albert gave me a secret nudge. I took it to mean to be cautious in my testimony.

"It was the drunken cowboy who ordered up his own fate," said Albert. "He threw down insults on Ivory and Man Who Waits for no other reason than he was drunk and being sore about it. That cowboy over there stepped in and defended the honor of my two friends. He was brave in doing so."

One of the dead cowboy's friends shouted, "Liar!"

Muddbottom seemed uncertain, confused. He ordered the arrest of Julip Deeds and took from him the small pistol. Deeds gave a sigh, looked my way, and smiled, and then was marched from the room.

I could not help but think what a strange breed is the cowboy.

THIRTEEN

The sudden violence and the arrest of Deeds, had caused me to lose more than my appetite; it had cooled my ardor as well. And with it, my desire to spend the waning hours with Jasmine, for I felt I would be no good company to her.

But a promise was a promise and so I went to the cafe and waited for her to come out and meet me. Whilst waiting, the German waitress, Hilda, once more appeared, carrying with her her usual loaves of bread.

"So, once again, you have come, ya?" I could only nod that indeed, I had.

"Not so perky tonight! What's da matter, cat got your tongue?" Her laughter was like creaking doors blowing in a stiff wind. But in spite of her callous manner, I wanted to throw myself into the large pillows of her bosom and rest my weary head against the pain throbbing within. For the image of the drunken cowboy, lying upon the barroom floor with a hole in his face, had dogged me like nothing else ever had, and the banging of the two pistols still rang in my ears even though more than an hour had passed. Then, too, there was the arrest of Julip Deeds who had all but saved me and Albert and the Indun from certain harm.

I felt badly for him having to spend the night locked up and without a friendly voice for comfort.

She stood there waiting for me to give her a smart enough answer, Hilda did, but I had none to offer.

"Poor kiddo," she clucked and headed off down the sidewalk.

In a few minutes more, Jasmine was there by my side.

"Well what on earth is the matter with you?" she asked.

"Don't ask," I said.

"Why not?"

"Because I have just witnessed something terrible."

"What?" She was happily curious.

"You don't want to know."

"I do." She elbowed my side and pinched my cheek and took my hat and waved it around.

"I have just seen a man killed not two feet in front of me! Shot through the face!"

"Oh . . ." She stopped waving my hat around and looked at me with her large brown eyes.

"Was it really that awful?"

"It was."

"Was it one of them friends of yours?"

"No. Nothing quite that terrible, but terrible enough."

"You wasn't hurt was you?" she said, examining me all over.

"No. But, just as easily," I affirmed, "it could have been me and that's what's so troubling. He wasn't nothing more than a mean drunken cowboy, but it could have been me that got shot through the face, or Albert, or the Indun. It happened just that quick."

Something about just the telling of it to her caused unwanted tears to well up in my eyes and spill down my cheeks and burn hot upon my face. I felt immediately embarrassed, and as such, the tears flowed harder.

I quickly took her by the arm and stepped into an alley so as not to be seen crying openly in full view of the public.

"Ivory, you is hurt."

"No. No, I told you I wasn't."

"I don't mean in that way, I mean inside you."

How could I deny it?

We walked along the edges of the town, along the less-traveled sections until we found ourselves beyond the town itself; it had grown dark and the sky was beginning to fill with stars. We found us an old cottonwood that had fallen over and sat with our backs leaning against its rough trunk.

She was soft and sweet and gentle and understanding and said that if I wanted to cry I should: "There ain't no need to be ashamed 'bout it," she said. "Crying's a way of washing out all the hurt in you and makin' you new inside again."

I leaned my head on her and she cradled me and it was the first time anyone had ever done so. I felt a comfort come over me that I had never known before.

We stayed like that for a long time, her cradling me

and both of us staring up at the stars without saying much.

After a time, she said: "I bet you ain't even ever been kissed before, have you?"

"I reckon not," says I.

"Well maybe it's time you was."

"Maybe so."

How can I explain what it was like, Jasmine's kisses? They tasted like wet sweet rain drops, or sugar candy. They were soft as rose petals falling on my mouth. They were exciting, like nothing else could be exciting. I quickly found that I had a natural understanding of it (kissing), for I was soon giving as good as I was getting, and she was whispering to me how good I was at doing it.

It didn't take me long after that to know why prairie chickens dance, and antelopes hop around, and horses bite and kick one another over mares. I surely would have done any of those things right there and then if I'd had to in order to maintain Jasmine's affection.

"We better stop before we come to trouble," she warned after about fifteen minutes of us kissing each other. What I was feeling running through all parts of me sure didn't feel like trouble at all.

"Huh?"

She pushed me back, but in a gentle way, and straightened parts of her hair with the palms of her hands and pushed down the skirts of her dress that had risen up past her knees somehow.

"I mean what we is doin' is startin' to feel too good."

"What's wrong with that?"

"Plenty, specially my pa was to catch us!"

"Well," I state, looking all around in a smart sort of way. "He ain't anywhere about."

"Likely he'll be comin' lookin' for me, since it is so late and I ain't home yet!"

Jasmine stands and smooths and straightens those parts of her that have become dusty and wrinkled from our having sat on the ground.

"Point is, Ivory Cade. A gel like me could get in all sorts of trouble over a feller like you and where would I be if that was to happen? You is goin' to be gone soon enough and Lord if it is likely I will ever see you again. I ain't goin' to give myself to no man that ain't goin' to be around come mornin'."

It wasn't plain as paint, her little speech, but it was plain enough.

"You mean if we was to do it?"

"Doin' it's what causes babies," says she with high determination.

"I guess I know that much," I state. My only course in biology was delivered by the big-boned presence of Mother Magdalene every afternoon at three o'clock when the westerly light filtered through the tall beveled glass windows of the orphanage and fell upon her countenance, which was notable because of her mustache which she made no effort to shave or otherwise hide. Most of my attention was paid to the hairier parts of her person, but not all. I did, with great fascination, pay strict attention to the lectures on human reproduction. Now, I was glad I had.

"Well then," says she. "You can understand my point in us stoppin' our foolin' round before it is too late!"

It was a disappointing announcement.

"I will walk you home," I say.

"You ain't mad?"

"No."

With that, all her sweetness returns, as does her smile.

"I thought maybe you'd be mad," she said.

"What for?"

"For me teasin' you like that and then not doin' it with you."

"Was you teasing me?"

"No. I was feeling sweet on you."

"I like kissing," I say.

"Me, too. You is good at it, Ivory. Too good."

We both laugh.

I leave her at her door, which is a small one-room shingled dwelling with a fence around it that needs repair.

"We is common folks," she states, noticing my attention to her happy home.

"It looks warm and cozy."

"I have to go in," she says.

"I reckon."

"You hurry up, you can steal one more kiss." She glances at the door and the window to see if her daddy is looking out. I steal the kiss and bid her good night.

Albert and the Indun are waiting up for me upon my return. They both have expectant looks on their faces, but neither says anything.

"Well?" I say.

"Well?" Albert states.

I look over at the Indun. He remains mum. "Ain't what you're thinking," I tell Albert. He seems disappointed.

I ask Albert for a hand in pulling off my boots and he obliges. We turn out the oil lamp and the room fills with darkness. It is only eight o'clock in the evening, but it seems later. A lot has transpired.

We are all reluctant to talk about the events of earlier. Me and Albert take the bed, the Indun the floor. Soon he is snoring.

My thoughts turn to Julip Deeds. I imagine his loneliness sitting over there in the jail.

"We ought to go break him out," I say, lying on my back, staring at a ceiling which I cannot see.

"Deeds?"

"Yes."

"How did you come to know him?" Albert asks.

"We met this morning out on the prairie. He offered me a job herding horses back to Texas."

"I imagine you was tempted to take it after all what's happened. Especially now."

"No," says I, "I was not tempted to herd a bunch of horses clear on back to Texas. I suppose that fellow is sorry he ever laid eyes on me, for look what it has cost him."

"I thought by now, we would have already caught up with Rufus Buck and his bunch and have served justice on them," Albert said with a forlorn sigh. "It seems we have been gone from home a long time."

It did seem that way, but actually we had been gone for little more than three weeks.

"Maybe you ought to wire your ma back in Texas," I suggest. "Let her know that you are all right."

"That's a good idea, Ivory. That's a good dang idea. I'll do it first thing in the morning. You always seem to know the right thing to say to pick up my spirits. A fellow couldn't ask for no better friend."

"Same here," says I and mean it. I have grown fond of Albert's company, and even that of the Indun's and feel they are like family to me. I think of Preacher in that maudlin moment and wonder how he is faring (better than the three of us, I suspect).

In the morning, I go straightaway to the jail. Deputy Muddbottom is drinking a big tin cup full of steaming coffee at his desk when I enter. He gives me a cold stare.

"I am here to see Mr. Deeds," I state.

For a long full moment, he does nothing more than stare at me, his one eye wandering around in his face like it is lost and looking for something that ain't there, while the other one bores a hole through me.

"You sure are some uppity nigger boy to be coming into my jail and making demands," he growls. I am not about to give up easily in my effort to visit Deeds.

The door suddenly opens behind me and an older

gentleman enters; he has stone-gray hair and faded blue eyes and walks with a limp.

"Officer Muddbottom," he greets the deputy, then gives me the once-over. "Who are you?"

"My name's Ivory Cade," I inform him. "And I've come to see a prisoner, Julip Deeds."

"He's one of them fellers involved in the shooting last evening, Sheriff," states the deputy.

"In what way?" inquires the old man.

"Saw it all. It was the cowboy who jumped to this here nigger's defense!"

"Watch your tongue, Turnel. Ain't no use to calling folks names in my presence. You know I'm a Christian man and don't hold with such ugliness."

Deputy Muddbottom flushed red from the warning, but did not speak out further, as is common with a man of low qualities who has just been put in his place by a better man.

"Are you a friend of Mr. Deeds?" asks the sheriff.

"I am."

"Well, he is in the back there, through that door. I am sure he will welcome the visit."

"Can I ask how long he will be here?"

"A grand jury will be impaneled later this morning to hear the facts and circumstances of the shooting. He could be bound over for trial. If that be the case, who knows his fate or time here, or on this earth."

"There's plenty that seen what happened," I protested. "I don't see how a man who defends himself can be considered guilty of anything!"

The elder man sat heavily in a chair and rested his faded blue gaze upon me.

"Son, I ain't a judge or a jury, I'm only a lawman. Whether or not your friend in there is guilty or not, isn't up to me. You want to do him a good turn, go on in there and pay him a visit. Maybe in a few days, you two can go have a beer together and celebrate the joys of life."

Deputy Muddbottom seemed to enjoy my consternation at this unforeseen circumstance: It was beyond my belief that Julip Deeds might be found guilty of murder, or anything other than that of being a good samaritan!

Glumly, I made my way to his cell. He was lying on a cot, his eyes open, staring up at the barred window above him; the light coming through was a blade of pearl; it reminded me of a painting I had once seen on a trip to the art museum in Dallas where the Sisters took us to bear witness of man's God-given creative talents.

In the painting a shaft of light poured through a window and fell upon the praying figure of a man who knelt down on a stone floor. I remember it as gloomy. So, too, the scene I now witnessed of the cowboy upon his bunk there in the shaft of free light falling upon an unfree man.

He smiled and sat up when I came near.

"Ivory," says he. "I sure am glad to see a friendly face!"

"How are they treating you, Mr. Deeds," was all that I could manage to say.

He smiled fully, then laughed, and said, "Ivory, I ain't but a few years older than you. You don't have to be putting no mister on the front of my name."

It was true, looking at him now without his hat pulled down on his head, that he was hardly any older than me or Albert, but that the wind and sun had weathered his face some (and I suppose the hard life of herding cows up months long trails). Now as I stood near studying his features, I could see Albert or me in another year or two.

"I . . . I just want you to know how grateful we all are for what you did last evening," I begin, for I have been up most of the night thinking of the words I want to tell him. They are words that have laid heavy in my belly like a bad meal all the night long.

"I didn't kill him for you, Ivory. I killed him because he pointed a gun at me and would've taken my life had I allowed it. That's the plain and simple fact of the matter."

"The sheriff says they are putting together a grand jury to hear evidence in that matter," say I joylessly.

"It don't matter," says he, seemingly unfazed by the bad news. "They will find me innocent. Everybody saw it. Ain't no use worrying when you've got the truth on your side."

"I figure maybe that's right, Julip," I say. "And I will be there to tell my side of the story."

"I still wish you'd consider joining our group to take them horses back to Texas. I reckon you'd be a good hand for you are of good cheer and pleasant disposition."

"I wish I could, Julip," says I. "But I have already thrown in with my other partner, Albert. If it weren't for that, I'd give your offer serious consideration."

Then deputy Muddbottom clangs on the door and says it's time for me to git, that visiting time is up. Julip sticks his hand through the bars and says, "I'll see you later on at the hearing."

I shake his hand but have run out of words to offer him.

"I'll sure enough be glad to be shed of this place and get back to Texas," he says in a chipper way as I leave him there in his tiny cell of gloom. Was it me, I think, I can't say how awful I would feel. But cowboys are different from all other of God's creatures.

FOURTEEN

I meet Albert and Man Who Waits at the cafe. Jasmine is there to wait on us. We share coffee and biscuits. Again, Albert is watching our financial resources—as he calls them. He is hoping that this is the day that Augustus Monroe will return from his hunting party and wants to be able to offer him every spare penny for his services. Neither the Indun or me complain about the meager victuals, however, for beggars can't be choosers.

Jasmine looks and smells fresh as spring flowers and offers me special attention which causes Albert to roll his eyes round in his head in mock fashion.

"Well," says Albert chewing on his biscuit that he

has loaded up with butter and honey. "When will Mr. Deeds be released from jail?"

"Don't know," I say. "The sheriff says that a grand jury will be impaneled to hear the evidence of the shooting."

Albert looked puzzled.

"Well everyone saw what went on last night. Don't seem like there'd be much evidence to dispute."

"I know," says I. "But something gives me a bad feeling about all this."

We talk about it for a time, the shooting, the way Deeds most likely saved us grief from the drunken cowboy, Kelly, and how unfair it seemed that Deeds was right this minute locked up in a jail cell and probably eating worse than us for his trouble.

We agreed that we would go to the grand jury hearing and give our own testimony and felt somewhat better knowing that it was now our turn to save Deeds from further grief.

Albert and the Indun allowed me a few private minutes to say my goodbyes to Jasmine, although the big German waitress, Hilda, eyed us from behind the counter with a scowl on her face. I reckoned, catching a glimpse of her over Jasmine's shoulder, that such a woman had never had a sweetheart, or been shot through the heart with Cupid's bow.

We stopped off at the jail and was told by the kindly sheriff that the grand jury hearing would take place in the Golden Palace Saloon just across the street in less than an hour. We went there, took up chairs near the front, and waited.

Soon enough, twelve of the local male populace strode in and took up chairs provided for them, and within minutes, Deputy Muddbottom brought in Julip Deeds, his wrists and ankles shackled in chains.

I tried to offer him a comforting look and he waved and smiled as though he wasn't worried about a thing. Muddbottom made him sit down and stood by cradling a shotgun in the crook of his arm.

Then, a stiff-backed man in a claw-hammer coat and shiny black pants made his way into the room and took up a seat behind a small desk that two men had carried in from another room off behind the bar.

Upon the man's entry, Muddbottom shouted, "Everybody rise, this hearing's now in session! Judge Dewater presiding!" and we did until the judge took his place behind the desk and ordered us to take our seats as well. He had a dry crackling voice and seemed to stare at no one in particular, as though he had gone through this business before, which he most likely had plenty of times.

"We are gathered here to hear evidence into last night's shooting in the Jezzebel Cattle Company Saloon of one Ike Kelly by one Julip Deeds. Let the proceedings begin."

First Deputy Muddbottom told his part of how he had heard the shots and come running and how when he arrived, he found Ike Kelly lying dead as "a coon" on the floor with a bullet hole through his face and out the back of his head and how when asked who had done the shooting, was told that it was another cowboy named Julip Deeds, which he pointed to sitting there in the chair manacled.

Then, several of the dead man's friends sat in the chair and testified how it was Kelly and ". . . that colored boy and Injin" sitting over there in the front row who was having an argument when Julip Deeds stepped out of the crowd and shot Kelly before he could even know what was happening. Several of them testified as to how Deeds had had it in for Kelly over past differences and how Deeds had sworn a vengeance oath on Kelly.

It was all lies of course and I was anxious to be called forth for my side of it. All the while the cowboy friends of the dead man are telling their lies, I watch to see what effect it is having on Deeds, but all I can see is him smiling pleasantly like he is sitting at a piano recital being polite and enjoying it some.

Finally, after the lies are all told, I am called forward and told, after swearing an oath of truth on a thick black Bible, to state my case.

"Julip Deeds did nothing wrong," I say firmly. "Unless you would consider one man coming to the defense of others as a wrongful act. It was Mr. Ike Kelly, although I did not know his name at the time, who began the show by calling me and him (I pointed toward Man Who Waits) hard names and questioning our presence inside the saloon. This, followed by him pulling one of his guns on us. All Mr. Deeds did was step forward and call him a drunken mean son of a bitch and that he should leave off on me and the Indun, to which he acted as though he would, having been called down like that. But then, he suddenly turned and aimed his pistol at Mr. Deeds and that is when Deeds shot him."

The judge had, the whole while I was stating the truth, been working a thumbnail between his teeth and generally acting as though he was bored. I waited— the whole room did—and then he turned his grave attention toward me and said: "So, Mr. Deeds called the deceased a drunken mean son of a bitch?"

"Yes sir he did, and yes sir, he was—Kelly, I mean. For he was drunk and being mean and, I'd say, a son of a bitch for the way he was treating us. All we was doing was eating a lunch meat sandwich and some beans!"

I was excused from the chair and some other cowboys came up and pretty much said the same thing that I had, all of them friends of Deeds, but the stiff judge didn't seem to care much one way or the other, or so it seemed.

Finally, all the witnesses and spectators were asked to leave the room while the jury convened among themselves. We waited outside and in less than ten minutes were let back in.

"I am binding over for trial, one Julip Deeds, for the murder of one Ike Kelly," was the judge's announcement. Then he explained that the jury's determination had been based on the fact that Deeds had inflamed the situation by having called Kelly a drunken son of a bitch and thereby causing the man to defend his own honor.

It seemed faulty reasoning from where I sat.

The trial would be held the next day, same place, at ten o'clock in the morning. There was a lot of noise raised on both sides and the judge slammed down his gavel to quiet the crowd, then ordered the bar open.

I glanced at Deeds. He was no longer smiling.

We waited all the rest of that day for Augustus Monroe and his hunting party to return, but dusk found us still waiting with no sighting of the famed shootist.

Topeka had proved a troubling place as far as I was concerned. Had it not been for the presence of Jasmine, I am not sure that I would have stayed there one more day. The fact that the citizens had chosen to try an innocent man was as equally disturbing to me as was the death scene the night previous inside the Jezzebel Cattle Company Saloon. I had now witnessed violence from both the black man (Rufus Buck) and the white (Ike Kelly), and the only thing I knew for sure was, it seemed to be drawing closer to me every day.

I went to spend an hour at noontime with Jasmine during her meal break and promised that I would return that evening for our usual stroll, but she informed me that her daddy was feeling poorly and would have to go straight home that night. I was not sure that she was not just telling me such in order to avoid more temptation. Anyway, I felt blue because of it.

Albert and me and the Indun spent the rest of that evening playing whist. Man Who Waits caught on to the game quickly saying that the Comanches played a similar game but used bones instead of cards (how that was I cannot say, nor did I ask for fear of another grisly tale).

The next morning, we left off having any breakfast at all and went straight away back to the makeshift courthouse at the Golden Palace Saloon. Already a large crowd has gathered, but we manage to squirm our way inside, though we had to stand, for all seats were taken.

The trial had convened much as the previous day's grand jury hearing with Judge Dewater entering wearing the same claw hammer coat and shiny pants and stiff formality.

Everyone stood, then sat back down again except for those of us who did not have chairs.

Once more, Deputy Muddbottom led in Julip Deeds, manacled the same as yesterday and ordered him to sit in a chair near the front.

It took all of an hour to convict Julip Deeds of murder. The judge called the killing wanton, and stated that the citizens of Topeka had a right to demand their safety from the wild cowboys that invaded their hamlet every summer!

"Young man," he stated in that dry crackle of a voice as Muddbottom made the prisoner stand up. "This court, having found you guilty, has determined to set an example to all cowboys and wild drovers who choose to bring their cattle to our town, that Topekans will not any longer tolerate or condone the murderous behavior of a few! I thereby sentence you to be hanged at first light, tomorrow morning! Do you have anything you wish to say to this court!"

The judge's pronouncement rang in my ears more loudly than pistol fire. *How could this be!*

My own hot anger pushed me to my feet.

"You have convicted an innocent man!" I shouted. I rushed to the jury box and repeated my accusation to twelve white startled faces. They blinked their eyes and let their jaws fall open.

I could hear Judge Dewater shouting that I should be restrained and saw from the corner of my eye, Deputy Muddbottom making his cautious approach. But now was no time to fake a seizure.

I turned my attention to the stern old man who sat behind the spindle-legged desk.

"It ain't right!" says I. "It ain't right to convict and hang an innocent man! It would be worse than murder!"

"You will shut your mouth and sit down!" says he. "Or I will have the deputy knock you in the head and retain you in his jail for contempt of court!"

"I don't care what you do to me!" I state, my voice breaking with all the anger welled up inside me. "What sort of place is Topeka, Kansas, that would hang an innocent man?"

"Deputy!" shouts the judge. "Do your duty and arrest this boy for contempt! Use any means necessary to bring him under control!"

Deputy Muddbottom, cautious about approaching too close, leveled the twin barrels of his shotgun at me and said: "Give it up boy, or I'll air you out like a bedsheet!"

I was no match for the judicial system as imposed by Judge Dewater and Deputy Muddbottom.

I looked hopelessly at Julip Deeds who was slumped in his chair. He tried to smile but couldn't. It had been my good fortune, I suppose, to have left the Navy pistol, that Albert had presented me, back at the hotel. For had I been armed, I might just as well gone to violence myself in that mad moment.

Deputy Muddbottom marched me off to jail, and I never did hear Julip Deeds's final words to the court. In a little while, he was brought back and placed in the cell next to mine.

"I guess you two can spend the rest of the afternoon and evening sticking up for one another," laughed Muddbottom in obvious delight over our circumstance.

For a long while, neither Deeds or myself spoke. Finally, he said: "I appreciate everything you said on my behalf today, Ivory. I appreciate, too, the way you stood up to all of them."

"It didn't do any good," I said.

"No. It did not. But it was the gesture of a true friend."

"I should have kept my mouth shut and just busted

you out of jail tonight," I told him, my heart in my boots.

"They'd a probably killed you for trying."

There was lots of things I wanted to say to him, but what do you say to a fellow that is just hours from his own death?

"Ivory," says he after a long time more of silence. I find it hard to look into his sad face.

"I have a ma that lives near Sweetwater, not far from Chili Pepper down in Texas. I know that she will never hear about me if someone don't tell her. I would not want her to know that I was hanged, for she would see it as my having turned out bad and it would only break her heart to hear such news." He then sighed greatly and I could tell by the way his voice sounded that he was fighting back tears.

"Ivory . . . I would appreciate it if, when you could see your way clear, you'd take her the news that I had lost my life crossing a river, or maybe in a lightning storm, or even stomped by a horse. I'll let you choose whatever story you'd care to make up. Knowing I died at the hands of nature would not leave her so sad and brokenhearted, as it would if she knowed I passed from this earth as an innocent man hanged by wrong-informed citizens."

He then partly turned away from me and I knew the reason why. I wanted to tell him what Jasmine had told me: that there is no shame in a man shedding tears. Who would blame him for the inconsolable circumstances he now faced?

"I will deliver whatever news you want me to," I say softly. "If you'd care to write a last letter, or have me take your belongings to her, I will."

After a few muffled moments, he screwed up his courage once more and said, without turning to look at me there in that dim light that is part of the gloom of such places as jails: "I knew you was a good fellow the first moment I laid eyes on you out on the prairie."

I remember once back at the orphanage of being "switched" for some trouble I had gotten myself into and then being placed in the "Silent Room" by Sister Waldo, a dedicated bride of our Savior without an ounce of mercy or understanding of the mischief that boys is bound to get into.

The room was dark and forbidding and damp and cold. And so silent that I could hear my own heart thumping down inside my chest and the air passing through my nose with each breath. It was the most forlorn I had ever felt, sitting there on the cold stone floor of that room waiting for someone to come let me out. To know you ain't got a ma nor pa nor kin to love you and rescue you is about as bad a feeling as you can have in this life.

But now, sitting there across from Julip in the other cage, knowing what would soon be his fate in a matter of hours, I can't says I've ever felt worse about a thing and that my time in the Silent Room was nothing in comparison to the helplessness and hopelessness of the moment.

Albert came that afternoon to visit me, and so did

the Indun, but Muddbottom would not let the Indun come into his jail and made him wait outside on the walk.

"How are you being treated, Ivory?" Albert inquired. I could only turn my eyes to Julip Deeds's cell. Julip had taken to his cot and had flung his arm over his eyes (in order to block out all things, I reckoned).

"I am okay," I informed Albert.

"I have inquired as to your release, and Deputy Muddbottom says he will let you go in the morning, right before . . ." Albert almost said the words that nobody wanted to hear, but held himself when he realized it.

"I don't much care if they keep me in here forever," I say with anger. "It would not surprise me if they did!"

I could see by the troubled look on his face, that Albert was just as much at a loss over words to comfort me as I had been with Julip.

I softened my own voice.

"How is the Indun?" I said as a way of skirting the present condition of us all.

"He's hungry, as usual," says Albert with a weak smile.

"I ain't surprised. Tell him he can come and take my place in here and eat whatever grub is brought to prisoners."

"I'm sure he wouldn't mind. The old man could eat most anything, including tin cans, I suspect."

We talked on like that for a short while more until we both could see that there was nothing more could be done about my plight, or that of Deeds. Finally, Albert said goodbye and that he would be round first thing in the morning when I was to be released.

"I'll spring for a big breakfast," he stated. "It'll just have to come out of Mr. Monroe's portion." I thanked him and watched, clutching the cold hard bars of my tribulation, as he passed through the jailer's door and out into the evening. Julip sat up as soon as Albert had left and said: "You are lucky to have such good friends."

"Yes," I admitted that I was.

Deputy Muddbottom entered carrying two plates of beans and a loaf of fresh bread. Strangely enough, he said little as he placed the grub through the slots in our cell doors. He simply looked first at Deeds, then at me, and then turned and walked out.

"You can have mine if you want," said Julip, looking down at his plate.

"Naw, I ain't hungry either," I say truthfully. It has been all day since I have eaten anything, but I have no hunger and all I can feel in my belly is a knot.

We place our plates on the floor and ignore them.

"Ivory," says Julip after a long time of silence. "Will you pray with me?"

I feel off kilter at such a question, for I have never been a body of great faith even though (and maybe in spite of) the fact that the Catholics had a great influence on much of my, so far, life. The Sisters (the bulk of them, anyway), was mostly good-hearted and well-intentioned creatures of soft white skin worn under their black garments whose whole life was practically lived around praying and I can (honestly) say, I never seen where it done them all that much good. For theirs was a life of hard labor—scrubbing stone floors on their hands and knees, and plunging their arms clean up to the elbow into hot vats of soapy lye water whilst doing the daily laundry and so forth. Theirs was a life of being without things such as husbands and children and womanly gossip. Theirs was a life lived plain and without any earthly rewards such as a normal body would expect, or want.

No, I never did get the hang of prayer and its true meaning or see in any way, how it could work out as a worthwhile endeavor. I always figured that maybe if I'd been born female and entered the convent, I might've been let in on the great secrets that resided in the minds and hearts of the Sisters. But, I wasn't.

"Sure, Julip, I'll pray with you if that is what you want," I say. (What would anyone have done given the same request true belief or no?)

For a time there, it was sort of like being asked to dance and each one waiting for the other to take the lead. Me waiting for Julip to say something, him waiting for me.

Finally, he says, "Ivory, I never have prayed for nothing before in my life. I don't know how it is done . . ."

"Well," I say. "It is just like talking to your pa, or

ma, I reckon." (Although the Sisters oftentimes mumbled loudly when they took up the cause, or sometimes sang in sweet melodious harmony—which I preferred above the other way.)

Albert got down on his knees and leaned his elbows on his bunk, took a great breath and let it out again, and commenced. I won't reveal the details, for I feel now, even after all this time has passed, that he was and is entitled to his privacy in that sad circumstance.

I will admit, that what he had to say, and how he said it, caused me to wipe at my eyes several times and I could not have felt more pitiful than were he my own flesh and blood.

Upon finishing he said: "Did you pray, too?"

I nodded that I had, and I suppose, thinking back on it, I was praying inside, somehow, without fully knowing it.

It seemed enough for him.

"I feel relieved of my earthly burdens," he said. "And feel that the Lord has prepared a place for me in heaven. I ain't scared no more of dying tomorrow."

I looked into his face and saw a sweet serenity and knew that something special had happened to him.

"Julip," I say.

"Yes."

"I will be awake if any time during the night you care to talk."

"Thank you, Ivory, but I reckon I am all set."

FIFTEEN

I remember it as having been both the longest and the shortest night I ever spent, those waning hours there in the cell with Julip Deeds nearby, both of us waiting for the morning, but hoping that it would somehow not arrive. But, it did. The gray light seeping through the one and only window where us prisoners were kept. Gray light that seemed cold and uninviting—and, unwanted.

I tried rubbing the weariness from my eyes, for all night I had lain awake, unable to sleep a wink. Occasionally, Julip and me carried on small conversations that lasted no more than a few minutes at a time.

His voice was soft and sometimes broken, but mostly he held up as good and brave as could be expected of any man.

Deputy Muddbottom came in early jingling his big ring of keys and stated: "I'm letting you go, boy! You and your friends would be best advised to ride on out of Topeka and go somewheres else."

I looked at Julip as the door was swung open for me and Deputy Muddbottom stood there waiting impatiently with his big belly draped over his belt.

Julip didn't bother to offer me his hand, nor rise from his bunk. I understood. We had already made our peace with one another.

I walked past the deputy and out the door where Albert and the Indun were waiting for me.

"Do you want breakfast, Ivory?" Albert asked.

"No," I stated. "I have no appetite."

"How is your friend in there?" asked Man Who Waits.

"As well as can be expected," I said.

"It is a poor thing," says he, "to be hung up by the neck with a rope. That is no good way for a brave man to have to die."

"No, it ain't!"

"Ivory, I hope you're not thinking about trying to break him out!" says Albert. "There are a number of armed deputies on their way here now—me and the chief saw them on our way over."

I had been thinking about just such a thing.

"You would be shot down and killed," said Albert, reading my thoughts. I felt like cussing him for doing so.

"And, Mr. Deeds would still be hung. There is nothing more we can do for that poor fellow." I felt like cussing him for telling me I couldn't do anything to help Deeds. I felt like cussing him for telling me the truth: There was no way to help my friend, Julip Deeds.

"I will not leave him die without a friend looking on," I state.

"I understand, Ivory," said Albert. "We'll stand with you, me and Man Who Waits.

The armed deputies passed us by and marched into the sheriff's office just at that moment. There were all darkly dressed and somber men who carried shotguns cradled in their arms. It seemed to me madness that it would take so many men to hang a boy not much older than myself. But then, I guess that is what outright murder is: Madness!

A sizable crowd had gathered around the jail. Out back, beyond a high fence, there stood a gallows, and the crowd was working its way into the little space beyond the fence.

I was surprised at the number of women and children that had come to witness the gruesome spectacle and felt a bitterness toward them because they had. I felt bitter that they had not stayed home and baked breads and cooked and cleaned and played in their yards and chased puppies and done all the things normal folks should be doing at such an hour. I felt bitter that they had not come to save Julip Deeds from having his neck broke by a hemp rope, but instead had come to be entertained by it, to be startled and shocked by it, to witness a spectacle they could talk about for days to come and then forget when the next terrible thing would come along in their lives.

I was bitter at just about everyone and everything.

Soon enough, the yard surrounding the small simple gallows was filled to overflowing with Topekans. A candy butcher worked his way through the crowd, and another sold lemonade and both did a brisk business. A photographer set up his box camera on a tripod to record the event. I felt sickened and saddened by it all, and would have fled had it not been that I wanted Julip to be able to look down in that crowd of (uncherished?) faces and see at least one who deemed him a friend and comrade. It was the least I could do for him. It was the most I could do for him.

I could not bear to think of poor Julip as I stood there waiting for the deputies to bring him forth. I thought instead of Otero and wondered just what he was doing this very moment.

I imagined him to be shoeing one of his horses, or mucking out the stalls, probably cursing me with each breath for having abandoned him and his kindness after having rescued me from the Sisters and the orphanage. Or perhaps, he was constructing a new coffin for some unfortunate citizen (like Deeds himself), the whole while sipping at his greasy liquor and letting the pine sap stick to his fingers and the sawdust cling to his arms.

I thought, sadly, that maybe he was dead. Maybe the liquor had killed him, or he had fallen from a wagon, or simply died in his sleep. It was all possible.

No matter how hard I tried not to think of it, death seemed all around me, seemed to reach down in my bones.

A stir from the crowd brought my attention to the back door of the jail. I could see the tall hats of the deputies bobbing up and down, weaving their way through the gathered mass. I knew that Julip was between them, being led toward the gallows. A lank, bearded man had climbed the steps and now stood passively by the lever that would spring the trap door.

His pants were too short and several inches above his shoes.

I found myself holding my breath as the sea of people was parted by the shotgun-toting deputies. I closed my eyes for a minute against the glare of the morning sun and asked one last time that God not let this thing happen. I waited for thunder and lightning and the sky to be rent apart, but knew down in my soul that no such thing would happen.

I noticed when the deputies aided him up the first few steps (for his ankles were in shackles still, as were his wrists), that Julip had taken care to fix his bandanna neatly around his neck and had brushed the dust from his clothes.

As he neared the top step, he stumbled a bit and the deputies caught him up by the arms and lifted him onto the platform. Then, he was made to stand over the trap, while the sheriff read a statement that somehow got lost on the wind and amid the "huzzing" of the crowd.

"He has a calm and peaceful countenance," whispered Albert.

He seemed smallish between the armed deputies.

"I should have tried breaking him out," I said with all due regret that I had not.

The Indun began humming a low chant that caused several of the crowd to turn around and stare at him. His own eyes were closed, however, and he continued his plainsong unabated.

"I think it is some sort of death chant," said Albert.

"In honor of Mr. Deeds's braveness." I tended to agree that it most likely was.

I stared up and into the peaceful face of my friend and after a time, his gaze came to rest on me. Without knowing how, or understanding unseen forces, I can only state that the face that should have broken my heart, that should have brought me to tears and more anger, did not, but instead, somehow (amazingly so), brought to me instead, comfort.

The faded blue eyes of the young cowboy spoke to me in ways that no words could and told me not to worry about him 'cause he was going on to a far better place than any of us could know.

There was forgiveness in those eyes. There was hope.

I felt the tears slide down my cheeks as the lank man with the beard stepped forward and placed a black hood over those faded blue eyes, over that peaceful countenance, and then stepped back and placed his hand upon the lever.

Albert muttered: "Damn!" And the Indun kept up his mournful hum.

And then, with unexpected suddenness, the lank man pulled the lever toward him and the trap door banged open. I closed my eyes against the terror.

Me and Albert and the Indun followed the wagon that carried the plain wooden coffin holding Julip Deeds's mortal remains out to the cemetery. None of the crowd, except for the cowboy friends of Deeds, bothered with that part of the proceedings, having lost interest beyond the sensationalness of a public hanging. (I was just as glad they had for I was in a fighting mood and ready to bloody the high spirits of any spectator.)

There was no words spoken for Deeds, for no minister or Bible-carrying man of the cloth, bothered to show up. None of the cowboys spoke up either, but that was not uncommon on their part, being mostly quiet men except when drunk or drinking. We all just stood for a time holding our hats in our hands and allowing the wind to swirl the dust around our feet before lowering the coffin into the hole that had already been dug.

As a way of expressing our regrets, we each took a shovelful of dirt and scooped it down into the grave, and one cowboy, upon completion of our efforts, threw in his makins, saying that maybe Deeds would appreciate a smoke now and again.

Then all but me and Albert and the Indun drifted back toward town.

I have to be honest with Albert.

"I don't know how much longer I can stand waiting for Mr. Monroe to show up," says I. "I'm of a mind to leave this place and all places like it. Kansas has been nothing more than misery and uncertainty to me. I hope you can understand that."

Albert shuffles his toe in the dirt for a few moments, then says: "I understand, Ivory. And, if you don't feel you can go on, I don't blame you. Most would have already turned back. You have grit, no one can say different."

I know that what's inside me can't be consoled and am just feeling rambunctious for things to want to change. I am grown tired of having things happen to me instead of the other way around. I am anxious for either a fight or a change of scenery altogether. I am no longer willing to be laid at the doorstep of fate (as has been the story of my life thus far).

"I will make this agreement with you, Albert," says I after several more minutes of reflection. "If Mr. Augustus Monroe has not returned by tomorrow noon, I will be on my way. Where, exactly, I do not know. Or, you and me and the Indun can go after Rufus Buck ourselves and get this matter settled. Whichever you decide. But, I ain't going to just stand by and see misery rain down on me and my friends any longer."

Albert thrusts forth his hand and says, "You are absolutely right, Ivory Cade. It is time we make matters happen instead of what we have been doing. Come noon tomorrow, if Mr. Monroe has not shown his face, we will either go home or go to our glory. I could not ask more from you than that!"

We shake hands warmly and firmly and at once I feel the heavy weight of waiting lift from my shoulders.

The Indun finally halts his plainsong and shudders slightly as though a cold wind had passed through his blood.

"I think that our journey has not ended yet," he says.

"But, a man can not travel far on an empty belly." I am up to spending the last of my own money to see that we have a good meal and lift a glass of beer to the memory of our departed friend and ally, Julip Deeds. Later, I hope to see Jasmine. And there, in the midday of a blue and clear sky, I say a last silent goodbye to the cowboy who had turned friend without my asking.

SIXTEEN

I whiled away the rest of the day by riding the prairie on Swatchy, letting him run full out by giving him his head. The wind sang past my ears and whistled through my clothes and it felt like as though I could ride forever and not stop. My only thoughts were of Julip Deeds—the one who should've been riding the prairie instead of me. He had every right.

I rode Swatchy until he near gave out and then brought him to rest by a little stream and let him drink his fill and catch his wind. I didn't want to ever go back to Topeka again, but knew that I must. I had made a promise to Albert that I would wait until noon the next day for Augustus Monroe to show his face. I had hoped strongly that he would not, and that I could be free of my promises of revenge, for I'd had dearly enough of killing and murdering and dying in general.

I stayed out there amongst the sweeping grass all the day long and lay on my back and stared up at the clouds that passed overhead like big sailing ships floating in a blue sea. And if I could, I would have flown up there and ridden on one of them clouds clear across the country and maybe into the next.

Then, too, there was Jasmine to think about. Whether she cared for me or not in the same way as I had cared for her remained a mystery still.

She tugged at my heart one way, the death of Deeds the other.

I found the events of that morning, and the previous night in which I slept not at all, had left me completely wore out. I closed my eyes and let sleep take me. It was a gentle sweet feeling to slide down into the darkness and away from the tragic events of earlier.

I awoke in time to ride back to town and wait in front of the cafe for Jasmine. As usual, the German waitress, Hilda, showed first carrying her tote full of breads, her big feet stuffed into carpet slippers. I noticed then, she seemed to have no ankles.

"So, you're still here, ya?" she said, staring at me with her steely gray eyes that matched her steely gray hair that was pulled up into a loose bun atop her head. She was big and horsey and her opinion of me was no longer of concern—my mood being especially insociable that evening.

"Yes'm, I still am, and I reckon I will be for as long as I want and I reckon further, it should be of no concern to you!"

She took a faltering step backward, for it was plain that in the past, she had taken her enjoyment from causing me great discomfort by her mere presence, and now I had stood up to her bold as a brass monkey.

"You are a smart aleck with a wicked tongue in your mouth!" she declared.

"Maybe so, Miss Hilda," I tell her right back. "But I ain't no longer going to let you cow me!" With those words, she did a quick shuffle off down the walk, the cheeks of her backside fighting one another for a place under her skirts.

Jasmine showed forth just then and wondered aloud what I had done or said to Hilda. I said nothing more than what I should have done the first time I took wind of her. Jasmine declared me uncivil but laughed anyway.

We took our stroll out to our where the town gave out and the prairie began, out to the fallen cottonwood where I had gotten my first kiss stolen.

There were few words spoken between us and I wondered if she had heard the news that I had spent the night in jail, or that I had stood helplessly by and watched Deeds get hung. It was not something that I felt like discussing.

She told me that her daddy was feeling somewhat better. I said that was a good thing. Then she started kissing me in a way that I would describe as sudden and "hungry." It felt good, the passion of her and the way she held me.

"I can't help myself 'bout you, Ivory Cade," she breathed into my ear between those hungry kisses. "I tried and tried to tell myself to stay clear of you, but, I got a fever for you!"

I don't know exactly how or just when it happened, but before I knew it, we was both naked rolling around on the grass in each other's arms. It was the first time

I ever did see a girl naked (except for Junebug Watts a cross-eyed little carrot-headed gal back at the orphanage who one day ran down the corridors without a stitch on yelling at the top of her lungs that Sister Piquat was trying to kill her with a butcher's knife. Everyone knew that Junebug didn't have all her senses). It was a great pleasure, what I saw.

Our union was a natural thing, is all I can say. There couldn't have been anything more natural on this earth, than her and me at that moment. I still think of her often. And whenever I do, I still hold a special place in my heart for Jasmine Winfred Lucille Pettycash. I hope she still thinks of me occasionally. It would be nice to know that she did.

And for once, in all my life, I forgot all the bad things of this world and thought of only one thing: Jasmine and her sweet sweet love.

Afterward we sat and talked and held hands and she said: "Ivory, that was the first time for me."

"Me, too," I stated.

"Honest?"

"I wouldn't lie about something like that."

"I's glad then that you ain't had no other girl other than me."

"I'm glad, too," I say, and mean it.

"I know I should be shamed of myself for doin' it with you out here in the open, but I ain't. Not at all."

"I don't see why you should be," I say. "Or me either. What we done seemed like the right thing to me."

"You won't tell nobody, will you?"

"No. Nobody needs to know."

"Not even those friends of yours?"

"No, not them either."

She sighed deeply and leaned her head against my shoulder.

"What will become of you tomorrow?" she said.

"Well, I don't know. We have agreed to wait for Mr. Monroe until noon tomorrow. If he don't show by then, I'm not sure what will happen to us, where we will go, or what we will do."

"But most likely you will go somewhere?"

"I expect so."

"I know my heart will break in two if you leave," she said.

"Maybe if I do leave, I will come back," I said.

"No. I don't reckon you ever will. You don't look like the sort of boy that will ever come back to Topeka, Kansas."

"Maybe because of you, I will."

She kissed me again, but this time tenderly and on the cheek.

"Whatever gel winds up with you, Ivory Cade, will be doin' good by herself."

"Maybe I *will* come back and take you away from here with me," I said. "Maybe after me and Albert's business is concluded, I'll come back."

"I'd like to think that you would, but I won't go holdin' my breath waitin' on you." She laughed sweetly, as she did everything sweetly and I could not help but tell myself how much in love I was with her.

"You better walk me home," she said. "At least partways, it is gettin' late and my daddy will be worried."

"I'd like to meet your daddy sometime," I told her.

"He sure wouldn't like to meet you," she said.

"Why not?"

" 'Cause he could see right off that you was a heart thief."

"Well I don't know nothing about that," I said, sort of feeling both embarrassed and proud that she would think me so.

"No, it's best that you don't come around in front of my daddy, he'd sure run the likes of you off, and with good reason, I suspect." Then she laughed again and stood and straightened herself and offered me her hand.

I found my companions still up waiting for me at the hotel.

Man Who Waits looked me directly in the eyes and smiled that nearly toothless smile of his and said: "It is done, you have become a man."

"Is it true?" asked Albert.

In spite of my desire to sing Jasmine's praises, I could not break a trust that I had made to her there on the prairie. It wasn't in me to tell low tales of a private nature.

"I reckon I don't know a thing about what he is talking about," I say with a stone face.

Albert simply offers me that innocent smile of his and says, "I understand a man not wanting to discuss delicate matters that involve his beloved. It is a trait I can respect and won't ask you any further about the subject."

I can't say, looking at the Indun's rugged old kisser, that he would offer me the same privilege. I knowed him to be indelicate about most things but assigned it to his wild nature as opposed to simple mean-spiritedness.

We rose early and waited outside the hotel and within an hour of doing so, were not disappointed. A rising cloud of dust far out on the west road signaled the arrival of the hunting party led by Augustus Monroe.

Within minutes, they were sweeping past our hotel: Augustus Monroe (as pointed out to me by an excited Albert), riding a dappled gray stud with flowing mane and tail, lead the procession of wagons and riders that included some mighty fine dressed gentlemen, the finest of whom I supposed were the dukes and one tall gentleman wearing a black and red jacket and a curly hat, I assumed to be the Russian prince we had heard about.

The wagons were being driven by bullwhackers who made a big show of it by cracking their whips into the air and making them sound like pistol shots. One wagon contained several hides of bear and antelope and mule deer and mountain lion and wolf—all with the heads still attached.

My attention was mostly drawn to Augustus Monroe. He appeared awfully old, but a man who seemed to possess much flair anyways. He was sort of heavy around the middle, had long, faded brown hair that spilled out from under a cream-white Boss-of-the-Plains Stetson, and a long auburn mustache that dropped below his chin. He was dressed in fringed and beaded buckskins much like the Indun wore, but of a better quality. He rode the trotting stallion like it was a natural part of him.

We fell in behind the procession, Albert, me, and the Indun, all the way to the Brassfield Hotel which, with its tall windows and porticos, appeared the finest in Topeka.

There, Mr. Monroe, and his party of fancy dressed gentlemen, dismounted and strode inside. We followed them in. They took their liberty in the bar, which was equally ornate, and talked loudly to one another, shaking hands all around and slapping one another on the shoulder in a congratulatory manner.

"We'll wait until he gets off by himself," said Albert. "I would not want my business known by everyone."

Augustus Monroe seemed to be the center of everyone's attention: his own party—the dukes and the Russian prince who seemed not much older than either me or Albert the employees of the hotel, and several of the guests who came up and shook the famed man's hand repeatedly.

I noticed, paying close attention to his countenance, that he possessed a weariness about him, like a man that had labored long and hard at something he didn't care much about, but did it anyway.

His smile seemed easy enough toward the others, but insincere, at least from where I stood.

Several hours passed, hours that were filled with conversation of the just ended hunt, and rounds of cognac being lifted in small delicate glasses, and the smoking of long green cigars. And then, slowly, as if the talk had worn them out more than the hunt itself, the men began to break up and drift off up the stairs to their appointed rooms.

Until at last, Augustus Monroe sat by himself in the tufted red velvet chair with the curved arms and legs and high back. He seemed a lonely king.

Albert said we should go up to him now that he was alone and we could discuss our business in private. Albert said that maybe we ought to remove our hats out of respect and to show him we wasn't there for trouble, and further, were not carrying pistols in our hands. Albert said his daddy had once told him that Augustus Monroe was a very dangerous man when approached by strangers. I said to Albert that maybe he ought to have mentioned this fact a little earlier in the game. He merely grinned and asked me if I was not being overly sisterly in my caution. I said that it was no shame for a man not to want to be plugged full of holes by a dangerous killer of men.

Mr. Monroe seemed not to notice our approach at first, for the wide brim of his Stetson had fallen low over his brow and his chin seemed to rest nearly on his chest, as though he were dozing, or having suffered the effects of the cognac, of which he seemed to have consumed his share with ease in the several hours of celebration of his hunting party.

But then, as we got to within five feet of where he was sitting, he snapped up his head and leveled his clear-eyed gaze at us like an old bull that had just noticed us crossing his pasture.

"Who are you boys? And hold it right there!" His voice, for all its command, was surprisingly high-pitched, almost womanly, I thought. It was, unnerving.

Albert said: "Mr. Monroe, I am Albert Sand, and this here is Ivory Cade, and that there is Man Who Waits for Winter, Comanche, of the Antelope Eating band."

His gaze narrowed at the introductions.

"Who are you?" he said again.

"I just told you who we were, Mr. Monroe," said Albert.

"No! I mean who do you represent?"

"Oh," said Albert with a sigh of relief. "We represent ourselves."

"I suppose you have come to get my autograph," said Monroe after a long full moment of studying us, then leaning back once more in his chair and giving us a sloppy look of indifference.

"No sir," said Albert, then seeing as how that answer evoked a look of slight disappointment on Mr. Monroe's face, he quickly retreated by saying: "I . . . mean it would be an honor to have your autograph, but that ain't why we come."

"Then why did you come?" said Monroe, looking

disinterested in the three of us, which I cannot say that I blame him, for we don't represent ourselves well in our run-down appearance, nor do we match up to his equal.

"We . . . I came to hire you to help track down my pa's killers."

Mr. Monroe arched his left eyebrow at the good news we had brought him.

"Who's your daddy, boy?" says he.

"Joe Sand, constable of Last Whiskey, Texas, Deaf Smith County—or at least he was until Rufus Buck and his cutthroats rode in and murdered him!"

The old bull leaned forward slightly and clicked his teeth.

"Joe Sand, you say?"

"Yes sir."

"Seems I have heard that name somewhere before."

"Yes sir, my pa knew you back in Abilene."

"Abilene? Son, Abilene was a long time back."

"Yes sir, it was."

You could tell by the way his eyes shifted around in his head that he was trying to remember. Finally, he shook his head and said: "I don't recall your father."

"It don't matter," said Albert. "I have come to hire you regardless."

"Rufus Buck you say is the man who killed him?"

"Rufus Buck and the men with him."

"That's bad people," said Monroe. "Down in Texas was it?"

"Yes sir, down in Texas."

"That's funny," said Mr. Monroe. "I have never heard of Rufus Buck's bunch going that far south. They mostly are known to terrorize the Indian Nations and on east into the Oklahoma Territory, and once in awhile over into Arkansas, but not much so more with Judge Parker's court and marshals handling that section."

"Well sir," said Albert. "They did come to Texas and they did murder my father and I aim to see them dead for having done it. I have brought along three hundred and fifty dollars reward money, my own savings, that is yours if you will help us."

Upon the announcement, Augustus Monroe looked from Albert to the Indun to me, spending enough time on each of us (I suppose) to make his assessment of our little bunch.

"You ain't but boys," says he.

"We're carrying my pa's Navies and know how to use them," says Albert. "And I reckon it don't matter whether it is a young finger or an old one that pulls the trigger, for if the aim is true, him that is aimed at will die just as dead!"

Monroe smiled at Albert's little speech. I nearly did myself, for it was a good one in my book.

"Boys!" he hoots. "Three hundred and fifty dollars would keep me in cards and good whiskey and good whores for about a week, then after that, I'd be no better off than I am today. I just brought back a hunting party of dukes and a Russian prince, and for that I was paid one thousand dollars! What do you think of that!"

The disappointment was plain on Albert's face. Mr. Monroe wasn't for hire, at least not at what Albert could afford.

"I thought you was a man of honor, that stood for justice and righteousness," he said to Mr. Monroe.

The old bull laughed even harder, laughed and wheezed until his face flushed dark red as beets.

"Hell son, that's right!" he states between wheezes. "It says so in them Dime Novels that DeWitt writes about me, and that pasty-brained Ned Buntline and all them reporters from the *Police Gazette* and *Harper's Weekly*!"

I could see Albert's disappointment beginning to turn to a shaky anger at the unsympathetic way Mr. Monroe was behaving.

"Albert," I whisper to him. "Maybe Monroe's had too much cognac and ain't his usual self."

He whispers back, through gritted teeth, that intoxication should not be used as an excuse for discourteousness.

"I figured you as a man that would want to right a wrong and erase evil from this world!" declared Albert in a more sober way than I had ever seen him before. "But, I reckon I figured wrong. Come on, Ivory. Let's be on our way, for Mr. Monroe is no salvation at all!"

Mr. Monroe stopped his laughing then, and eyed Albert with a serious nature.

"Are you trying to insult me?" he said, his voice growing even higher still.

I could see that he was well armed with a pair of Navies of his own, whose pearl grips caught the light and shone prettily. He was also armed with a dagger—a long-bladed variety with a bone handle. There was no telling what was hidden inside his pockets.

Albert (to his credit, I suppose) stood his ground, locking gazes with that of the shootist, hunter, and man killer.

"No sir, I am not trying to insult you. I thought you was the man I needed for a job. I made a mistake and won't trouble you further."

Monroe stood up from his chair then. He was well over six feet tall and broad shouldered and heavy chested. He seemed, to me, dangerous just standing there like he was; like as though he could kill you just by standing there staring at you.

"I am somewhat drunk and tired, having just returned from a successful hunt," says he. "You don't know what it is like to sport around Englishmen and a Russian prince. They take their sport of hunting seriously and with much passion. And when they ain't shooting critters, they are fond of drinking hard liquor and arm-wrestling and jawing the whole night long to where a body cannot get much rest.

"Now I sympathize with you, son, over the loss of your daddy, and I wish I could say truthfully that I could recall knowing him, but I can't. And was I ten years younger, and a good deal poorer and didn't have Englishmen and Russian princes paying me big wads of money to sport them around on hunting parties, I might just take up your offer of three hundred and fifty dollars' reward money and go after of Rufus Buck and his bloodletters—for it would be fun to raise that kind of hell again!

"But the plain and simple fact is, I am content to stay right here where I am at and be a hunting guide and a celebrity to the well-heeled foreigners and gents from the East. It suits me just fine, this style of living. Now, if you'll excuse me, I feel the necessity of a hot bath, a fifty-dollar whore, and a good night's rest afterward."

And with that, he touched a forefinger to the sweeping brim of his Stetson and made the spiral staircase to the upper rooms.

"Well," said Albert. "I guess we have ridden a long way for nothing." He was cheerless.

"The way I look at it," says I. "We've got two choices left to us: we can either turn back and give up the chase, or we can try and bring Rufus Buck to his end ourselves. I'm with you either way you want to go, Albert." It is brave talk on my part for someone who has had his fill of death and destruction of the human being. But, I wish nothing more on the other hand, than to cheer poor Albert's spirits. For he, maybe more than any of us, has suffered his loss greatly and with dignity.

"I don't know, Ivory," he mutters. "It would seem too much to ask you to continue on with me without us having an experienced gun to help us go up against

Rufus Buck. I would not like to see you dead on my behalf."

"Well, Albert," I say. "I would not like to see me dead either. But, I reckon my days are numbered in the good book and whether I go with you or not, my number will stay the same and on the appointed day when I'll be called. It don't seem to me to make a difference on that particular day, whether it is shooting it out with Rufus Buck, or peeling an apple on a widow's porch—either way, come my time, I don't stand a snowball's chance of seeing one more sunrise. So you decide whether you want to go after of Rufus or not, and if you want me along with you."

Albert lets a slow grin spread across his lips that are much like his mother's in their fullness.

"You give me hope, Ivory. Hope and unwavering friendship. We will spend the remainder of today getting the supplies we need to carry us into the Indian Nations and start out first thing in the morning. And I can promise you this, now that I won't be paying Mr. Monroe the reward money, I'll make sure there is plenty for us to eat, including canned peaches if you like and plenty of sugar for our coffee. You won't ever have to be hungry again!" (It is good to know that if I do die, it won't be on an empty stomach.)

All around, it seemed the best choice, for I would, if nothing more, have one more evening to spend in the loving embrace of my sweetheart.

If I was going to the Nations to be killed by the ugly Rufus Buck, I'd just as soon do it knowing I had spent my last full days on this earth tasting the carnal pleasures of Miss Jasmine Winfred Lucille Pettycash, and that she knew she had been loved by a signified man!

SEVENTEEN

I won't go into details about my final evening's pleasure in the warm embrace of Jasmine Pettycash. Suffice it to say it was wondrous and plenty tearful when it had come to an end, for I told her afterward, that come morning, me and Albert, and maybe the Indun, would be leaving Topeka and going in search of Rufus Buck.

Her final words to me were: ". . . you has a beautiful soul, Ivory, and lovely teeth. I reckon myself lucky you come along. Don't let that mean old nigger shoot you in the brains—or nowhere else!"

I waited outside her poor little home until she had disappeared within and turned out all the lights. I reckoned then, standing there in the dark, that Topeka had its bad side, but it had its good side, too.

Come morning, me and Albert and the Indun began packing our personals and then went out front of Dick's Emporium Hotel and began loading our supplies on to the small dove-gray burro Albert had purchased from a failed prospector (whatever he could have been looking for on the open prairies of Kansas was beyond anyone's guess) who had been standing outside the livery with a sign tied around the burro's neck: DONKEY CHEP $15. Albert thought it a good deal and so did the prospector. "Her name's Ivy," said the prospector.

I liked the looks of her and she stood the load we was putting on her back. The Indun stood there looking at her as though she might be a good meal for him to eat somewhere down the line in case we was to fall on hard times. I vowed not to let that happen.

We had nearly finished our preparations when Augustus Monroe approached our small party. Albert did not seem inclined to pay him much notice as he tightened down this rope and that over Ivy's load.

"Well, I see you boys are the type that like to get an early start on things," says Monroe as way of casual conversation. Albert tosses him a sidelong look but does not reply.

"We figure that every moment spent around here in Topeka is a moment wasted," I say.

"I can understand that," says Monroe. "That's smart thinking. Last evening, I paid my friend, Sheriff Bo Dean, a visit and asked him to send wires to his counterparts down in the Nations inquiring about the man you seek, Rufus Buck." Albert halted his progress on the hitch knots he was laying in on the pack.

"Got back several replies this morning. One from a local sheriff in Tahlequah said that Rufus Buck and some of his members robbed a bakery there of twelve dollars less than a week ago. They shot the baker's dog out of frustration—at least according to him. And another wire, this from Checotah, stated that a man fitting the description of Rufus Buck . . ." Here he paused and produced forth a telegram from inside his shirt pocket, held it out at full arm's length, studied it, then read, ". . . a big negro with scarred face, did on this date—July the thirty-first—rape and murder a Cherokee woman named Alice Bluewalker. And, that he and the men with him, held at gunpoint, the owner of a grocery store and did rob the man of eighteen dollars and change and wounded him in the side. No doubt," said Monroe, "they must've thought him dead."

Augustus Monroe, lowered the paper and offered us a pleased look. "I guess that pretty much puts the feller where you can find him easy," he stated.

Albert stepped away from Ivy and toward Mr. Monroe.

"That's all very interesting," says he. "But why are you telling us this and why did you go to all the trouble?"

Then, Mr. Monroe throws him a wide smile and states: "Because it's important if we are to catch up with him and see that your daddy's death is avenged."

"We?" says Albert.

"That's right," states Monroe. "You come and asked me yesterday if I'd hire on and I pretty much told you I wouldn't. And, I wasn't going to until I got to telling Alexy—he's the young Russian prince—your story. It was him that turned the trick in your favor. Said he'd much enjoy the hunt of a man. Says he's hunted most everything there is to hunt in this world, including something he calls rhinoceros in Africa. He's a young eager buck with plenty of money and states he is willing to fund the whole expedition and pay five thousand dollars for the privilege to boot!"

Albert looks my way, unsure of the offer.

"Excuse me while I confer with my partner," he says to Monroe, then walks over to me.

"What do you think, Ivory?" he asks.

"It all sounds sort of sinister, in a way," I tell him. "Sort of like they want to turn this into a sport instead of what it is—revenge!"

He hesitates, looks at me with those warm dark eyes of his in which I can see two little me's reflected in them.

"I know it does," he says. "But, we could use the help, and the extra guns, to say nothing of the experience Monroe would bring with him. It was him we come here to hire in the first place because of his experience in such matters. And besides, what difference does it make as long as we accomplish what we set out to do?"

I have no good argument against what he is saying, for it is true that Rufus Buck deserves his just due, one way or the other. But still, there is something about it that bothers me.

Albert turns and faces Monroe once again.

"How good is your man, the Russian?" he asks.

"Oh, he's damn good, son. He can hit most anything he aims at up to three hundred yards out."

"You'd do it for the money, then?" says Albert. "You do it for the Russian's money."

"I believe I would," states Monroe. "Or else I would not have taken the trouble to catch up with you this morning. Five thousand dollars is a ton of money."

"Ivory?" says Albert.

"Might as well," I say truthfully, for the wisdom of the offer seems to outweigh the morality of it no matter how the pie is sliced.

Albert nods and turns back to Monroe once more. "How soon can you and the prince be ready to leave?"

"Within the hour, son. Within the hour."

Monroe extends his hand to shake the bargain to a deal and Albert accepts, and so do I, and so does the Indun, who (as I have stated before) would shake any man's hand for the sheer delight of it.

I said, "Excuse me," to my two comrades and made my way quickly to the cafe to say one last farewell to Jasmine. Augustus Monroe and his Russian prince had bought me an hour's time which I hadn't previously counted on. I was determined to take advantage of it.

Jasmine was there, waiting tables as usual, a glisten on her face and arms from her quick agile movements around the tables and carrying the heavy dishes. She looked as sweet as ever and when she spotted me, she stopped what she was doing and took a whole long second to just stare at me.

I quickly found a seat at one of the tables and waited for her to come my way, which she did soon enough, carrying with her a tin of hot coffee and a slice of apple pie and placed it in front of me.

"I thought you would already be gone," she said.

"I thought so, too," I said. "But an unusual turn of events has delayed us for another hour. Can you get away?"

Her eyes were puffy from crying (no doubt) the previous night over my impending departure. It made me feel at once saddened and pleased to know that someone would cry over me.

She looked around nervously, then said: "No, Hilda did not come into work today, she has the grippe, and I am all alone in serving these gentlemens their breakfasts."

My hopes, of yet another few moments alone with her, fell to the floor.

In a clandestine manner, I reached out and took her hand.

"I love you, Jasmine Pettycash," I whispered. For a moment, her own sadness seemed to flee from her, for she offered me a toothy smile, but then, just as quickly, it was gone again.

"You is goin' to get yourself killed out there, Ivory. I know it . . . I just know it!"

"No I ain't," I try reassuring her. "Not now, especially."

"Why not?" says she, the soft cinnamon oval of her face dropping into a mask of glumness.

"Albert has hired on Augustus Monroe to go with us—and, a Russian prince who Mr. Monroe states can shoot a man at three hundred yards out! It ain't going to be just me and Albert and the Indun no more— we've hired professionals to help us see the job done!"

It seemed to cure her some, the news of us hiring professional man killers (although the Russian prince hadn't been proved yet, but then, neither had me or Albert. The Indun, I had no doubts about).

"Still . . ." says she.

"You are just wasting your worrying over nothing, gal," I tell her. "I reckon me and Albert made it this far without getting our brains blowed out, we'll do fine the rest of the trip. I feel that we have angels riding with us."

She smiled some more and it lifted my spirits to see her do so.

The cook started yelling out from behind the counter for her to come get more of the meals; several pairs of eyes have gave up their interest in the hash and eggs and slices of ham on their plates and turned their attention to us.

"I got to git," she says sorrowfully. "But I will wait on you to return to me, Ivory—if you ever git around this way again."

I make a hasty promise that I will be back and she pecks me sweetly on the cheek and then returns to her labor. I linger as long as is possible and then rejoin my companions out front of Dick's Emporium Hotel.

Waiting there also are Augustus Monroe and the Russian prince.

As stated before, the prince is wearing a bright red coat, a curly black hat, black velvet trousers stuffed down inside highly polished riding boots, and further, has a brace of long-barreled pistols about his waist.

The bullets in his cartridge belt are as long as my finger and just as big around.

I am introduced to him: "This is Prince Alexy Rachmanikoff, of the royal family." Alexy has bone-smooth hands and neatly trimmed fingernails (the kind I had only seen on some women before).

"Howdy!" he said brightly, shaking my hand almost as vigorously as the Indun would do. He speaks good English, and Monroe explains that he was educated in that country at a place called Oxford.

"Please to meet you, your highness," I state with all due respect for his high station in life.

"Please," says he. "You call me Alexy, only. Like Mr. Monroe, eh?"

He surprised me with his pleasantness, for I figured a man such as him that has lived all his life the pampered individual would be full of himself; but he seemed a regular fellow.

He was carrying with him a magnificent repeating rifle that had brass fittings and a special-built rear sight. Carved into the hardwood stock was a scene of cavorting stags. He noticed my interest in it and held it forth.

"Please. Try it if you like."

It was the sweetest rifle I ever did see or hold and I was sure that it could shoot a mile accurately. I hefted it to my shoulder, sighted down its long octagon barrel, aimed it at the prairie, aimed it at blue sky. I was sure even a lesser shot such as myself would do well by such a gun.

Handing it back to him, I knew instantly that I liked the prince. He had a warm generous open manner about himself. Unlike Augustus Monroe, who I had the opinion would not do much, if it first did not serve his own purpose.

Alexy seemed much curious about the Indun, and was now asking him if he ever "scalped" anyone, a question I thought was pretty personal, and did not believe Man Who Waits would care to answer. But he did.

"Yes!" declared the Indun. "Plenty of times, but mostly in the old days when there was some fighting going on."

Alexy brightened at the news.

"Really!"

The Indun nodded that it was true. Alexy seemed satisfied. Man Who Waits eyed the fancy Henry. "Do you wish to try it?" said the prince.

"Yes. It has been a long time since I held such a gun," said the Indun.

The old man took up the rifle in both hands, held it in front of him for a time like it was a peace pipe or a war lance, turned it over slowly in his hands, his wet eyes examining it. Then, he lifted it to his shoulder and aimed it at a sign far down the street that advertised: LADIES' BONE CORSETS & MILLINERY.

The big gun exploded in our ears and a trail of blue smoke curled from its barrel. The sign, which had been hanging by three links of chain, bucked, then swung cockeyed for a few seconds before settling back down again.

The Indun smiled, pleased with himself, no doubt, but Monroe snatched the rifle from his hands and said: "That's a damn foolish thing to do!"

Man Who Waits simply eyed him with a dull stare. "I thought it was a pretty good shot," he said.

Albert cleared his throat and said: "Since this is my party, I say we get started."

It was agreed that such was a good idea. I could not help but wonder silently, looking at our little parade of mixed blessings, if Rufus Buck knew what was in store for him. We rode past the cafe and Jasmine ran out to me and placed a red scarf around my neck as I bent down to kiss her.

"Let this be your good luck charm," she said. I hoped with all earnestness, it would be.

EIGHTEEN

For the next nine days, we rode south across the grasslands and rolling prairies. Along the way, time out was taken by Augustus Monroe and Prince Alexy to shoot at wild game for our supper. Antelope were the most difficult to come by, although we spotted plenty of nice fat herds in the distance. They are a nervous animal that are skittish, even when standing still.

On a warm afternoon of the third or fourth day, we spotted a small herd of the white-rumped creatures at a distance of about a quarter of a mile.

Up till that time, our repast had consisted mostly of

prairie chicken which were good roasted over an open fire.

"The prince wants to show off his skills," said Monroe at having spotted the distant herd of antelope. Albert was impatient and wanted to keep going, but the possibility of something other than the little game hens in our nightly pot, caused him to assent.

We dismounted and held our ponies while Alexy took up a sitting position there on the grass. He flipped up the rear sight of his fancy repeater, made some adjustments to it, and took aim at the thirty or forty antelope.

I didn't see how no man was going to hit anything at that distance, but he did. One loud bang that caused our ponies to jerk up their heads in a start, and I watched one of the tail-twitching pronghorns topple over—the rest bounded off in unison and disappeared over a little rise as if though they had never even been there. It was all just that quick.

That evening, after having spent an hour butchering the beast, we ate until it felt as though our bellies would pop. I don't ever recall being that full before (or since, for I have learned, in older age, to take all things in moderation, including the pleasures of food, drink, and women).

I watched Monroe wipe grease from his mustache, then roll himself a cigarette there in the firelight of burning cow flop. He seemed, somehow, much older a man there in that flickering light of evening; it had to do something with the way the skin folded in around the corners of his eyes, and the way his jowls seemed to sag.

It was easy to see that he was once a handsome man and most surely lived up to his reputation as a womanizer (at least according to the stories Albert related to me as having been printed in the *Harper's Weekly* and the *Police Gazette*).

He had clear eyes, but ones that seemed lifeless in a way, as though he saw only what he wished to see and little else. I had no doubts that he could and had killed men without ever concerning himself with the plight of their souls, or his own.

(Sister Mordicai was, in my experience, the true expert on the plight of souls once they have departed their earthly vessel. She was fond on lecturing the many directions our souls had a way of going once we bit the dust. As far as I could figure it, there were three different routes a spirit could travel: Heaven, which all good Catholic boys and gals hoped for; purgatory, which no one seemed to want; and hell, which no one wanted less, except for a fellow orphan, Virgil Boot, who said he wanted to live a life of sin and didn't care whether or not he wound up in hell 'cause it would be well worth it just to live the good life for once. I, later in life, heard that Virgil Boot wound up becoming a bank robber—a poor one at that and was shot to death in a parlor house by a posse of farmers whilst in the ample arms of a fat redheaded woman who possessed only her molars in the way of teeth. To me, it was proof that Virgil practiced what he preached and was not at all worried about the plight of his soul.)

At one point, Augustus Monroe looked my way, and I shunned his gaze, for it gave me the same cold chill as had that of Rufus Buck.

In nine days of travel, the prince shot plenty of birds, one gray wolf, several rabbits (with something he called a needle nose rifle of small bore), and a sickly coyote. Man Who Waits went and prayed over the dead coyote—it seemed that coyotes held some sort of special place with the Indun, maybe all Induns as far as I know—and he paid it its just due and did not seem at all happy that Alexy laid it low. But, it was full of mange and scrawny, and the way it limped in near our camp, we all figured that it was just begging to be killed and put out of its misery for no good coyote would get that close to a man or let a man get that close to him.

Upon seeing the Indun's concern for the creature, Alexy spoke his apologies and offered the Indun a taste of a clear liquor he called vodka. The chief smacked his lips and gave up praying over the prairie wolf.

We was each then offered some of the vodka to try. I didn't care for it, nor did Albert. Only the prince, Monroe, and the Indun seemed to take to it. Fact was, they took to it real well.

Pretty soon, the Indun turns drunk and begins dancing on one foot in circles around our little fire. He takes to hollering like he has been scalded or cheated out of something. But we learn later that it was only a war song he was singing over his enemies, which was many, considering that his enemies consisted of practically everybody that wasn't a Comanche, and of the Antelope Eating band in particular.

He kept that up for some time, then took to weeping openly and blubbering about a woman named Standing Stalk. In so doing, he wandered far out onto the prairie and into the night speaking the woman's name over and over again. It was a sad and pitiful scene to watch the old man so drunk and suffering. It reminded me of Otero on some of his return trips from Ulvade, how he would suffer the effects of his encounters with Ulvade women.

Albert suggested that we go and retrieve him off the prairie for fear that wolves might get him and eat him up, but I voted for leaving him be in order to work out whatever suffering he was having to deal with—that I didn't think any wolves would want to make a meal of him once they caught a good strong whiff of his buckskins.

The next morning proved me right for the Indun was in camp, smudging himself with sage and seeming as though nothing was troubling him—except that he did hold his head at an angle that I have seen Otero hold his when suffering a severe hangover.

The prince seemed cheerful as ever, and Monroe taciturn, as would befit a man of his profession, although the later in the morning it got, the more agreeable was his nature. I figured that the most dangerous time to approach Mr. Monroe would be in the morning, before he had his coffee and cigarette. I wondered of the many men he had killed, how many had been in the morning before he'd had his coffee and cigarette.

We rode into a small settlement called Young Ida toward the middle of the fourth day and folks come out like we was a circus passing through. We might just as well have been in their eyes for what other little parade had they witnessed that contained an Indun, a Russian prince, a man killer, and two boys packing Navies?

It seemed like all the Kansans in that particular town were towheaded and blue-eyed and wind-burned. Didn't seem like none of them wore shoes, either, for they were all barefooted, as many as I could see.

Monroe stopped and asked directions to the nearest whiskey tent of a long-bearded man whose straw hat was busted out at the top.

"This here is a dry county, mister," said the man.

"There's nowhere a man could get himself a drink?" inquired Monroe, as if he had not heard the old man correctly.

"Didn't say that," said the man. "Just said this here is a dry county. You want a drink, you could ride yourself out to Miss Mossey's place. She's got whiskey to sell you, I reckon."

"Well, which way does she live?" said Monroe.

The man pointed out the direction with his nose. It lay farther on south, in the direction we was already headed. "Go to the first trace off to the left, take that, and about a mile more," instructed the elder.

Albert complained that we must not forget that we were on a mission, and not on a journey to see how many liquor dens we could find. Albert could have a stern tongue in his mouth when he chose.

Monroe gave him a cold stare because of it. Alexy smiled brightly—didn't seem to have no other way of smiling—and rode over to Albert and begged his patience.

"It will only be for a very short time," he said. "It is nearly on our way in any case. I will insist that we do not stay very long . . ."

Alexy could charm a snake with his humble manner.

Albert traded looks with me and I simply shrugged: it was better that we leave Monroe a little slack in the rope than have him give up the cause over something as simple as whiskey.

Miss Mossey's was a long soddy with windows all across the front. What impressed me was that the windows had real glass in them. There were several gals sitting around out front on chairs in various stages of dress. Mostly, it appeared to me, they were dressed for the weather, which was uncommonly warm, which meant to say, they wasn't wearing all that much.

Alexy, the Indun, and Mr. Monroe all grinned like possums at the sight of the soiled doves. Albert flushed red at the sight of the lightly clad women. Embarrassed, but not enough so as to avert his gaze, it was plain to see that his attention mostly rested on one little freckled-faced gal that had hair the color of honey and cat green eyes. She teased him with those eyes and I saw him swallow hard.

Miss Mossey proved to be a sturdy-built gal with bramble-bush hair and face round as the moon.

"Welcome, gents," says she with a voice that was deep and hollow as a well. "Welcome to Miss Mossey's; it's Miss Mossey you're looking at!"

"We was told you sold whiskey," said Monroe.

"Whiskey and anything else that ails you, stranger," she said, sweeping one large arm around to indicate the reclining women.

"Well, that might be of interest to us, your gals might," said Monroe. "But whiskey will do for the present."

"By the bottle or by the glass?" Miss Mossey wanted to know.

"Does it make a difference?" said Monroe.

"Hell no, it's all the same price!" I have heard horses that didn't laugh as loud.

She invited us to step down and ordered some of the gals out of their chairs so's we could recline in comfort: "Agatha, Mirinda, Jesse! Git up and let these gents sit a spell!" she ordered. Three of the homeliest gals stood up and slunk off like cats, but not any farther than the well-kept yard. Me and Albert chose to sit our horses and allow Monroe, Alexy, and the Indun to take up residence in the gal's chairs.

Albert was still captivated by the honey-haired little gel who was now inspecting the toes on her right foot.

She had very little feet and I wondered why she would pay them so much attention.

Miss Mossey brought out a cider jug and several tin cups and began to pour. She noticed then Albert's attention to the gal inspecting her toes.

"Honey," she said, opening her mouth wider than a picket gate. "That there is Zypherilla and she's young and sweet and ain't hardly used none at all. It'll cost you one dollar to take her inside."

Albert blinked suddenly, realized that he had been caught looking into the cookie jar, and offered me an embarrassed stare.

The Indun was already holding forth his cup for a second pour and Alexy and Monroe seemed somewhat amused at Albert's innocence.

I ride my horse over next to that of Albert's.

"Why not?" I say.

"Why not what?" he asks.

"Why not pay a dollar and go on in there with that gal?"

He blinked more surprise at me.

"What'd I want to do a thing like that for?"

"It seems to me you're sort of stuck on the looks of her," I say. "So why not go on and find out what it's like?"

"It wouldn't be right," says he.

"What wouldn't be right about it?"

"You know . . ."

"No, I don't. It seems to me that sooner or later you are going to find out what it is like to be with a gal.

Why not now while the opportunity presents itself?"

He worked his tongue around inside his mouth like he was trying to find some words with it in order to give me an answer.

"What difference does it make as long as you like the looks of her?" I say as a way to buck up my side of the argument. There's no way I can tell him what it's like, being with a gal in that way; it is just something he needs to experience for himself, as does every man.

"It'd be morally wrong," he stutters finally.

"No more so than killing a man," I remind him.

"I ain't never killed a man either," he states.

"No, but you're bound to when we catch up to Rufus Buck."

The gal, as though knowing that Albert is indecisive, smiles pertly and brushes her lips with the tip of her small pink tongue.

Still, Albert is reluctant to let sin overtake him.

"Let me ask you this," I say. He looks at me with those warm brown eyes, only full of confusion and doubt now. "It says in the Bible that if you are thinking about sinning with a gal, that it is just the same as if you was to do it. Are you thinking about sinning with that gal?"

Albert swallows hard again. "I reckon I can tell you," he whispers. "I was."

"Are you still?"

"I am."

"Then you've already done as bad as you're going

to. Might just as well give Miss Mossey the dollar and go on in there with Miss Zypherilla."

I wait, and so does Albert. I have but one dollar left to my name stuck down inside my shoe. I reach down, pull it out, and ride over and give it to Miss Mossey.

"That's for him," I tell her, then ride back to Albert. "There, you don't have to feel so dang bad about it," I say. "I've paid your freight, so that if there is a wage to pay for your sinning, we will both share in it."

He offers me a slow, relieved grin.

"Dang, Ivory, if you ain't the best companion a fellow ever had, I don't know who is."

"Go on," I say, before Monroe, or Alexy, or even that of Indun decides to take up with her first."

He dismounts, and I hold the reins to his pony. With much care and deliberation, he approaches Zypherilla, who seems to be very proud of the fact that she, amongst all them gals is the first to be chosen even though it ain't but ten o'clock in the morning. (Sinning has never been a sport that takes much notice of the time.)

Albert pulls the hat off his head, and the little gal stands up and takes his hand.

"Is this your first time, boy?" she asks. Albert merely flushes more red as she leads him inside the little soddy. I notice then, that Monroe has taken to eyeing a big-bosomed gal with black hair and a mole on her cheek. And Alexy has been approached by one of the homely gals that earlier gave up her chair; he seems intrigued.

Even the Indun is getting a good amount of attention from a woman that Miss Mossey has referred to as Loletta, a happy-faced gal that outweighs the chief by a hundred pounds. I can see where all this is leading, and decide to take my leave for a little ride, for I am not inclined to want to cheat on my sweetheart, Jasmine Pettycash, with women that only cost a dollar. (Even orphans have their morals.)

Later on, as we continue on toward the Indian Territory, I urge my horse up next to Albert's and inquire as to what he is thinking, for he hasn't seemed himself since leaving Miss Mossey's. I am concerned that maybe I struck him a bad bargain and caused him to do something he wasn't ready to do.

At first, he only mumbled that he wasn't thinking any one thing in particular. I said, I thought he was and that if I was the cause of his moral decline, then he ought to at least lay the blame at my feet and get it over with, for I did not want to see him in a low condition—if, that was what he was in right now.

"No," he said. "I ain't. It's just that I never would have believed how different and wonderful a pleasure sinning can be. I am worried that I have purchased my way into hell because I like it so much."

"It is an easy thing to like," I say. "I reckon that is why so many do it. But, I reckon even the Lord Almighty would understand that we're just boys with weak minds when it comes to such things, and will forgive us once we grow to manhood and can gain control over our senses."

"You reckon so?" said Albert.

"Yes, if my understanding of Sister Fister's teachings is correct."

"Who is Sister Fister?"

"An expert on sin and redemption. She's the one that gave me these scars on my knuckles. Her's was a hard class not to pay attention in."

NINETEEN

On the morning of the eleventh day, we reached Checotah, having been decided by Monroe that we should bypass stopping at Tahlequah since Checotah was the last place where Rufus Buck's gang had left their stamp of terror.

Checotah proved to be a well-kept little place with green grasses, plenty of trees, and much good water. We pulled in at the small squat building housing the sheriff's office and were greeted by a square-built man wearing a white cotton shirt, black homespun trousers, and a nice fresh haircut.

"I am Homer Creek," he said, as way of introduction. "And you must be Augustus Monroe from up in Kansas."

"You have heard of me?"

"Yes, only recently, when Sheriff Bo Dean wired an inquiry and stated that you and some others would be on your way here in search of Rufus Buck."

Monroe seemed slightly disappointed that Homer Creek had not otherwise heard of him.

"I guess you all don't read the *Police Gazette* or *Harper's Weekly* down here," said Monroe as way of a jibe.

"Huh?" said Homer Creek.

"Never mind," said Mr. Monroe with a show of impatience. "This here youngster is Albert Sand, and that one there, is Ivory Cade. And the Indian is someone who calls himself Man Who Waits for Winter. And this," Monroe said, pointing with a slight flourish of his arm and wrist and hand, "is Prince Alexy of the royal family of Russia!"

Homer Creek appeared to be unimpressed, but smiled pleasantly anyhow and showed us his good white teeth in so doing. He had a darkness to him that caused me to believe that he was of mixed blood: white man and Indun. He had hands that were well veined and shapely enough to appear to have been carved from stone.

"Well, you have got yourself quite a little party," said Homer Creek. He wore a small nickel badge that was no more the size of a silver dollar.

"Yes we have," said Monroe. "And we come here to kill Rufus Buck."

"Well, good luck to you sir," said Creek in an amused sort of way.

"Luck won't get it done," replied Monroe, somewhat stiff over the light manner Creek was taking our business.

"No sir, it surely won't," offered Creek in return, then leaned and spat and straightened up again.

Homer Creek wore a pistol of large bore inside the rope belt of his pants.

Augustus Monroe and Homer Creek spent a few seconds more marking their territory before Prince Alexy spoke up in that charming manner of his and said: "Mr. Creek, would you mind if we asked you for more detailed information on the tragedy Mr. Buck brought to your community?"

That seemed to take the starch out of the air, for Creek allowed us a half grin and said for us to step down and come on in his little office, which we did without further comment. He had the blackest hair of any man I had ever seen.

The air inside was tight, the light poor, the furnishings sparse. A shotgun hung on the wall by a rope lanyard, as well as a photograph of several men standing around a butchered hog that was nearly as large as the men themselves. I thought it strange, what some men keep as mementos.

Homer Creek sat himself in the chair behind the small bare desk and said: "Now exactly what is it you want to know about Rufus Buck?"

"Everything you can tell us," said Monroe, but in a way that was no longer sounding like a challenge to the sheriff.

"Well, he and his bunch come through here nearly two weeks ago, after having robbed a bakery up in Tahlequah a day or so before. They come across a Cherokee woman between here and Honey Springs. It was unlucky for her that they did. Raped and killed her. Her boy, a tad of seven or eight years old, saw the whole thing from the bushes she had hid him in when she saw them coming up the road. She must of known by the looks of them, they were trouble. Anyway, the boy described Rufus to a tee. Big and black and ugly! Said all the men with him were ugly, too. The boy's uncle brought him in to give a report. Said the boy was still having nightmares over it.

"A day later, they rode right into Checotah and held up the grocery store and shot poor Kelly Price in his side and left him for a dead man. Which, he nearly was. All they got was eighteen dollars and some pleasure from it . . ."

"Nobody tried to stop them?" said Monroe with an assured air that let the sheriff know he did not think him brave and willing.

"Don't lay it at my doorstep," said Homer Creek stiffly. "I was escorting a pair of prisoners over to the constable in Eufaula that day—a whiskey peddler and a pimp who were wanted for crimes in that place."

"Convenient," said Monroe.

"Please," said Alexy, trying to keep the dust down between the two men.

Then, Homer Creek said something in Indun tongue to Man Who Waits. Man simply looked at him and said nothing.

"Don't understand Creek?" said the sheriff. "I thought maybe you would. You look like my wife's grandfather."

"I guess all Indians look the same," said Man Who Waits. "Even to other Indians."

Homer Creek was more white than Indian in his ways. At least he spoke and dressed like a white man.

Then, having lost his interest in the Indun, he turned his attention to me.

"What they bring you along for, these men, you ain't nothing but a colored boy, and neither is he, except he's white," he said, nodding toward Albert. "Him I can understand, but not you."

Albert started to come to my defense, but by now, I had learned that I must come to my own, or forever be without respect from such men as Homer Creek and Rufus Buck and Deputy Muddbottom.

"I am known as the Kansas Kid," I said with cold dispassion. "I have killed several men, including men of color as well as white, and all in between. I am a deadly fighter with pistols, and can shoot with either hand. I especially don't take to insults, nor do I go about looking for trouble, but will handle it wherever it may find me!" (I had learned much at the orphanage—some of which I knew, at the very time I was learning it, would do me no good later in life, but was required to at least make an attempt, or be subjected to broth and bread and no recess. However, the one thing that I did learn, that now served me well, was the ability to act. For I had been selected to perform in several of the plays as directed by Sister France, because of my natural ability to make up stories—some referred to it as my ability to lie—a mean-spirited misinterpretation.)

Homer Creek stiffened in his chair, unsure whether or not I was who I said I was, for I said it without flinching nor removing my gaze from him.

"It's the truth," said Albert. "I hired him, along with Mr. Monroe here, and the Prince and that Indian. They are all man killers of great skill and nerve. I would be careful as to how you address this . . . colored boy."

Augustus Monroe himself must have surely appreciated the fabrication (he being a man whose own reputation was stretched and bloated by the yellow journalists of that day with full knowledge and approval of the principal—Augustus Monroe, himself), for he confirmed it with Homer Creek.

"I have personally witnessed the Kansas Kid here, kill four men in a gunfight over the insults they cast on a fallen women in a saloon in Hays City. He is quick to anger over slight things."

It was getting to be such a good lie, that I had the urge to believe it myself.

Homer Creek looked pale and stricken and when he found his voice, he said: "I'm sorry if I have slighted you. I didn't mean to."

"What is the latest you have heard of the movements of Rufus Buck and his bunch?" said Monroe.

"Little," said Homer Creek, still suffering the effects of near death at the hands of the Kansas Kid. "In the past, it has been rumored that they are known to hole up between criminal activities at a ranch outside of Childer's Station run by a woman named Tulip Belle.

She, herself, has been several times accused of illegal activities and been brought before Judge Parker's court in Ft. Smith. But, nothing has ever been proved about her except that she is an exceptionally ugly woman, and has no trouble gaining suitors—Rufus Buck among them. Or so it is rumored."

"How far?" said Monroe, determined.

"A full day's ride south of here. You get as far as Childer's Station, then just ask around how you get out to Belle's Bend. That's what she calls the place: Belle's Bend, named after one of her several husbands. I don't know which. She is rumored to have had four or five, some legal, some not. As I said, she seems to have no trouble gaining suitors. Why, I don't know. For I have personally seen her one time in Ft. Smith, and would not believe she could call a hog to come to her."

It was a colorful description but of no concern to Monroe for he promptly turned and left the little office, stirring behind him motes of dust in the dim shaft of light filtering through the single window.

The prince said a graceful thank you to Homer Creek, then followed Monroe out into the street, followed as well by me, Albert, and the Indun.

Alexy and Monroe had already mounted their horses and were heading down the south road.

"He does not waste time," said Albert, finding his stirrup.

"Except on whiskey dens and parlor girls," I reminded.

"Oh, that," said Albert, his cheeks streaking crimson.

It is strange how much my opinion of Augustus Monroe has changed since that first afternoon in Albert's home when he talked about hiring the famous gunman. It is one thing to read about a person of fame, and another to actually meet them. To me, Monroe was a thoroughly dangerous man without hint of the romantic character that had been assigned him in the pages of *Harper's Weekly*, DeWitt's Dime Novels, or the *Police Gazette.*

To me, Mr. Monroe lacked any of the qualities I would seek in a friend: Compassion, humor, and kindly eyes. I could only hope that once we caught up with Rufus Buck, that the lack of such qualities served us well in combat. For if not, we might all be doomed.

We arrived at Childer's Station at dusk. It wasn't much. A scramble of buildings, a few barking dogs, an old man leaning on a cane hobbling down the road.

We pulled up alongside him, and he stopped long enough to look up at us. Looked us over a couple of times.

"Are you boys lost?" says he. "You must be lost, or you would not be here. The only people that come here that don't live here, are usually lost."

"No, we are not lost," says Monroe. "We know exactly where we are. Can you tell us the way to Belle's Bend?"

The old-timer cupped his hand to his ear and said, "Huh?"

"Can you tell us the way to Belle's Bend?" Monroe said louder.

"Belle's Bend?"

"That is right Belle's Bend!"

"What the hell do you want to go to Belle's Bend for?"

"We want to go," said Albert, "to talk to Tulip Belle."

He twisted his neck around to see where the new voice was coming from. He had thickets of white hair growing out of his ears. I assumed that was the cause of his hearing difficulties.

"Well, son," he crackled, "that is a damn foolish thing to want to do. Belle's Bend is full of thieves, and killers, and horse stealers and just plain trash. You don't look like that sort," says he, giving us all the once-over again. "But then maybe I am wrong. It's down that way until you reach the river, then follow it west until you come to it Belle's Bend."

Alexy took a coin from his red coat and handed it down to the man.

"Thank you sir for your valuable information."

The old man eyed the coin carefully, it was gold. He turned it over between his fingers, then closed his hand around it.

"I'd be careful going around Belle's Bend carrying gold money on me, mister," he warned the prince. "Them there will cut open your throat for less than this!"

"We will be careful, sir," said Alexy.

Monroe said, "Night is no time to make our approach. We will ride as far as the river, then make camp and leave for Belle's Bend first light."

There was something about that place that lent me little comfort, as though I could almost smell the nearness of Rufus Buck and his killers, the way the damp heat pressed in and the creatures of night sang forth from their hidden lairs.

As we rode toward the river under the rising full moon of that warm humid night, Albert came up alongside me and said: "It feels like it won't be much longer before we find Buck."

"Are you anxious to kill him?" I ask.

For a time he didn't answer. Then, he said: "Yes, I reckon I still am."

"We have come a long way just to do that," I said. "If it had to be another thousand miles, it wouldn't bother me," he said.

We rubbed down our ponies with handfuls of grass and fed them apples from our supplies as way of a treat. Beans and more antelope hump was the meal of the night, and afterward, Monroe, Alexy, and the Indun sat around the campfire sharing some of Alexy's vodka.

Monroe had taught the Indun how to roll a cigarette, and Man Who Waits seemed to take as much pleasure in that as he did in shaking someone's hand.

It was one of them deep black nights where the sky is almost creamy in some places because of all the stars. Then, suddenly, the stars started falling.

"Look at that!" I declare. "The stars are falling."

Everybody but me has taken their amusement in watching the Indun roll his second cigarette.

All eyes turn skyward.

"They're meteors," says Albert. "It's what is known as a meteor shower!"

Man Who Waits said: "This happened in the time of my grandfather—he told me several times about it. My grandfather said that after the stars fell from the sky, our people were plagued with bad fortune for a while. My grandmother died, and her sister. Then, their herd of ponies got sick and many of them died, too. And for a long time after that, they could not find any buffalo to kill for food, and that winter was a very hard one for them."

I noticed Augustus Monroe, his neck craned, squinting toward the sky It was then that I knew he had poor eyesight. How poor, I could only guess, but it was plain as anything that the man could not see well. There was something ominous about learning that the most famed gunfighter of the time had flawed vision. Nobody counted on Mr. Monroe not being able to see very well.

In my book, that made him even more dangerous, but to who?

It was one of those little secret things you learn by accident and wished you hadn't. (Like the time I had to use the privy one night at the orphanage—it lay clear across the other side of the courtyard from where we boys slept and was near a grove of old cottonwood trees—and I saw something then going on between Sister Latrell and Sister Felice, which I hadn't wished I'd seen: They were kissing one another on the lips. It troubled me for several days afterward. But then, I got to realizing just how lonely a place the orphanage could be, and that the Sisters didn't have no men around, except for Father Gumpmiller who was old and brittle as a twig and couldn't hear too well anyhow.

It seemed to me, after thinking on it hard, that the Sisters needed love and affection just as much as us orphans and was happy to take it in whatever form it might present itself—at least it seemed so for Sister Felice and Sister Latrell, and I can't say that I blamed them if that was the case).

I guess maybe Augustus Monroe couldn't be blamed either if he had bad eyesight but it sure wasn't a thing I wanted to get up and dance a jig over.

I just wished I hadn't of noticed it.

Somehow, after having noticed it, the frogs seemed to croak louder and the mosquitoes took a greater toll on us, as if though they was preparing us for what was to come, as if though, what discomfort we was having to deal with was nothing compared to what we would be dealing with.

Even the Indun foretold of hard times after a night when the stars fell out of the sky. It was one of those moments when the idea of mucking out stalls and digging graves didn't seem so bad a thing to be doing right now. I promised myself that if I lived through whatever terribleness awaited us, I'd go back and visit the old man, Otero and see how he was making it on his own and apologize for my hurried departure from his employ.

TWENTY

After a meager breakfast—with the exception of a tin that the prince opened and passed around among us of something he called caviar, which is no more than black fish eggs, and too salty for my blood—we mounted our horses and followed the river west to Belle's Bend.

A long log house with several chimneys, two or three corrals and chicken coops, outhouses, hog stys, a hay mow, and a corn crib. That is what Belle's Bend proved to be.

The place swarmed with barnyard animals and good-blooded horses.

We was greeted by several individuals, all well armed, and with slothful faces and slack ways of standing around. I didn't see where a one of them looked like he knew a thing about farming, or raising stock, or even gathering eggs from the chickens. These men looked like they might be more comfortable slitting a body's throat and picking the pockets of dead men.

Augustus Monroe whispered, upon our approach, that we should prepare ourselves, meaning, don't let our pistols be too far from our hands. "Be prepared boys," he said. I could see that Alexy's eyes were wet with excitement over the possibilities of a shootout. I guess the man lived for danger.

But, by the time we rode up into what could be described as the front yard, for it was littered with tin cans, a horse-faced woman stepped out of the log house and onto the fancy porch that had been added the whole length of the front.

It was true, what Homer Creek had told us: she was an ugly woman.

She wore a black getup of velvet jacket and riding britches and horseman's boots. Upon her head, a black silk hat decorated with posies; around her waist, a pair of silver pistols.

"What can I do you gents for?" she said in a deep throaty voice.

Monroe had warned us that he should be the one to do the talking since he had the most experience at extracting information from a reluctant mouth. None of us took issue with his reasoning.

"We are just passing through your territory," said Monroe. "Possibly we could do with a meal and water and feed for our animals."

"Are you the law?" she asked, balling her fists against her surprisingly slender waist. "If you are the law, you have wasted your time in coming here. I know most of the Federal marshals over from Ft. Smith. Ha! I've been arrested enough to know all them boys pretty damn well. You ain't from over there are you? You ain't new boys that Judge Parker has hired?"

"No, ma'am, we ain't," agrees Monroe.

"Well, I ain't never seen any of you boys hereabouts before," she states with an air that gives no indication whether she might order her men to open fire on us or not, for she is cautious in her questioning of our visit.

"We are from Texas," Monroe says. "Have you ever been to Texas before?"

"Yes, plenty of times. I married a Texas man once. You don't talk like a Texas man."

"How so?"

"They talk mostly without moving their mouths too much. You move your mouth a lot when you talk."

"Well," says Monroe, cool as a cucumber. "I wasn't always from Texas. I am originally from Ohio."

That seemed to satisfy her curiosity on that particular subject, for she smiled enough for us to see that she had long teeth to match her long face.

"Well, you could be lawman from Texas, I don't know any of them . . ."

"Ma'am, if you will take a good look at us, you can plainly see that we are not lawmen from anywhere, for what lawmen do you know that are young boys, old Indians, and a Russian prince?"

"A Russian prince?" says she. "Which one?"

"This one," says Monroe, sweeping his arm out to the side that Alexy is sitting on. "He is Prince Alexy, from the royal family of Russia."

She placed a hand to her throat, her long slender fingers lightly stroking the notch just below her Adam's Apple. She seemed to almost sigh at the introduction.

"Is it true?" she asked.

Alexy nodded in modesty. "I am afraid so," he said.

"Well, my my. I can't believe a Russian prince has come to visit here at Belle's Bend. I never would have thought in all my days that such a thing would happen!"

Alexy removed the curly hat from his head and held it over his breast, charming the woman to no end.

"I am Miss Tulip Belle," said she in a breathless sort of way that reminded me of stage acting. "And these are my boys," she indicated with a wave of her hand that was bent at the wrist.

"Henry," she said to one particularly rough-looking fellow who had, by his shaggy appearance, forsaken shaving, and probably regular bathing, too. "Go and kill several hens and see that they are plucked and put in the pot. I'd say we're having guests for dinner."

Henry offered us a look like as though he had sore feet and someone had just stepped on them.

"These fellers could be bounty hunters," Henry protested. "Or worse!"

Tulip Belle gave him a sour look of disapproval.

"Can't you see that they got a nigger boy and a white boy with them, and that old Indian that looks like he might just fall off his horse and die at any time. Does that look like bounty hunters to you?"

Henry said, "You just never know about bounty hunters, Tulip. I've seen them in all sizes and shapes."

"God damn it, Henry, go and kill them chickens and clean them!" Then, turning her attention to us once more, she said: "I apologize for my coarse speech, but Henry can be bullheaded and hard to direct at times."

Henry slunk off like a kicked dog.

"Won't you step down and come sit up here on the porch whilst we wait for Henry to clean and prepare them chickens?"

She had one of the other men, a fellow named Pepper, go and bring us bark tea from a storm cellar and a fellow named Raggs, bring us cigars.

"You boys care for a cigar?" she said to Albert and me. "Or, are you too young for such vices?" She spared no part of herself in her laughter. Me and Albert declined the invitation to smoke, but Man Who Waits found it a delightful endeavor, as did Augustus Monroe and the Prince. Tulip Belle bit the end off one herself and smoked as readily as a man. Had it not been for her bosoms, I might as easily thought she to be a man.

Monroe talked all around the subject of why we had come to Belle's Bend, saying that we were merely passing through, and that we might be in the business of buying some good horse stock if the right deal was to come along, that we were of no particular mind to do this or that, but would be open to whatever proposition that might present itself; that we were not regular hands as such, nor looking for any sort of regular work. In otherwise, painting a picture of us as men that would be open to criminal activity if there was money to be made at it, and the risks were low.

The whole while, Tulip Belle doted on Alexy, which she had sit right next to her there on the porch. Alexy didn't seem to mind the attention of the nefarious woman as much as I might have thought.

"Well, that is all very interesting, Mr. Jones," said she. Monroe called himself that, figuring that his own reputation might well have spread this far south of Kansas. The rest of us, however, were introduced as ourselves. I guess he figured we didn't have any reputations to worry about. Which was true enough, but nonetheless, I suspect we would've felt more like true detectives if we had've been give aliases.

"But, if you don't mind, I'd sort of like to take the Prince on a tour of my place, show him around a little." She said it with a wink that looked like the blinking of an owl.

"I don't mind, if he don't," said Monroe.

"Prince Alexy, would you do me the honor?" says she.

"It would be my pleasure, madam," barks Alexy. And I thought for a minute she might swoon there in the storm of his civility.

They went off toward the corrals together, Alexy and Tulip, she locking her arm through his, which I suppose foreign men do as a matter of common cour-tesy—offering a woman your arm like that, even the ugliest women.

"Well, boys," says Monroe after they are out of earshot. "I think we have struck on a good thing here. She seems to have taken a shine to the Prince and that is a good thing for us. For if it is true that Rufus Buck is in the area, she would know."

"I feel sorry for Alexy," said Albert. "For she is powerfully ugly, that woman."

"The Prince loves a challenge," said Monroe. "That is why he wanted to come along on this little foray to begin with. I know that if I state to him the importance of eliciting the information she has about our Mr. Rufus Buck, he will do his duty to see that we are successful in making of Rufus pay."

"That's a lot to ask from any man," I add.

"I know it is, son. But no victory is without its casualties."

Henry is quick with preparing the chickens and has killed, cleaned, and fried them in hot grease for our benefit. Along with the tasty hens is served baked squash, fresh tomatoes, and green onions and cold bark tea.

All of us, our bunch, Tulip, and her boys, sit at a long table out in the yard and fill our bellies with the good fare. Henry seems to be the only one not enjoying the festivities, for it is plain to see that he is Tulip's forgotten sweetheart, and that further, even a blind man, or one whose vision is as poor as that of Monroe (which I have thus far kept as a secret to myself, not wanting to upset the apple cart, or have Monroe prove to me the quality of his eyesight, and therefore his ability to hit what he aims at which could be me were I to publicly raise the issue), can see that he is heartsick at the sight of Tulip and the Prince, being so chummy the whole afternoon and on into our meal, as she is even willing to shake salt on his tomatoes and fork them up to his mouth.

After the meal, we stretch out on the grass and close our eyes against the warmth of the afternoon sun. Tulip has asked Alexy to go riding with her. She has a tall Morgan which she rides sidesaddle, having now changed into velvet skirts, but wearing the same jacket and a more practical hat with a stampede string to keep it from flying from her head.

Monroe sees this as yet another good sign in our favor. I wonder. Miss Tulip looks as though she could swamp poor Alexy under if she took it in her mind to do so. He might even become one of her husbands. Homer Creek clearly stated that Tulip Belle seemed to have an uncommon power over men, and that she never lacked for suitors, or husbands. And, judging by the way Henry was moping about (he kicked a dog in the butt for being too slow in moving out of his way after we finished our meal), I tended to believe that Homer was truthful in his description of the strange attraction she held over men. Except, like Homer, I could honestly say, I, too, could not see where she could even call a hog to come to her.

By the time Alexy and Tulip returned to Belle's Bend, the sun had crossed over the sky and now lay just above a copse of hardwood trees to the west.

"You will of course stay for supper and then the night," she announced brightly to our little group, but directed her comments by way of staring directly into

Alexy's eyes. He smiled somewhat weakly at the announcement, but Monroe spoke right up and said that would be fine with us and a damned nice offer on her part, to which she bowed and said: "Tulip Belle's place is always home to any man who ain't the law, Mr. Jones."

After a supper of collard greens cooked in bacon fat, buttermilk, slabs of fried ham, and turnips, Monroe got Alexy off to the side a ways and whispered instructions to him. I was too far off to hear what was said, but I seen all the color drain out of the prince's face.

But finally, he sort of hunched his shoulders in a gesture of pure resignation before the two of them rejoined the rest of us.

Tulip had disappeared for a time inside the log house, only to reappear shortly after Monroe gave his clandestine orders to Alexy. She was wearing a white cotton gown that, standing there framed in the light of the room behind her, showed that she wasn't wearing anything at all underneath. I did not stare long nor hard, for she held no interest with me. The Indun sort of smacked his lips, but then, I figured he'd been a long time without companionship of any kind and wasn't in his right mind.

Albert and Monroe simply gasped.

"Well, Alexy," said Monroe in a low sort of tone. "You know what you must do. Be brave now."

"Are you certain that this is absolutely necessary, Mr. Monroe?"

"I am, son. I am."

"Well then . . ." He marched resolutely toward the log house and the waiting Tulip Belle. Henry was sitting off to one side of the porch, and I could see the forlorn look on his face. His mustache dropped all the way to the ground, it seemed.

Tulip greeted the prince with a warm embrace and led him inside. Monroe blew air through his puffed cheeks and said, "I wasn't sure he'd do it, I give him credit for being a righteous individual."

"Do what?" asked Albert.

Monroe shook his head. "Do what he's got to do to find out the whereabouts of Rufus Buck and his bunch."

"What's that include?" I ask.

"Everything and anything, I reckon," said Monroe. "She looks like a woman that would demand much of a man in return for privileged information."

Then, Augustus Monroe did something I had never seen him do before: he laughed.

"All I can say boys, is I am glad that it wasn't me that Tulip Belle decided to spin her web around. I don't know that even for five thousand dollars, I could've done it."

We threw down our bedrolls there in the front yard and were troubled by the mosquitoes again, but not so badly as before when we were nearer the river.

Albert whispered to me after a time, "I wonder what they are doing in there?"

"I reckon the same thing you and that little honey-haired gal was doing back at Miss Mossey's place, but only the prince ain't enjoying it nearly as well."

It was Albert's turn to laugh then before stating, "I shouldn't be enjoying the thought of it—Tulip and Alexy—but I am."

"I know," says I. "I'm enjoying it, too. Only I feel sorry for him, for it is something that he will always have to live with."

Monroe, having rolled himself his nightly cigarette, said: "It won't be that bad I imagine. Look the lights have been doused. At least he won't have to look at her."

I looked over at the Indun who was staring at the house; he looked nearly as forlorn as Henry, for I believed he saw it as a missed opportunity that Tulip had not chosen him for her evening's companionship.

Then, he slowly turned to me and said, "She is a good-looking woman and has strong bones and teeth."

I could only guess that he was seeing things through the eyes of a man who had once maybe died and come back and not through the eyes of any mortal person to have made such an observation of Miss Tulip Belle's qualities.

My last thoughts were of Jasmine—a truly lovely gal.

TWENTY-ONE

The following morning brings stormy weather; the sky is dark with heavy clouds and the air so damp you can smell the rain coming even though it had not actually begun.

I awake to the sounds of a stirring camp, many of the men around Belle's Bend are already up having their coffee, and eating plates of hash.

One man stood on the front porch brushing his teeth—an uncommon sight among the bunch, for most, as I have stated, were ill-kept in their personal habits.

Monroe is already up, a tin of hot black coffee in one hand, a rolled cigarette in the other. He looks as though he is enjoying himself. The Indun is still asleep, his hands clamped between his knees. I reckon he has a right to sleep in as long as we are not on the move to anywhere.

I noticed Henry staring over our way from where he sat on the far edge of the porch. His countenance had gone from dejection, to pure hatred. Some of his companions sat nearby and he spent some energy talking to them with occasional nods our way.

"I think that fellow has it in for us," I tell Monroe.

He gives only a cursory glance toward Henry and his friends.

"He does not look like much of a fighter to me," states Monroe, taking careful sips of his coffee. "Any man that would let a woman as homely as Tulip Belle order him around and make him fix chickens for strangers and then see her carry on with the prince the way she has, cannot be considered much of a fighting man."

"Maybe he just loves her so much he's willing to put up with anything," suggests Albert.

"That ain't love, son. That's being hen whipped!"

Monroe seems to pay it no more mind than that, the fact that Henry and his friends are tossing hard looks our way. I feel uneasy about it, myself.

Soon, the door to the log house opens and Tulip and Alexy make their appearance. It begins to rain. Alexy seems glum, but Tulip offers him, and us all, proud, happy smiles that show off her long curved teeth. She cuts him loose at last with a peck on the cheek and then joins the others in getting a dish of hash and some of the hot black wicked coffee that has burned my tongue.

She is dressed much like a man: shirt, britches, boots, and a flop hat with her hair pinned up under it. I would not have believed, seeing her yesterday, that she could have performed any trick to make herself less attractive to the human eye. But, seeing her now, dressed in men's clothing, I can confess that I was wrong. She wore over her shirt, a leather vest, which concealed her bosoms—the last parts of her that would indicate she was a woman. She could've easily been mistaken for one of the other men in camp, so plain and mannish was she in appearance.

Seeing her thus, my sympathies for poor Alexy only increased.

"Well?" says Monroe, after Alexy came and joined us in our little circle under a tarpaulin fly we used for cover against the sad weather.

Alexy only shrugged, sagged a bit, and sat himself down on an overturned pail.

"It wasn't as bad as I first thought it might be," he said.

Monroe clapped him on the shoulder.

"I figured you'd get the hang of it after a time," said he. "I figured she'd grow on you, and I guess I was right."

"She knows things," said Alexy, in a slow, deliberate manner of speaking, "that few other women know."

Even the Indun, having awakened to the smell of hash, had taken an interest in what Alexy had to say about the previous evening spent.

"Such as?" said Monroe.

Alexy flushed red from that line of questioning.

"Oh, a gentleman should never speak of such intimate details," he insisted. "I will tell you, however, that there is one performance that she gave that could not be equaled, not even in the Orient, where I have been and have had the pleasure of the very finest in the way of feminine pleasures. I can fully understand now, why men would seek after her. I suppose that the American frontiersman would be much more inclined to pass on such carnal tales to their cohorts than would I. That being the case, I can see how such news might bring the men a running to her."

"Wow!" said Albert. The Indun was uncertain as to exactly what the prince was talking about, but nodded his head in an approving way anyhow.

There wasn't a one of us who wouldn't have bitten off our own tongues to have heard the details.

I looked over long enough to see that Henry had taken to falling in behind Tulip and her every step and was now trying to talk to her in an earnest way.

She seemed to be enjoying it, having Henry follow her around like that, like a duck will follow you around once you train it to.

"Well, did you at least get what you went in there for?" said Monroe. "That is news on where Rufus Buck can be found?"

"Yes," said Alexy. "It was all very difficult, you understand, for all that Miss Belle seemed interested in was, hmmm . . . other things. Things of the night."

"Well?" insisted Monroe.

"She states that Rufus Buck was here as recently as a week ago . . . She further stated that she and Mr. Buck shared more than mere pleasantries, practically bragged about it. I was not interested, of course, in hearing the details, but prodded her along to the part of where Mr. Buck said that he would be going upon departure from this place.

"At first, she was reticent as regarding the whereabouts of Mr. Buck, saying that she never liked to discuss one man while with another. I assured her that it was okay with me to do so. Then, a bit of suspicion overcame her, and I had to delay further probing until a more opportune moment presented itself. Which it did, shortly." The prince paused, took in a deep breath, and wiped droplets of sweat from his forehead.

Albert and me and the Indun clung on every word.

"Take your time, Alexy," said Monroe. "I know this ain't been the easiest on you."

"I have a strong craving for a good bowl of borscht," said the Prince, "for my insides feel empty, and my strength all but gone."

We all traded looks not knowing what was borscht.

"A sort of beet soup," says Alexy, reading the confusion on our faces. "Whenever I think of home, I think of cold winter nights and hot bowls of borscht and big loaves of black bread." The mention of bread loaves caused me to think of Hilda, the hateful waitress.

"Would hash do?" said Monroe. "I will send one of these boys over to fetch you a plate of hash."

Then before the prince could answer, Monroe turns to me and says, "Please go and get Alexy a plate of that hash and a cup of coffee. He has earned it."

I do not want to depart from the story that Alexy is telling, but, looking at his gaunt nature, I figure that I would be mean by not doing so.

I wander over to the hash steaming in a large black kettle over an open fire. I grab a tin plate and load up, then do the same with a cup of the coffee. But before I take two steps back toward my companions, Henry and several of his slack jawed friends have blocked my path.

"I reckon you are taking that grub over to the foreigner," says he, gritting his teeth. I notice then, just how far his ears stick out under the slouch hat he is wearing. The hat is in no better condition than my own. I figure he has not been much of a success in life to be that much older than me and not be wearing a better hat.

"I reckon I was," I state. "For it appears that he has had a tough night and deserves the victuals." I knowed I was rubbing salt into the wounds by such commentary, but I didn't care that I was, for I found the manner of Henry to be surly and not worth taking up my time by asking such obvious questions as to who I was carrying the hash over to.

He gets almost cross-eyed with anger at my comments to him.

"You're a black little sumabitch, that I ought to buggy whip!" says he.

"You ought to try," I say, dropping Alexy's plate of hash and coffee unto the ground where it is immediately lapped up by a mangy black dog.

From the corner of my vision, I can see Tulip Belle and some of the rest of her boys standing on the porch, out of the rain, where she is grinning over the way me and Henry are getting ready to bust each other good.

As a way of show, I reckon, Henry snatches the cheap rundown hat off his head and flings it away.

Taking up a fighter's stance, he waves his fists at me and says, "Come ahead, nigger boy!"

But, before I can even move to bust him one, Augustus Monroe is there with his pistol drawn and cocked and coolly says: "I would not molest this boy was I you." The front sight of Monroe's Navy is no more than a few inches from Henry's nose, and now his eyes have crossed in staring at it.

I watch him swallow hard, the cuss words caught up in his throat, the ones that he can't let out for fear of the natural consequences that would occur, cussing a man like Augustus Monroe whose pistol is drawn and ready to be fired, even though he is known only as Mr. Jones and not who he truly is.

It would still be the same thing as suicide.

"Ivory, go and get Alexy another plate of that hash, would you," says Monroe calmly. I knew right then that he might not be able to see well, but that it did not stop him from asserting his presence among lesser men.

I pick up the plate, scrape it off some, and pile on more hash from the kettle.

"Now son," says Monroe to Henry. "What is your choice? Do you want to go on about your business and leave my people alone, or will you have it another way?"

Henry has lost his color and his nerve. I reckon most men would under the circumstances.

Henry continues his cross-eyed stare at Monroe's big Navy for a second longer.

"Well?" states Monroe impatiently.

In something that sounds like Henry is trying to swallow his own tongue, he mutters, "I . . . wouldn't . . . stand no . . . chance at all . . . against that . . ." meaning Monroe's cocked Navy. And, he was right.

"Then go mind your own business," says Monroe, and waits till Henry does, before lowering the hammer of the Navy and replacing it inside his waistband.

I look over to see Tulip Belle grinning above her plate of hash. I had no doubts that she enjoyed blood-letting, regardless of whose blood it might be that was getting let.

Handing Alexy his plate of hash, he offers me a grateful smile.

"As you was saying," says Monroe. "Where did that woman state Rufus Buck and his band to be?"

"She stated that she wasn't a hundred percent certain—because Rufus Buck didn't always go where he said he was going—but that there was a small bank in Ardmore that he was thinking about robbing. She further said that Mr. Buck commented, several times, on his impoverished condition, and that the last few folks he had robbed were nearly as poor as himself and that he didn't understand why the government of this country didn't do more to help folks to be better off than they were, complaining the whole while, according to Miss Belle, about the Democrats who were ruining everything."

"Ardmore, eh," states Monroe. "Well, that's good news for us, but bad news for the folks of Ardmore."

"Mr. Monroe?" said Alexy.

"What?"

"You are not planning that we spend another night here?"

"No need to now that we got what we came here for."

Alexy looked more than relieved.

Tulip Belle drifted over our way, only this time Henry wasn't following on her heels.

She was all pleasantries in greeting us.

"Mr. Jones," she says by way of greeting. "Poor Henry is concerned that you are out to kill him, and that he does not think you are who you represent yourself to be, and that he further thinks that maybe you are the law in spite of traveling with these two boys and that there Injin."

"Henry has mush for brains, miss," states Monroe without even bothering to stand up. She is carrying a small parasol to keep the rain off her.

"Yes, I am afraid that is true, but he is loyal to me and hopes someday to be my husband."

"Well, you could get a dog for that," says Monroe in a cold manner. "I have heard tell that down here in the Territory, almost anything goes." It was a heavy insult.

For a long full moment, Tulip Belle simply stared at the notorious pistoleer, known to her only as Mr. Jones, but plainly a dangerous man regardless of who he was.

"You don't find me attractive, do you Mr. Jones? Most men find me attractive. They come all the way here because they have heard about me and think me to be a woman they'd like, to be with. But not you."

Monroe looked all around us, looked to see that Tulip's men were looking to see what might occur between her and him. The men, for the most part had finished their hash, but were still working on their coffee because the rain had put a chill in the air and hot coffee was the one thing that stood off the chill.

"Ma'am, I did not come here looking for a woman or anything else," said Monroe, leveling his clear-eyed gaze at her. "I have already told you that all we are doing is passing through on our way to someplace else. Whether or not I find you attractive has no bearing on anything. It looks to me like you have plenty of male company to last you a lifetime."

"Henry thinks I should have my boys shoot you and bury you all among them trees over yonder."

"Like I said, Henry's a damn fool. It would seem to me, if you are thinking about marrying that man, that you have made a poor choice."

Then, Tulip Belle smiled her horse-tooth smile and said, "I tend to agree. My first husband, Jim April, would turn over in his grave at just the thought of me and Henry Barns. Jim April was a tall man from Mississippi, full head of hair and big hands. He would've thought Henry Barns somewhat of a sisterly type—if you know what I mean." She offered a wink with the comment.

"Jim April was shot by a constable down in Dallas over the ownership of some horses Jim had in a string he was bringing north. That constable was an old, old man and no one in this world could've guessed that an old, old man would've shot and killed a man like Jim April, as handsome and robust a man as he was. But it happened. Just like that. I cried for three days when I got the news, still cry sometimes whenever I look at Henry and think of Jim April. They're as different as night and day.

"But, Henry has his good points," says Tulip, brightly. "He don't lift a hand to me; Jim April sometimes did; he was a man of quick temper and short patience. And, Henry, like I said, is loyal, whereas, Jim April had an eye for the ladies and though I knew he was not faithful to me in that way, I could not help it because of him being such a handsome man. Handsomest man I ever saw, except for the Prince here. You are a handsome man, Alexy!"

Gentleman that he was, Alexy, gave a slight, if weakened, bow of his head, and murmured a thank you. It seemed to please her to no end, his princely ways.

I looked and saw the Indun staring at her—he was in love; anyone could look at him and see that much. My intention was to tell him not to waste his time, for I saw nothing outstanding about Miss Belle, and that she would, in most likelihood, not give him the time of day if she owned the only watch in the world and he was offering to pay a dollar a minute.

But, one thing I had already come to learn about Induns, once they got their mind set on something, there wasn't much that was going to put them off. So it was with Man Who Waits's lustful nature toward Tulip Belle.

"If you want a real man," he said of a sudden. "Then it would be good if you took a Comanche brave into your robes."

"Huh?" said Tulip.

Man Who Waits smiled boldly. For the first time since our arrival of the previous day, Tulip Belle had let her attention rest fully on him.

"I could show you what most white women do not know," he said.

She took him in from head to toe. The toes of his moccasins were worn through and showed the yellowed horny toenails of his gnarled feet.

"You look old enough to be Moses's cousin," she said, with a half laugh.

"Who's Moses?" he said.

"Oh, I forgot, you ain't a Christian man. Jim April wasn't either, but then he wasn't an Injin—he was a Cajun."

"I think you look like a good woman to me," said the Indun. "I always have liked a woman with a face like yours." If it was some sort of compliment, the only one that took it as such was Belle, herself. The rest of us had to bite the insides of our cheeks to keep from laughing.

"Well, thank you, chief," says Belle. "I reckon you have as much manners and good sense as some of these white men around here."

Now it was the Indun's turn to seem pleased—his face bunched up into a wider grin still.

"Well, it all sounds wonderful," said Augustus Monroe. "The two of you complimenting one another this way and that. But, we must be on our way."

"I could stay behind," Man Who Waits told Tulip.

"What for?" she said.

"I could stay here until winter comes," he stated. "I could show you what the white women don't know. But, after that, when the winter comes, I'll probably die again."

"I don't think the boys would take too well to having an Injin around here. They's mostly boys with particular ways as to the company they keep." She could see the disappointment in the old man's eyes.

"Don't take it personal, dad," she said. "I wouldn't so much mind trying an Injin for a lover—even an old one such as yourself, for you are an interesting old coot and I would dearly enjoy seeing what it is that white women don't know. But, me and Henry is planning on being married soon, and he wouldn't stand for me being with no Injin in that way. The prince, I reckon I can explain, but not an Injin. Henry's folks was killed by Injins. It'd be hell to pay all the way around. You best go on with your friends and dream of me at nights and what might've been rather than risk murder and bloodshed over something so scabrous as me and you rolling around in the blankets."

The Indun looked crestfallen, for his fires had been

dampened in a rain of words, some of which he did not understand, and others, which he understood all too well.

"Mount up!" said Monroe.

"We'd best be on our way," Albert consoled the Indun.

"You don't have to go, Alexy," said Tulip.

"I must," said Alexy.

"I'd get rid of Henry if you was wanting to stay," said she. "I'd tell him to get gone."

"No . . ." said Alexy. "I could not in any case stay on. I must ride with my companions." He was clearly uncomforted by her efforts.

I could see from across the way, the anxious face of Henry Barns as stood under the protection of the porch roof, for the drizzle of rain was now beginning in earnest.

"If we do not leave soon," said Monroe, "we will all be drowned, sitting out here like this with our mouths open." And with that, he spurred his horse into a trot.

The rain dripped off the leaves of the trees and off the eaves of the porch and off Tulip's parasol as we departed Belle's Bend and rode toward Ardmore. I refused to think ahead of what might lie in wait for us there.

TWENTY-TWO

Ardmore was no good-looking place. It was muddy streets and raw lumber buildings and whiskey tents and whore tents and full of low-looking types. But, that is just my opinion.

We found the local sheriff's office, a man named Billmore, and announced ourselves to him.

He looked us over like we was a circus come to town, or a three-legged toad.

"Do you have a bank in this town?" asked Monroe.

"Are you here to invest?" inquired Billmore.

"We are here to save you grief," said Monroe.

"Of what sort?"

"Have you ever heard of a man named Rufus Buck?"

"Everyone has heard of Rufus Buck if it is the same nigger bandit that has crisscrossed this territory and is also known for banditry and murder down along the border and on into Mexico."

"One in the same," said Monroe.

"Well, what about him?"

"We have it on reliable sources that he will come here soon to rob your bank."

"Which one?" said Billmore. "We have three."

Monroe rubbed his jaw for he had not counted on three banks.

"That presents a problem," says he after a time of rubbing his jaw.

"What is your interest in bringing me this news?"

said Billmore. He had a tic just below his right eye and it appeared as though he was winking at Monroe, which in itself seemed funny enough, for Augustus Monroe was not the sort of man that another man would dare wink at.

"We have come to finish him off," said Monroe. "To end his days!"

Billmore looked at the lot of us again, saw that we was boys and old Induns and Russian royalty and could not seem to grasp that we were a match for such as Rufus Buck and his murderers.

"Well, if it is true what you say," said the constable, "that Rufus Buck is on his way here to rob one of our banks, I reckon that we are in big trouble!"

"How many men do you have?" said Monroe. "How many deputies work for you?"

"None," said Billmore. "I am the only lawman around here."

"Well, I figure it won't matter in the long run," said Monroe. "For we intend to wait here in Ardmore until he arrives and then put an end to him, and to the others that ride with him."

Billmore seemed relieved to hear it.

"When do you suppose he will show?" said Billmore.

"Have no idea," said Monroe. "Why do you ask?"

"Well . . . it's just that I was about to leave for Boggy Depot this very day. I have an aunt that is dying over there of the bloody flux and thought that I'd go and pay her a final visit before she passed on."

"An aunt! The bloody flux!" said Monroe, his high voice a whine of disgust. "You have picked a poor time to abandon your station!"

"Can't be helped," shrugged Billmore. "I'd like to stay, in case Rufus Buck shows up . . ."

It was clear to everyone there that the man had little backbone. (For such men were paid only thirty or forty dollars a month and board, and what was the point of dying for that?)

He looked at all of us with a troubled stare.

"We are wasting our time here," stated Monroe, and with that, turned and walked back out the door. "Now what?" asks Albert.

"We will just have to wait," says Monroe. "We will just have to wait and see if Rufus Buck does show up and try to rob one of the banks here. I am hoping that he does, for I miss Kansas and the lay of the land and other things, too."

I knew that the other things he missed were the women and the gambling dens and being known as a local celebrity about town. Here in the Nations, no one seemed to know who Augustus Monroe was, and I knew that he probably missed that more than anything else.

"Let's get a drink," says he and marches off down the muddy street, trailing his horse behind him. We all fall in line and march down the muddy street as well.

He stops in front of a whiskey tent that has a painted board sign hanging over its opening. The sign is well lettered and reads: THE ROAD TO RUIN. I think that is a correct thing to advertise, for such places usually are—the road to ruin.

"Let's go in," says Monroe, and we do.

There are several bearded and rough-looking types lounging both outside, and within. They roll their eyes at us, and watch our movements. A few are armed. They look like slackers to me.

Inside, standing atop the plank bar that is laid over two whiskey barrels, is a yellow bulldog with slobber running from its ugly mouth.

A bald-headed man behind the plank announces that we should not be disturbed by the presence of his pet, Elmo. "He is all I have in this world," states the barman. "I usta have a wife and several children and owned a grocery store in Pennsylvania," says he.

"I usta have money in the bank and owned several good horses and everyone knew me as a generous and loving man to my family." As he talked on, his features took on a greater and greater sadness.

"I usta read the good book and attend church and once was a deacon." I couldn't help but believe by the sound of his quavering voice that he was going to begin bawling.

"I usta ride the train to Denver . . ." Not a one of us knew the significance of that.

"But now, all I have left is me bulldog, Elmo. Was I to ever lose him, I'd take me own life!" Tears leaked out his eyes and unto his sallow cheeks. He did not look a well man in my book.

"We only came in for whiskey," said Monroe.

"Oh . . ."

Then, blinking several times and swiping at his eyes with a rag he carried in one hand, he said: "Is that an Indian you got with you?"

"It is," said Albert.

"I cannot serve Indians in here. It is illegal."

"I wouldn't worry about that, my friend," said Monroe. "Your constable is right now packing to go visit his aunt in Boggy Depot who is dying of the bloody flux."

"An aunt!"

"Pour us whiskey all around," said Monroe, and the man did.

Man Who Waits smacked his lips, drank his whiskey down in one gulp, and tapped his empty glass atop the plank.

"Another," he said.

"Pardon me," said Alexy, polite as usual. "But is there an establishment where we might obtain rooms that have baths?"

"Baths?"

The prince nodded.

The man scratched at a spot between his eyes. "Only one place in Ardmore that has baths," says he. We waited for another few seconds for him to tell us which place that was.

"Ma Mayweather's Chance Hotel is the only place in Ardmore that has baths."

"Do you think she might have vacancies?" inquired Alexy in his soft pleasant voice.

"If she does," said the barman, "it would be a damn miracle!"

"Why is that, sir?"

"Because Ma Mayweather is as dead as last year's posies!" He seemed to take great delight over his little joke with us, the fact that whoever Ma Mayweather was, she was no more and thereby could not possibly have any vacancies.

Monroe took it upon himself to lean in real close to the man and said: "You have an ugly dog, mister, and a poor sense of humor. Now which way is that hotel?"

We waited three days for Rufus Buck and his men to show, but we waited in vain.

"What now?" said Albert on the afternoon of the third day.

"We wait some more," he said. We did, two more days.

By chance, I bought a copy of the local newspaper, *The Democrat*, for a penny which I had found in the street just lying there. I had thought of buying a stick of hard candy with the penny, but a stick is all that I could have purchased, and that I would have to share with Albert and the Indun and it didn't hardly seem worth the effort for a stick of hard candy that wasn't much longer than the longest finger on a man and split up three ways didn't leave enough to satisfy a sweet tooth in my book.

Our waiting days in Ardmore had been hours of boredom for me and Albert and the Indun, and even Alexy. Only Monroe could find any entertainment in

such a place as Ardmore. Of course he took his pleasure in the whiskey tents and the whore tents and did
what little gambling was available to him, mostly on
spread-out blankets with a pack of dog-eared playing
cards that some trashy type would produce from a
frayed coat pocket. Did I mention the fact that
Augustus Monroe was a poor gambler?

One day, he lost nearly a hundred dollars in a game
of monte to a fellow with a glass eye and who only
had three fingers on his left hand and two on his right,
and sported a wooden leg.

"How did you lose all those parts?" Monroe had
asked the fellow, somewhat brazenly for he had been
drinking hard that day over the fact that he had lost
fifty dollars the day before.

"I just sort of lost them along the way of life," stated
the man. "It's funny," said he, "you lose a part of yourself here, and a part of yourself there, and before you
know it, most of you is gone."

The man seemed not bothered at all that he was
down to his last five fingers, one eye, and a leg to give
before he would find himself in a real fix. He was a
good gambler, and from having watched him closely,
an honest one, I believe.

I thought surely, that Alexy would be disturbed by
the fact that Monroe seemed to lose as much money as
he could lay out on a blanket in as quick a time as he
could lay it out, but the prince merely spotted him
more and stated that probably next time, he would
come up a winner.

I only glanced through *The Democrat* with idle curiosity, looking mostly at the sale advertisements of ladies corsets, coffee grinders, and funerals. One place in town would bury you in a good oak coffin for fifteen dollars (I thought it to be a bargain).

Then, like a snakebite, on page two, inside column, there it was: MURDEROUS GANG ROBS TEXAS PACIFIC RAILROAD. THREE ARE KILLED. The story was a lurid detail of how the flyer had been derailed and robbed of several mail sacks but little else. The engineer and the fireman had been killed in the crash itself. A third man, the mail car clerk, a man named Davis, had been blown up inside the car from several sticks of dynamite having been used in an obvious (according to *The Democrat*) miscalculation of the gunpowder's prowess. Davis, it is reported, was blown nearly fifty feet into the air and was a dead man by the time he landed.

Eyewitnesses to the event all stated that the ringleader of the bandits was a large negro man with a scarred face and plenty of white teeth, and that all the others were of similar cut in their evil appearance. A Mrs. Truly Benoit was quoted as saying, "It is only through the grace of Jesus that all the men aboard were not murdered and that all the ladies were not subjected to depredations that no decent woman would care to find herself thinking about."

Since all available men were on a posse chasing another gang of bandits, there was no pursuit. *The Democrat* stated that the robbery occurred just north of Bonham and south of the Red River and closed the article by stating: *The bandits got clean away!*

I carried the news to my companions and they in turn read it with the same interest and dejection that I had.

"Well, so much for him coming here and robbing the banks," said Augustus Monroe.

"They only got some worthless mail sacks," said Albert.

"They are better at murdering folks than they are at robbery," said Monroe. "That's plain for anyone to see."

It was true. Mr. Monroe could lose more money in one hour of gambling than Rufus Buck and his men could rob in a month. They were just poor at everything except killing.

"If we hurry," stated Monroe, upon finishing his part of reading the article—a great effort on his part, because of his poor vision and the way he had to keep bringing the paper up close to his face—"we can maybe get on their trail before they get lost again. I think that Bonham, where this train was robbed, is not more than forty or fifty miles northwest of here. We could be there by first light tomorrow was we to ride all the rest of today and through the night."

It was not an appealing thought to ride for forty or fifty miles and through the night without sleep, or the benefit of a warm bed. But, I had grown as tired of dutchy little Ardmore as I had anyplace on this earth, and was eager to be on my way to some other place—even if it was on the warm trail of Rufus Buck.

We left immediately. My one regret, and Albert's as well, was that we had to leave Ivy, our little burro behind, for as much as she was capable of carrying her load of supplies, she had not the speed in her short legs that was required to ride hard and fast as our grown horses.

We gave her to the one-eyed, five-fingered, wooden-legged man that had won the hundred dollars from Mr. Monroe, for we felt sorry for him and his declining condition and thought it would be nice that he had a good burro like Ivy to share his company with.

TWENTY-THREE

It was a terrible long night that all but wore us out, the ride from Ardmore to near Bonham where the Texas Pacific Train had been robbed and its mail car blown to bits.

For the last twenty miles of our ride, we followed, easterly, the railroad tracks themselves, until we came upon the wreckage of the mail car.

"That is it," said Monroe, halting his horse near a pile of splintered lumber. Still resting on the tracks were a quartet of steel wheels supporting what was left of the flooring of the mail car. All around the area, could be seen splinters of wood siding, several pieces of which had stuck themselves into the ground like arrows.

"That mail clerk must have not felt a dang thing!" said Monroe, upon inspection of the wreckage. "Lucky for him, for I was in the war and seen men blown apart, but not enough so's they were killed. They screamed the loudest, the men that were blown apart!"

I thought then of the gambler, with the missing parts of himself that had won the hundred dollars from Monroe. It did seem that it would be more terrible to have some of yourself torn away, than it would be to just be outright killed.

We spent several minutes scouting the scene, Monroe was busy looking for the tracks of the outlaws.

"Mr. Monroe," says Alexy in a somewhat apologetic tone. "I think this would be a good place for a brief rest in order that we may recover ourselves sufficiently. A small meal, perhaps, in the way of sustenance."

Monroe seemed irritated with the suggestion. I believed him to have gotten the blood scent in him, much like a hunting hound will get, and did not want to quit the chase or delay it.

"Please," said Alexy. "These young men could stand the rest, as could I."

We all looked around at one another, and at the ground near our feet, for no one wanted to appear weak or unwilling. The Indun, to our surprise, slept upright on the back of his horse. How he had remained in that manner without having fallen off, could only be guessed at.

"All right," said Monroe. "We'll rest for twenty minutes, long enough to swallow some grub and air the horses. But, if we want to catch them devils, we should not linger."

We gathered some of the splintered wood of the rail car and built a small fire over which we fried up chunks of bacon that was near rancid from the ever-present heat. It was small relief from the hunger that crawled around in our bellies, but relief nonetheless. I could barely keep my eyes open, nor could Albert. Alexy seemed equally fatigued, but maintained his composure well enough. (I suppose that being of a royal blood, meant that it would be undignified to show the effects of hunger or fatigue or any other form of privation. I had to give him credit, for I was so tired I could've bawled and would not have cared who would've seen me if I had.)

I found myself in a doze with a mouthful of half-cooked pork bacon when Monroe announced loudly that it was time to move on. It seemed as though we had stopped for barely a minute.

He picked up the faint trail, for it was already two or three days old, but plainly that of a large group of riders heading south, toward the border. It was not uncommon for killers and thieves and every other sort of malfeasant to head for the border after a crime. Borders just seemed to attract such types; always had, always would.

Our horses were nearly spent, but Monroe insisted that we push on as hard as was possible; I felt sorry for poor Swatchy, for his head was drooping nearly as bad as my own by the time we struck out from our little camp amid the debris.

Ten miles more brought us to what appeared to be an abandoned adobe, for its condition was run-down. It sat along the branch of a near-played-out little stream and we looked down upon it from a slight rise we had topped.

Upon closer observation, we could see several saddle horses tied up around back.

"There they are," announced Monroe in a whisper.

"How do you know that is them?" asked Albert. "It would seem to me that they would have been a lot farther away from the scene of their crime than this."

Monroe turned to him and winked. It was an uncommon thing for a man like Monroe to do, wink, but he did it anyhow out of a sense of great satisfaction.

"The thing you don't understand about criminals is," he said with much authority, "they are commonly stupid people. You or I was to rob a train, blow it up, we'd be a hundred miles away. But criminals are stupid and vain individuals for the most part. The only criminal I ever knew that was halfway smart was Jelly Jim who used to steal horses and rob a bank on occasion.

"Jelly Jim was as nearly as smart as a professor and read books written in Latin and could carry on conversations with rich folks. He could plan out a crime like some men could plan out the building of a barn.

But even Jelly Jim was vain, and it was his vanity that got him caught and hung. It took two ropes to hang him because he was such a big man . . ."

"How was it that his vanity got him caught?" I was curious.

"He believed that he was so smart that he couldn't get caught by no lawman. And, it was true, no lawman did catch him. He was caught by a farmer."

"A farmer?" said Albert.

"That's right. He got caught diddling the farmer's wife and the farmer caught him and forced him to hang himself from the hay pully of his barn. Either that, or the farmer was going to shoot off his man parts with a black shotgun. Jelly Jim went for the hanging. The first time he tried, the rope broke. The farmer gave him two ropes the second try and that did the trick. It was only after the deed had been done that everyone learned it was Jelly Jim, the horse thief and occasional bank robber. No one was sorry to see him go. As I said, criminals are mostly stupid and vain and will sooner or later meet their just end, just as those boys down there are about to do."

Monroe instructed us on taking up our positions there on the little rise two hundred yards from the small crumbling adobe.

"Alexy, you can have the first shot with that sporting rifle of yours. If it happens to be Rufus himself, all the better."

"I would consider that my chore," said Albert.

"Well, son," says Monroe. "Do you think you can

hit a man at this distance with that repeater of yours?" Albert looked unsure, but screwed up his courage and said that he thought he could.

"For if you miss," warned Monroe. "You might not have another shot at him."

Monroe said that if more than one man came out of the house, then we should fire at will and drop as many as we could. Most likely, he said, if we shot a few, the others would surrender themselves and we could take them to the nearest settlement with a jail and apply for any rewards on them.

I felt that within my own heart, that I could not shoot any of the men. Not like that I couldn't.

Monroe said that they'd most likely come dribbling out in order to relieve themselves; there was a little privy not far away. "No man can hold his water for long in the morning," Monroe said. "That is when we will have our opportunity, when they come out to make water."

No, I told myself. Even though they had it coming, I could not bring myself to shoot down a man in cold blood.

"Albert," I say. "Can you and me have a private talk?"

He looks wide eyed at me, blinking back his own fatigue. His eyes are red and weary.

Monroe and Alexy are busy watching the house below us.

"Sure," says Albert.

We go off a ways, me tugging at his elbow.

"What is it, Ivory?"

"I need to be honest with you, Albert. I don't believe that I am killer enough to shoot men who are doing nothing more than going to make water. It is not the way I imagined that it would be. I thought that there would be a fiercesome battle between us and them, and that in fighting for my own life, I would have no trouble in shooting the whole bunch of them. But, not like this. Not shooting men who are just on their way to making water."

For a time Albert just looked at me with those innocent eyes of his.

"I'm not sure I can do it either," he said. "Not even if it is Rufus Buck himself who comes out. When I think about how he killed my pa, I get mad enough and believe that I could shoot Rufus Buck a hundred times and not bat an eye. But, I can't say's I carry that much madness around in me most of the time. At least not enough so that if Rufus Buck comes out of that house holding nothing more than himself, I could shoot him."

"That's exactly how I'm feeling," I say.

"Well, what do we do, Ivory?"

"Let's talk to Monroe and tell him we've changed our minds, at least about the killing part, and see if he will assist us in the capture of Rufus Buck and his men, and help us transport them to the nearest town with a jail and a judge. I'm sure that once all the evidence against them comes out, Rufus and his boys will hang for sure."

"We could have the satisfaction of seeing them hung," says Albert.

"Yes we could, and that should be enough, to see Rufus Buck and his cutthroats swinging from ropes of justice."

"Well, all right. Let's go ask Monroe to help us," said Albert.

When we told Monroe our feelings, he said: "It is too late for that, for here they come out and it looks like some are getting ready to ride!"

True enough, two men were heading toward the privy, but several others were putting saddles on their ponies.

Before we could speak, Monroe leveled his Henry and fired off several shots down unto the little scene. Two of the saddle horses fell over dead and the men scrambled back inside the house, except for the two that had been heading for the privy, for they ducked inside, slamming the door shut behind them.

"Damn this gun!" said Monroe, inspecting the Henry as though it were not rightly made. "I did not mean to kill good horses."

I knew why he had: he was aiming for the men and hit their animals instead. He would not admit to his poor eyesight, but instead, blamed the Henry rifle.

"Well, we have them now," said Monroe. "Alexy, I suggest you train your rifle on that outhouse where a couple of them boys run to. They will be easy pickings if they get to where they can't stand the stench of their accommodations, and they won't be able to stand it long in this heat, I am willing to bet."

"I had thought," said Alexy, directing his words

toward Monroe. "That I would enjoy the hunt of these criminals. But now that they are down there at our mercy, I don't think that I can shoot them, either. Were they to fight, that would be a different story . . ."

Monroe looked exasperated.

"We rode all night for this?" He seemed thoroughly disgusted at our behavior, for he was a man used to a good fight to the death, and I believe he saw us in a lesser light as individuals now that we refused to shoot our helpless enemies.

"Why don't we just wipe them out and be done with it?"

It was a good question, but one that none of us had an answer to. It was just something none of us, with the exception of Monroe had in us, to kill men like that. He was born one way, we another. Although, having been awakened by Monroe's rapid gunfire down unto the adobe, the Indun was in agreement with Monroe.

"Mr. Monroe is right," said Man Who Waits. "If you do not kill those men, they could find a way to come back and kill you. That happened to a cousin of mine along the river you white people call the Big Sandy. He had caught some Mexican women and their children down there one time and was going to kill them and take their blankets. But, he saw those little children laughing and playing and felt sorry for them and refused to kill them that day. Two years later, near that same spot, he was killed by Mexican bandits. If you let your enemy live, they will sometimes come and find you and kill you. Or, some of their people will."

The whole while, Monroe nodded his approval of the Indun's theory. Before he could say more about it, however, a white flag was waved from one of the windows in the adobe. It looked to be a piece of torn underdrawers tied to the front sights of a rifle.

"Look!" said Albert. "They are giving themselves up!"

"It could be a trick," cautioned Monroe. "Bandits are stupid and vain, but they are not above suckering people!"

Pretty soon, a second flag of truce—this, an arm or a leg of the union suit appeared in yet another window. (I figured they must have been in earnest to give themselves up, if one was willing to offer his union suit as a flag of truce.)

Someone from within shouted: "We give up!" and "Don't shoot us!"

Monroe yelled down that those inside should come out unarmed and ready to die if this was a trick. Several come walking out with their hands in the air. They didn't look so mean or terrible now.

Monroe ordered the two men who had dived into the privy to produce themselves or be subjected to a rain of lead. His manner of speech had now taken on the flowered prose of *Harper's* and the *Police Gazette* and I could not help but wonder if he had read stories about himself and had been swayed by them.

A rain of lead!

The two men came out and went and stood with the

others. We counted eight in all. A few I remembered from that fateful day in Last Whiskey. But one face was not among them, that of Rufus Buck himself.

Albert noticed it, too.

"We've got them all but Buck," he said, disappointed.

We made our way down to the desperadoes, training our guns on them the whole while, for Monroe said even if we wasn't willing to shoot them, we ought at least act as though we were, or what would be the inducement to them to stand there like they was— some in nothing but their underdrawers and boots— and not take up arms and fill us full of holes!

"At least point your damn guns at them and make them think you are raw killers and bloodthirsty types!" We couldn't find no reason to argue with him on that point and therefore did as he requested. It seemed to have the desired effect on our quarry, for they did not take their eyes off our pistols and rifles the whole time.

Monroe had us tie their hands and then their feet once they was mounted upon their ponies. We looped the rope around their ankles, swinging it under the bellies of their horses so that they could not jump off. It scared them to be tied that way.

One man said, "What if I fall off? I will be drug underneath my own horse and have my head bashed in by the rocks."

Monroe said: "You should have thought of the risks of a life of crime, this is just one of them."

Up close, they did not look like a band of killers and cutthroats the way they had that day I seen them in Last Whiskey. Up close, looking at them now—their dirty faces and raggedy garments—they looked just like what they were: scroungy white men, and brown, with careless eyes and poor teeth and poorer haircuts. Men who would never make a thing out of their lives except to bring misery and trouble to themselves and others.

I could not have brought myself to shoot them in cold blood, but I had not an ounce of sympathy for any of them, either.

"Where is Rufus Buck?" asked Albert to one of the men.

"I guess you ain't never gonna know!" declared the man bitterly.

Albert struck him a sharp blow to the knee with the butt of his Henry. The man yeowled like a scalded cat.

"Maybe you think I ain't nothing but a boy and have no right to capture such trash as you!" said Albert in a tough tone. "But if you don't tell me where Rufus Buck is, I will pull you over and slap your horse to running and have him drag you to death!"

Then, turning to the others, he announced. "And if this man does not tell me where Rufus Buck is, I will do the same to each one of you until one decides that being drug to death by his own horse ain't worth the trouble to protect the whereabouts of murdering trash like Rufus Buck!"

The answer was not long in coming, for several of

the captured ducks shouted out that Rufus Buck had left two days earlier for Sacred Heart, a town two days ride north.

"What would be his business in Sacred Heart?" inquired Albert, determined to elicit the information from the now talkative bunch.

"He has a sweetheart there," said one. Several more agreed.

"What is her name?"

"She is called Bucktooth Sue. Ain't nobody knows her by any other name. Bucktooth Sue. Everyone in Sacred Heart has heard of her."

"Is there a jail and a judge there?" said Monroe.

The man who told us about Bucktooth Sue laughed and said, "Hell no!" The nearest jail and judge was back in Ardmore, he informed us, and he didn't mind going back there, because they fed their prisoners well and did not usually abuse them. Many of the others agreed and said, "We vote for Ardmore if you are to take us anywhere."

Monroe said, "This ain't a damn election!" But he had to admit that he would have to take their word on where the nearest jail and judge was.

"Well," says Monroe. "We are in a pickle it seems. For, if we are to deliver these boys back to Ardmore, then, it will take at least two of us. I figure me and the prince could see it done. You could go with us of course, but then that would take several days to go there and then two or three more to make our way back to Sacred Heart.

"I think that Rufus Buck would not wait around that long a time in any one place, sweetheart or no. For even sweethearts tend to wear thin on a man after a time. I don't think that Rufus Buck would be any exception."

"What do you suggest we do?" inquires Albert.

"Well, you boys are inexperienced when it comes to transporting prisoners. I have done my share of it and know how to do it. And besides, I am willing to shoot these boys if they try anything, whereas, I don't believe you would."

It was true, everything that Monroe was saying.

"I will write you a note to carry with you to the local lawman in Sacred Heart, telling him of who I am, and of who you are, and what your business is there. I will further request that he help you to locate and capture Rufus Buck. Three of you against Rufus Buck should be enough to get the trick done, if done right. It is all I know to do, unless you want me to let these boys loose and accompany you to Sacred Heart?"

It seemed we had no choice in the matter. Monroe could see the worry in our faces.

"A man who has taken time out of his criminal doings to go visit his sweetheart, does not sound like a man much concerned about capture to me. Especially capture from a pair of youngsters, no slight intended to either of you boys. You will have the greatest advantage: the element of surprise! Was I you," he suggested. "I'd wait until the exact right time to draw down on him."

"How will we know when that is?" I say.

"Oh, you'll know," said Monroe confidently. "There is always an exact right time."

He wished us luck, stating he was anxious to deliver his charge to the law back in Ardmore. I knew the real reason to be that he had been several days and nights without the companionship of gamblers and painted ladies, but I could not fault him for his braveness and help in bringing to arrest Rufus Buck's gang. Albert and I shook his hand, and that of the prince and watched as they rode off with gang in tow.

"Well, let's get started," said Albert. "We are nearly back to where we began, just the two of us . . . except for Man Who Waits."

We mounted our horses and started off in the direction of Sacred Heart. It was only after less than a mile that we noticed the Indun was not behind us. We turned round again and caught up with him. He was going in a direction that would take him north, but to the west.

"Sacred Heart is this way," said Albert.

"I know," said the Indun.

"Then why are you going that way?"

"Because that is the way that my horse chooses to take me."

"You're not going with us?"

"No. I am going that way," he said pointing to the north.

"Where to?"

"I don't know. My horse will know when he gets there. Probably he will go back to where some of my people used to live. Or maybe he will go in another direction later. I can only go where he goes."

We were losing a good companion in the Indun and did not want to see him go off alone like that, for he seemed barely able to care for himself.

"If you will go with us now," said Albert. "We will ride north with you when our business is finished in Sacred Heart."

"My horse does not want to go to that place," said he. "I think he knows that there is trouble there and does not want to go."

Albert fished out some of the money he was carrying and handed it over to the Indun.

"Here."

"I don't need it," said Man Who Waits.

"You've earned it," said Albert. "I'd feel better about leaving you, knowing I paid you for your time."

"Okay," said the Indun. "Then I will keep it."

Albert offered his hand and the Indun shook it with glee, then mine, too.

"You will someday be a great man, Ivory Cade," said he. "I had a dream that someday you would be a great man among the white people."

"I'd settle for just being alive long enough to grow old and fat," I tell him.

He smacked his lips and said: "It is too bad that Tulip Belle did not want me to be her man. I would have shown her what the white women don't know."

Then, he rode off toward the north just like it was something he had been doing all his life.

"Now it is just you and me, Ivory," said Albert. "Just like we started out," I say.

"I ain't sorry it's just you and me," says he. "Me either, Albert. Me either."

We turn our ponies in the direction of Sacred Heart. It did not fail my attention, that the name of the little town was exactly the same as that of the orphanage in which I had spent so many good years of my youth, and the one that the of Mexican, Otero, had come took me out of in order to teach me the business of taking care of the dead.

Was there something to it, that I was now riding toward a town called Sacred Heart? I was not one to believe strongly in omens or signs, but there seemed something dark and tricky by such coincidence.

I thought maybe it would not hurt me to try and remember one or two prayers I had learned while a captive at the Little Sisters of The Sacred Heart Industrial School for Boys and Girls.

TWENTY-FOUR

A rainstorm had swept down on us by the time we reached the settlement of Sacred Heart. It rained so hard, I thought me and Albert might be beat to death by it. It rained, and then it hailed, and then it rained some more. The rain and hail stung welts on our hands and faces. It knocked leaves off of trees, and some limbs as well. I am sure that it would have killed any small animals caught out in it.

Not only was there the rain and hail, but bright, jagged spurs of lightning flashed all around us and terrified our mounts and made them hard to handle.

It was a relief to arrive at Sacred Heart and duck inside the first building that was open to the public, which was a saloon called Cherokee Charlie's.

We trailed puddles on the floor behind us, but what did it matter, for Cherokee Charlie's appeared to be a low sort of establishment, judging by the rough trade that stood around inside taking their leisure in the embrace of sloe-eyed women and hard cheap liquor.

A tall black-haired man approached us and asked what it was we boys was doing inside his establishment.

"You must be Cherokee Charlie," I said.

"So what if I am?" says he in a gruff manner, as though I had done something to offend him terribly, like say that I wanted to court his sister.

"Well, we have heard much about you, me and the Whiskey Kid has," I said. "This is the Whiskey Kid himself, and I am Black Jim. You have heard of us ain't you?"

"No, I ain't!"

I laugh easily, like as though it don't bother me that Cherokee Charlie has not heard of the Whiskey Kid, or Black Jim.

"Well, you must be living in a hole," I say, "if you have not heard of either me, or the Kid here."

"What is it I was supposed to hear about you?" says Cherokee Charlie. His eyes and his hair are both black as pitch. He is missing some of his front teeth.

I look around, squinting as though I am unhappy about the dark and curious stares that our presence is bringing. Squinting, like I believe a cold killer would squint if he was unhappy with the way he was being watched at. Squinting, hoping that I would not see the scarred and evil face of Rufus Buck sitting in among the crowd. I did not, and thereby continued my little act.

"What you would know," I say to Cherokee Charlie. "Is that if you didn't spend all your life inside this little run-down shebang of yours, you would have heard the names of the Whiskey Kid and Black Jim."

"Well, is that supposed to mean something to me that I would have heard those names?"

I lifted aside the front flap of my coat and showed him the butt of my Navy.

"The Whiskey Kid wears one exactly like it," I state. "We are known all over the Territory and even down into Texas, where we hail from originally, for our ability to use these Navies. Do I have to paint you a picture?"

"Lots of men wear guns," he says in a devil-may-care sort of way.

"Lots of men is correct," says I. "But how many boys our age do? And how many of them have put men like Tall George Bledsoe, and Left Handed Irving, and Peaches Nebraska into their graves?"

That gives him pause. He ain't sure. He ain't sure of the names, and he ain't sure of us. He scratches the side of his head trying to decide if we are legit. He brightens a bit. He says, "I am sorry if I have in some way offended you boys."

"Now you are getting wise, mister," I tell him with a crooked grin purposely laid across my lips. "I was you, I would not flirt with danger any more by asking us to state our business. I was you, I'd get me and the Kid here a beer and make it a cold one. I was you," I said at last, "I might even make them beers as being on the house. It pays to have the right kind of friends, and, I'd say me and the Whiskey Kid are the right kind of friends to have—and the *worst* kind of enemies."

Cherokee Charlie wastes no time in drawing us each up a beer and setting it across his bar top.

"First one's on the house," he says with a wide gaping grin.

A bummer, or what looks to be one judging by the raggedy clothes he is wrapped up in, come from a nearby table and stands next to Albert and me.

"So, you're the boys that killed Peaches Nebraska, eh?" says he in a gravelly voice that comes out of a face full of bristly whiskers. (Was there really a Peaches Nebraska?)

"Yes sir," I state, unable to back away from a lie once told (That is the trouble with lies: once you tell one, you can't easily untell it).

"I knew Peaches," states the old stick. "Knew him in Oglalla. Mean son of a bitch, he was. I didn't reckon anyone would dust him off. You boys say you did, though?"

Albert and me trade looks.

Albert says, "If Ivory said we put Peaches in his grave, then that is what we done. You are right, he was a troublesome man to all them around him. He was abusing a widow and her children, and that is why we done it. He would not let off when asked." (Albert was gaining on me in the acting and lying department.)

"Well, I'd buy you boys a drink just knowing that you put an end to a no-account like Peaches Nebraska," states he. "But, fortune ain't been good to me as of late and I'm plum out of money." He eyes our beers like most men would stare at a seductress. He has made up his own lie about knowing a man that never existed just so he could maybe mooch a drink. It wasn't an uncommon tactic in those days—to lie about knowing one killer or another in order to get folks to buy you drinks. I have seen it many times since. It is an art that has not diminished with time.

I was ready to decline the old man's company when Albert takes two bits from his pocket and places it on the bar and orders the old man a beer.

I raise my eyes at the gesture, but Albert simply smiles his pleasant smile and hunches his shoulders as if to say, "So what."

Albert and me carry our beers to one of the empty tables and discuss the situation.

"Where do we begin?" says he.

"I say, we ask around for Bucktooth Sue," I suggest.

"We don't want to raise suspicion and put Rufus on alert to our presence."

"Maybe we ought to go find the city lawman first," says Albert. "Find him and give him this note from Mr. Monroe."

There are several men playing cards at the table next to ours. None are armed, and therefore seem a harmless lot to me. The type of men that would not take offense at being asked a simple question.

"Pardon me," I say. "But could you tell us where we might find the local lawman of this town."

The man I ask has a head as big as a pail.

For a full moment, the four card players look at one another and do that until they are all grinning.

"Sure," says the fellow I asked. "That's him up to the bar there—the one you boys bought a beer for." Then, as if unable to hold back their enjoyment any longer, they all laugh like horses.

Once more, my heart drops like a stone down a well.

"Well, Albert. It looks as though we are without benefit of a local man."

"Maybe we are too quick in our judgment," says he.

"I think not."

"We ought to at least give him a fair hearing," Albert insists.

"Pardon me," Albert says, tapping the grizzly fellow on the shoulder. "But those men over there say that you are the local lawman."

He squinted past Albert toward the table of guffawing gents and then grinned himself. "They's not lying to you, Kid. I'm Burns. Raydell Burns, city marshal. I got elected in May when the last man took off with several hundreds of dollars' worth of farm implements in a wagon. They was all stoled from Effrie's Mercantile. That man with the bucket head is Effrie."

"Why is he laughing?" said Albert.

"Well, for one thing, City Marshal Comeaux, the man that stole all that equipment and the wagon, wound up drowning in the Poteau River trying to cross it in his haste. That fact alone has always delighted Mr. Effrie. I can't say why else he is enjoying himself so much, other than he thinks my appointment a good joke to be played on the town committee who appointed Marshal Comeaux in the first place only to have him turn out a thief. Effrie spent a great deal of money to see that I was elected in his place. His way of thumbing his nose at the city fathers, I suppose.

"It don't bother me a twig. I get plenty of free drinks, thirty dollars a month, a bed over to the jail to sleep in. What could be wrong with that?"

"Can you read?" I ask.

"No. Do you think I should learn?"

"Do you know where we can find Bucktooth Sue?" says Albert.

He did not flinch from the question, as I thought he might.

"She's where she always is," says he. "Down the street in Gully's Number Nine Saloon. She works there."

"What sort of work does she do," I say innocently enough.

Marshal Burns looked at me like I was pulling on both his ears at once.

"Hell, what sort of work would you think a woman with the name Bucktooth Sue would be qualified for? She's a damn whore! Fact is, she come all the way from Chicago just so she could be a damn whore right here in Sacred Heart! She's the greatest whore that Sacred Heart ever had!" His laughter broke from the back of his throat like something terrible being torn loose.

It was all unwanted news, Bucktooth Sue's qualifications and high recommendations. We had agreed that if we found Sue, we'd most likely find Rufus Buck, and that was where our true interest rested.

We took our leave, each forsaking the idea that Marshal Burns would be an aid to us.

Our nerves were up on the way to find Bucktooth Sue and her lover, Rufus Buck. A dark stone of doubt rested heavily in my chest. It wasn't exactly fear, but something close to it. Both me and Albert had failed to use our weapons in the capture of Rufus's gang, but then that was another story. Would we have the nerve to fire pistols into the body of Rufus Buck himself if that's what it took to see the job complete?

Each step brought us closer to the ultimate answer as we came nearer and nearer Gulley's Number Nine Saloon, workplace of Bucktooth Sue.

Albert whistled a low tune, the way I sometimes

would do when of Otero would haul me out to the graveyard early some mornings before it got light, usually when we had more than one grave to dig for that day and needed as early a start as possible, or if it threatened rain early.

There is nothing as cold as a wind that passes over a graveyard. I am convinced of that.

The tune that Albert whistled was unfamiliar to me, but it was slow and it was sad and it seemed to fit the lonely rhythm of our boots on the boardwalk.

We passed several dark figures who idled in the shadows along the way. For what purpose, I could only guess, but I rested my palm on the butt of the Navy, just in case danger flew our way.

We paused outside the batwing doors of Gulley's Number Nine Saloon, paused there in the butter-yellow light that leaked out of the whiskey den, and peered inside looking for the ugliness of Rufus Buck. He was not to be seen.

Business was good inside Gulley's. So good, that no one even paid attention to me and Albert. We had to jostle our way to the bar.

"You boys want beer?" said one of the three bar-keepers working the other side.

"Yes, we will have a beer," said Albert. The bar-keeper gave me a second look, but poured us out each a glass and Albert paid him fifty cents.

We had barely wet our lips when approached by a scrawny gal in a red satin dress. She looked as though her feet hurt and she had dingy teeth and unkempt hair.

"You fellers want to go upstairs with Wanda?" she said.

"Who's Wanda?" said Albert.

"That's me," said the gal. Seemed she could only grin out of one side of her mouth, like as though she didn't have no way of controlling the other side.

"Why would I want to go upstairs with you?" said Albert. I poked him in the ribs and said it was obvious why she'd want him to go upstairs. His cheeks turned pink and so did his ears.

When she seen Albert's reluctance, she asked me if I wanted to go upstairs with her. I said no, I did not, but asked her if she knew of a gal named Bucktooth Sue.

"Bucktooth Sue ain't got nothin' on me," said Wanda. "I can do it as good as she can."

"We're not interested in your abilities, miss," I say.

"Bucktooth Sue is a sow who'd do it with a jack-ass!" says Wanda in a pouting, jealous manner.

"The thing is," states Albert. "We ain't come here to buy the services of Bucktooth Sue, or no other gal for that matter."

"Then why do you want her?"

"You see," says Albert with those big innocent eyes of his. "She is our dear lost sister whom we have come to collect and bring back with us to our farm in Kansas. For her dear old daddy is dying and wants once more to lay eyes on Sue before he passes from this world to the next."

"That's right," I join in. "Was we to want us a pleasure gal, you'd be the one. But, like Albert has said, that ain't the reason we want Sue."

She looks from one of us to the other.

"Well, you are different in color from one another to be brothers," she states. "And Suzy is yellow headed, not like either one of you a'tall . . ."

"Different daddies, miss," states Albert, with a face so honest men would deposit their life savings in to it.

"Oh . . ." says Wanda. Then in a tired sort of way, she rolls her eyes upward and says: "Sue is upstairs entertaining her gentleman."

"Would he be a black man with a long scar on his face?" said Albert.

"Do you know him?" she asks suspiciously.

"Yes'm," I say. "He is a cousin of mine." She looks puzzled.

"Your cousin is . . . with your sister?"

"He's a distant cousin," I state. "Real distant."

"Oh . . ."

"Could you tell us which is her room?"

"Last door on the right. Lucky number seven."

"Pardon us," said Albert, "while we go an get our sis."

"Good luck to you boys," says Wanda with that half smile on her lips. "I know Sue will be hurt to hear the news of your daddy."

"Yes, most likely she will," I say.

We climb the stairs, climb above the din, pass a gent and his gal coming from one of the many rooms that line the upper floor. They are both drunk and laughing.

"We had better pull our Navies and have them ready," I caution Albert.

He is tight-lipped and so am I as we pull the big Navies from our belts and ready them for action.

"We will give him every chance," says Albert.

"He will kill us if he thinks we are weak or afraid to use these," I say.

"I know."

My heart wants to thump out of my chest and is trying its best to do so.

"My legs feel weak," says Albert.

"Remember," I say. "You must cock that pistol in order to fire it."

He swallows hard and so do I as we near the number seven door.

Inside, we can hear the loud talk of a man and the loud laughter of a woman. They seem to be much enjoying themselves.

We stay like that for a minute more, our ears pressed to the door listening to their unbridled talk. "Well?" says I.

"Well?" says Albert.

"We might just as well break up the party!"

The door is unlocked and flies open in our hand.

Looking down the long barrels of our Navies, we see Rufus Buck, naked as a chicken, resting his big carcass in a copper bathtub full of soapy water. Buck-tooth Sue is reclining on a divan, wearing little more than her pantaloons and a toothy grin.

I had never seen that much flesh on one gal; her bare bosoms were . . . ample!

They both took a start at our sudden entrance. "What the god damn hell!" stated Rufus Buck in a voice that filled up the entire room.

"Don't move!" shouted Albert. He was holding the big Navy in both hands, but had not yet cocked it.

I trained my own pistol on Bucktooth Sue and said: "Miss, you ought to put something over you." She seemed not at all embarrassed about her condition, but I was having trouble holding my pistol steady, for the sight of her nakedness unnerved me more than the wet soapy appearance of the dangerous Rufus Buck.

"Is this somebody's idea of a joke?" Rufus Buck wanted to know, not quite sure if it was or not.

"It is no joke," I say, preferring to keep more of my attention on him than her.

"You boys put those pistols down before one of them goes off and blows a hole in me!"

"That would be exactly what would happen to you if you give us any indication of trouble," says Albert. He is also distracted by the shamelessness of Bucktooth Sue, for she still has made no effort to cover herself.

I clear my throat until he removes his gaze from her melons. But, coming out of the soapy tub of water is a pair of pistols held in the wet black hands of Rufus Buck. They are aimed and cocked.

"You damn whippers has bought yerselves a bunch of heartache!" says he. It is a standoff, nearly, for neither me or Albert have bothered to cock back the hammers of our single-action Navies.

He stands up, big and black and wet with soapy

water running off him. He stands up pointing his pistols at us and gives us a squinting look from his scarred side.

"I have never before shot children," says he. "This will be the first time!"

"Take them out back!" demands Bucktooth Sue. "For I don't want blood and brains on my floor!" She is as callous as she is naked, which is plenty, in my book.

"Well, to do that," says Rufus Buck. "I will have to get dressed in my underdrawers and that will take time, and I do not feel like wasting any more time with these cracker-headed boys!"

"I won't stand for you murdering boys in my room," she argues in a loud voice. "For I have just had that new carpet laid down, not two weeks ago, and will not have it stained because you don't want to waste time getting dressed!"

Rufus stared at her with that cold fish eye of his, the muscles in his neck were standing out like ropes.

"Bucktooth," declared Rufus Buck. "You is a fine woman with supple charms and the learnin' to know how to please a man in every way except one. And that one is your ability to make somethin' out of nothin'; such as whether or not I kill these boys in your livin' room and their blood and brains gets spilt on the carpet. Now what kind of craziness is that?"

His voice boomed off the walls and ceiling and off the window glass.

Of all the things me and Albert had been prepared for, a domestic dispute between the sweethearts was not one. We were to die in the arms of a squabble!

Bucktooth Sue stepped between us, her bulk, shielding Albert and me from Rufus's line of fire.

"I will shoot through you just to kill them boys!" says he.

"I would just as soon be dead as to have my new carpet stained with these boys' lifeblood!"

A sudden stir from behind us, a presence in the open doorway. The *POP! POP! POP!* of a pistol, smaller caliber than what any of us was holding, and Rufus Buck stares down at himself, down at the crimson holes dotting his chest that are now leaking out his blood.

He cannot believe, judging by the look on his face, that he has been killed.

He slowly sits down in the soapy water, water now tinged pink from his bleeding so. His mouth opens and closes like that of a fish tossed up on a grassy bank, but no words pass from his dark lips.

He is as surprised as we all are.

He finally gives up staring at his mortal wounds and turns his tragic gaze toward his assassin. Me and Albert and Bucktooth Sue all do the same.

"Why would . . . you come in here . . . and kill a man . . . taking a bath . . . ?"

Preacher removes his hat with the hand that ain't holding the smoking gun and replies: "First because you was raising such a racket that it was disturbing my pleasure in the next room. And second, because these boys are old friends of mine and I am happy to see them once more. And thirdly, because I have heard that there is a thousand-dollar reward on your head and can use the money. Amen!"

Rufus seems satisfied, for it is a good and honest answer and can't be faulted. He closes his eyes slowly, takes a final deep breath, as I have seen other men do, and bids the world farewell by letting his pistols clatter to the floor.

"Oh, poor poor Rufus," said Bucktooth.

"Look at it this way, miss," said Preacher. "At least your carpet didn't get stained."

It seemed some comfort to her that such was the truth. Her new carpet had been saved, even though her lover had been lost.

"I guess there are plenty more where he came from," she said, reclining once more on the divan. We all reckoned there was, too, for there has never been a shortage of the Rufus Bucks in this world. Not in my book, there hasn't.

TWENTY-FIVE

Upon the removal of Rufus's remains from the bathtub and room of Bucktooth Sue's, Preacher explained how he had been next door with a poor frail creature that was in need of spiritual guidance when he heard the loud outburst from Sue's room.

"I could not simply lie there in the tender embraces

of the fair maid, while in the very next room, another frail sister was receiving abuse. What sort of Christian would I be?"

Preacher sighed, took a pull on the bottle he was working on, the one Albert purchased for him, for as usual, Preacher was without his own funds, having spent the last of his money on Little Angel, the gal he was with upstairs.

"Her name had a certain meaning for me," he said. "Almost a calling.

"As it turned out, I was surprised to see the two of you being held at gunpoint behind the heavenly backside of Bucktooth Sue. She was a brave creature for having shielded you like that. I had no choice but to put an end to Rufus Buck for he surely would have shot all three of you had I not.

"I had heard rumor that he was in Sacred Heart as recently as yesterday. It was disturbing news."

"What are *you* doing in Sacred Heart?" asked Albert.

"Nothing much," said Preacher. "It was mere fate that I was passing through. My horse came up lame two days ago, and I have been resting here since, waiting for his recovery. He is a good horse and I would not trade him or leave him in the care of another man. You understand how it is, don't you, Ivory?"

I did, for I would have felt the same toward Swatchy; he had remained a faithful companion to me throughout our journey.

It had grown late, and the ordeal had left me and Albert drained of our energy; we both craved a safe place to lay our heads.

We thanked Preacher again for having saved us from eternal sleep, but he brushed aside our praises, stating that any decent man would have done the same. We thought not.

We rented a room at a boardinghouse from a nice Irish widow who fed us boiled potatoes and ham hocks and never was there a softer feather bed, nor a warmer quilt, than what she provided for our comfort. We slept like fallen logs.

The next morning found us saying our farewells to Preacher, who was on his way to claim the reward money for Rufus Buck.

"It may have been the only good thing Rufus Buck ever done for anybody else," said Preacher. "Letting himself get killed, so's a little church could be built with the reward."

"A little church?"

"You have heard right," declared Preacher. "Me and Little Angel have decided to wed and settle down and build a little church up in Kansas and preach the good news. We might even have youngsters. Wouldn't that be a nice thing?"

We thought it would.

We boarded our ponies.

"Now what?" said Albert.

"Now what?" I asked.

"I suppose I will return home to my ma," says he.

"I know that she will not believe that I have come home to her. I hope it will make her happy."

"I think that it will, Albert," I say. "I surely think that it will."

"What about you, Ivory?"

"I think that I will go back to Texas as well, if you can stand the company?"

He grins wide and so do I.

Albert's ma was so happy to see him she cried tears big enough to wet the shoulders of his shirt.

Otero had died a week before we arrived back in Last Whiskey. Some said he died of stinginess, that he was too tight with a dollar to want to spend any more money on living. Some said it was the greasy liquor that had stopped his heart. I don't believe any of that. I'd believe that he died of heartbreak from one of the painted ladies in Ulvade.

Some months later, I made a trip down south to the little town, Chili Pepper, and visited Julip Deeds's mother and told her the sad news that her boy had died bravely trying to save the life of a little calf whilst crossing a swollen stream.

She cried a great deal, but thanked me for letting her know and insisted that I stay over and fed me as though she thought I might not ever eat again. She was a kind and generous woman and it broke my heart to have to tell her about poor Julip. It was the one lie I have told in my life that I do not regret.

I never did go back and visit Jasmine Pettycash

again. I don't know why, I just never did, even though I thought of her often.

Later on in life I married a woman named Martha, and we was blessed with several healthy children. One of the girls I named Jasmine. She grew up to marry a lawyer. The first black lawyer in Texas. She named their first boy, Ivory, after me. It made me cry.

I never did hear any more about the Indun, but I supposed he died that winter, for it was a hard one that would have killed healthy men, and it did.

But then, that old man might not have died and is still out there somewhere roaming around on that old bag of bones pony of his. I wouldn't be surprised.

I read in the papers two years later that Augustus Monroe was assassinated in a saloon up in Montana, that a cross-eyed man had shot him in the back of the head whilst he was playing cards, and that the hand he was holding at the time contained four aces and a king and was good enough to have won the huge pot on the table, nearly two thousand dollars.

Nearly the same fate had befallen Tulip Belle, down in the Nations. She was shotgunned while out riding her horse one morning and for a long time it remained a mystery as to who done it. Later, Henry, her long-time lover and then husband, confessed that he had killed her out of jealousy for her liaisons with a drummer. They hung Henry in Ft. Smith under Judge Parker's orders.

Alexy became a czar over in his mother Russia and then was overthrown in some sort of friction among the people and went into exile and was never heard of again (at least by me, or none of the local papers I was privileged to read).

Albert got married to a young widow woman with three kids (he always had a soft heart) and then they had three more of their own, a boy and two fine girls, one of whom married the governor of Nebraska. We remained friends on and off through the years even though I had moved away to down by the Red River where I still am to this day, long after Martha has passed on and all my own children have grown up and moved along.

Now and then, I still get one of Albert's kind letters and save it in a shoebox with the others after giving it a good reading.

And now and then, whenever the world seems to get too slow, I remember back on Albert and the Indun and Alexy and Monroe and all the rest and think of the time when we became the last law there was. I think maybe that it was a good time to have lived.

Center Point Publishing
600 Brooks Road • PO Box 1
Thorndike ME 04986-0001 USA

(207) 568-3717

US & Canada:
1 800 929-9108
www.centerpointlargeprint.com